# WHEN SHE GETS HOT

## miriam
### ALLENSON

**Books by Miriam Allenson**

When the Duke Finds His Heart

A Duke for Dessert

For the Love of the Dame

"Miriam Allenson writes characters that leap off the page and into your heart, bringing love and laughter with them."—*Nancy Herkness, best-selling author of the Royal Caleva series*

"Miriam Allenson writes with heat, heart, and humor."—*Gina Ardito, author of the Calendar Girls Series*

"Hilarious, sexy, heartwarming...a fabulous debut! Miriam Allenson hits it out of the park in her debut novel, FOR THE LOVE OF THE DAME. Sofia and Car are proof that when opposites attract, sparks fly."—*Lisa Verge Higgins, author of Random Acts of Kindness*

# Justice, justice shall you pursue

Deuteronomy, 16:18 – 21:9

# What…you think I'm going to let you get away with that?

Tootsie Goldberg, January 21

*For Hannah Monheit*

# CHAPTER ONE

The phone rang before the sun came up and startled Tootsie Goldberg into dropping her tights on the floor.

"Happy half century, Toots," Arlo cackled. "Oh, and Raquel sends her best wishes too."

Awesome. Birthday greetings from her ex-husband, the Prince of Fools, and his 22-year-old Princess Bride. "Thanks. I think," Tootsie muttered. Sitting down on the bed, she snatched her tights from the floor.

"Raquel said I should buy you a gift."

"How generous." Tootsie switched her cell to speaker mode and put it down on her bed so she had two hands free to wrestle herself into what she hoped was at least one piece of clothing that would keep her warm on a too cold day.

"She makes me feel like a young man all over again."

"Mmm." She held the elastic waistband wide, stuck her right foot in, and stabbed a nail through a seam.

"Every day I ask myself how I got so lucky."

She threw her ruined hosiery on the floor.

"She could have had anyone she wanted. I don't know why she chose me."

Tootsie stared at the phone. Did Arlo think Raquel couldn't count, that she didn't know, to the penny what he was worth, courtesy of lightning striking and him being the sole winner of a $110 million mega lottery?

Did he think Raquel hadn't measured all that green against his 59-year-old ass, the major flab around his gravitationally challenged belly, and his disappearing genitalia, and like the smart second wife she was, kept her eyes closed when in a prone position?

"About your birthday…" Arlo cleared his throat. "The thing is, Toots, Raquel had no idea what to get for a woman your age."

Maybe Tootsie needed to check her thesaurus to see if 'woman your age' was a synonym for fifty?

"And you know me," he continued, oblivious to the silence. "I'm no good when it comes to getting gifts. So I decided what mattered was the phone call and the sentiment."

"Well good on you. Tell Raquel I'll send her a

suggestion list for next year."

"Yeah, next year when you're 51 and—"

Tootsie hit END before she could hear anymore. No one knew better than Arlo how much she'd been dreading this birthday. She shouldn't have cared that he did, right? He was out of her life. For three years since his little announcement at Ruth's Chris Steak House over her petite filet and his cowboy sirloin that he needed to move on without her, she'd sealed him in a box in her mind where she kept things that no longer had any value.

She stood, slid open the top drawer of her dresser in search of another pair of tights or even leggings. No such luck finding any, which meant today, her legs were going commando.

Once dressed, the coffee brewing, she ate a quick bite of the one thing left in her refrigerator: Fake American cheese and white toast with calcium propionate. After, she grabbed her warmest coat and hustled into her much-loved XC40 red Volvo SUV that she'd named Marge. That was short for Margarete, because what else? She *was* Swedish, wasn't she?

Minutes later, Marge was idling, nose first, on the yellow stripes in one of Glen Allyn's too many No Parking zones, this one in front of the cleaners. It was a quick drop off—three sweaters, not even that dirty—two minutes, no big deal. But two minutes was all it took for him to be there, doing his thing.

She rushed outside. "Oh, c'mon, Brian! Not

today."

He didn't bother to look up, just kept writing on his big, fat ticket book. "No parking means no parking. That's the law."

A gust of arctic air tore straight from the North Pole and spiraled around Tootsie's tight-less legs, raising goose bumps from her ankles to her knees. "But today is my birthday."

"I'm a cop, Toots, and part of my job is to write tickets for people who park in No Parking zones. Even if it happens to be their birthday."

She shifted from one foot to the other, not just cold, now. Freezing. "You can't cut me a little slack?"

"I might. If you weren't always parking in No Parking zones. Besides which, I'm already writing. You know what that means."

Brian was short enough she didn't have to reach too far up to poke his shoulder. "Oh yeah. There's no question about that one."

"You're breaking the no-touching-the-cop rule, Tootsie. And what do you mean there's no question about that one? That's not part of the script."

"I know. But I decided we needed to add something new." Giving her tickets was part of *The Game* she'd come up with and every game needed a change now and then.

"Okay I'll go along." He stopped writing. "What does the no question about that one mean?"

"It's the end of the month."

Giving her a look out of a pair of pale blue eyes

framed by wire rims, he raised his sandy-blond eyebrows. "Which means?"

"You haven't written enough tickets. You haven't filled your quota yet."

"That's a pretty weak one. You couldn't come up with anything better?" He began to write again.

"You're going to deny there's a quota?"

He sighed, shook his head, and kept writing. "Yes I am. Because there isn't one. Except in your fevered brain."

Again the wind whooshed in and reached under her skirt all the way to her tush. Last month, as if in anticipation of the birthday barreling toward her, her biological furnace decided it was time to flare to life. She'd been counting on that same furnace to warm her poor, bare legs on this cold January day. Which would have made menopause worthwhile.

Tootsie fidgeted. The game they'd been playing for months, the game that masked a serious purpose, him giving her tickets because she parked in No Parking spaces didn't feel like so much fun with hypothermia threatening. "Can't you write faster? I have to get to the radio station. I have a premonition."

"You had a premonition the last time I wrote you a ticket." He looked up. "Which was last Monday. Or was it Tuesday?" He shrugged. "I can't remember."

"Maybe you can't, but I can. It was last Monday." She held up a hand, fingers spread. "And five, Brian.

Five. That's how many tickets you've written me, just this month."

"Every single one of which you deserved."

Yeah, she had. But she'd needed to. It was the point of *The Game.*

No matter how many times she'd petitioned them, Glen Allyn's mayor and the town council kept refusing to expand the number of legal parking spaces in the town's business district even after it became obvious they were needed. Sometimes Tootsie, thought they refused because they could.

Finally, just before Christmas, when Brian had given her Ticket Number 475, the mayor and council had noticed. At last. Thanks God. Not that they'd done anything. Still.

Her being a thorn in the mayor's side? That didn't mean she was a militant activist. Nope. Never. She wasn't that type person, anymore. She was doing it because of *The Game.* "Okay, got it. Now, how about hurrying?"

"Patience, Toots. I'm getting there." He paused. "And about the radio station...I'll tell you what too many people in town won't."

"Really? Too many people? Are you speaking of Glen Allyn, where everyone knows your name plus what you had for lunch on Saturday?"

"Don't distract me. It's a nice station. If you like classical music. But from what you've told me? They don't appreciate you there."

She made a scoffing sound. "These days my boss

doesn't."

Brian made his own scoffing sound. "Just walk away from him and the job. It's not like you need the money."

"Money has nothing to do with it." It didn't. Not since Arlo won the lottery, he divorced her, and she got half of his $110 million lottery winnings, most of which she gave away to charity, reasoning how much money did one person need? Pride in doing her job well did. And having a purpose to her life. Or at least it had. Until Stan, who she'd worked for these past fifteen great years died, and left the radio station to his useless son, Robert.

"Meanwhile…" Brian smiled and handed her the ticket. "Add this to your collection. This time, try to pay it so we don't have to issue an arrest warrant for you."

Tootsie yanked it out of Brian's hand. "Thank you so very much." She stuck it in her purse. "And don't give me that arrest warrant thing. I pay *all* my tickets. On time." Though it was a game between them, there was that thing about staying away from cops, except for Brian, because of that day she—

She shuddered and not from the cold. How she wished she could forget that day.

Brian stowed the ticket book in his back pocket. "Oh, listen. Tim's Boy Scout troop is raising money for St. Brigid's Fund for Indigent Seniors. Can you help out?"

Tootsie pulled her car door open and slid into the seat. "If I wasn't so crazy about your family and especially Tim, I'd have no problem telling you to stuff it. But we both know that's not going to happen."

His fair skin chapped red with the cold, he placed a big palm on the top of the door and leaned in. "That's a yes, then?"

"Of course it's a yes." She pressed Marge's ignition button and her engine came to life. "Tell Tim to come by the house this evening with whatever form I need to fill out. And next time, do me a favor. Give someone else a ticket."

Brian stood away from the door and grinned outright. "And forget about our game? Where would the fun be in that?"

Tootsie gave Brian her own grin. Closing the door she began to pull away from the curb, but stopped when he knocked on the roof.

She powered the window down. "What, you're impounding my car, now?"

Brian leaned in the opened window and gave her a kiss on the cheek. "Happy birthday, Toots."

She laughed, gave Brian a little wave, and drove off up the hill to Fort Lee, her office, and her premonition.

By the time Tootsie arrived at the radio station and had pulled into her assigned space in the parking lot, she was no longer thinking about her latest parking ticket. She was thinking about what mess she'd be dealing with. Since Robert took over WCLS-FM, a mess was on her plate every Monday morning.

Juggling her purse, briefcase, and the latte she'd picked up at the Starbucks drive-through across the street, she shoved open the door to the station with her shoulder and ran into a soft body.

"Hey, Toots."

Tootsie gasped. "Fern!"

A bright, shiny smile wreathing her round face, Fern Burke planted a kiss on Tootsie's cheek. "I wanted to be the first one to wish you a happy birthday."

"If you'd called me in the middle of the night? Then you'd have been first."

"Huh?" Consternation marked Fern's rosy cheeks, and then cleared. "Listen, I know you've been dreading this birthday, but believe me, it's not so bad."

"The mere thought of today is like acid reflux after a bagel with lox and a shmear. And can you tell me exactly why we're hanging out in the doorway?" She took a couple of side steps past Fern into the radio station lobby and stopped.

Because... *They weren't alone.*

There on the couch in the reception area, a man. A silent man. All in black.

She gave Fern the look that said, 'who is this guy'? She got back an eyes-only 'I haven't got a clue'. Tootsie turned toward the visitor. "May I help you?" As the radio station's marketing director, part of her job was to be welcoming. Even with a man who gave off the 'I don't need your welcome' vibe.

He came to his feet and she did a double take. Folded up on the couch, he'd seemed normal-sized. Standing, he was no way normal-sized. He was more than tall. And holy moley, was he the whole package or what? Very fit. Wide shoulders. Narrow waist. Long legs. In a quiet voice, he said, "No. I'm good."

Goose bumps went skipping down Tootsie's spine. In his black windbreaker, open over a black T-shirt, black cargo pants—with all those little pockets to put things in that really should have been thrown out because it was just junk—and black laced-up boots, he was more than a man. He was a presence. With a capital P.

Which left her reeling, which she was not all right with because as he stood there, unblinking black eyes under black eyebrows fixed on her, it was like he was assessing whether she was a—

*Threat.* She blinked and her heat index went from medium to high and her curls melted on the back of her neck. Maybe because her hand had begun to twitch she righted her latte to keep it from overflowing and scorching her skin. Putting on her best fake smile, she said, "Well, I'm sure when our receptionist arrives he'll let whoever you're here to see know you're waiting."

As he nodded, she kept the smile pasted on her mouth. Without looking away from him and his black eyes, which seriously, she was *not* going to think of as smoldering, she nudged Fern. "Do you mind holding the door for me?"

Fern, who seemed to have been caught in the man's tractor-beam stare, jerked into motion. "Oh, sorry." She scooted up to the plate glass door that separated the lobby from the business section of the radio station, her tie-dyed, floor-length skirt swishing around her ample hips. She held out her keycard, and stepped aside for Tootsie to pass through. "Oh my God," Fern whispered. "That guy gives me the jitters."

Tootsie strode past the empty cubicles where the station's salespeople would be sitting if they were present, continued on past the general manager's office, and made a left down the hallway. The guy didn't give Tootsie the jitters. Jitters weren't the reason her nipples were pushing holes through her black mock turtleneck.

Nope.

He might be Mr. Sex on a Stick—and yes, he was—but between the time she spotted him and he came to his feet, she knew. He was a cop. Not a cop like good-natured, longtime friend, Brian. No, he was the kind of cop who did things to people. Not good things.

She stopped the thought before it could form. This was the second time today she was thinking about that day. It needed to end because *she wasn't going there, now...ever, if she could help it.* "Who is he?"

"I don't know and I don't want to talk about him

anymore," Fern said. "So I'm changing the subject. Did you get the application for your AARP card yet?"

Tootsie came to a halt in the middle of the hallway. "Did you just ask me if I went in for a root canal, this morning?"

"Very funny. You should have gotten an application in the mail."

Tootsie slogged on toward her office. "I should check, shouldn't I? You know, run right home, tear through my mail, find it, and fill out every little line." She stopped, swiveled on a heel, and narrowed her eyes at Fern. "I'll press really hard with my pen and carefully enter each number of the year I was born."

Fern sighed. "Would it be too much to expect you to lose the sarcasm, missy? You shouldn't be moaning about turning 50. It's not old."

Tootsie flinched. "I disagree. My hair is turning gray and my boobs are heading south. What should I expect next? Flabby arms and skin tags?"

"What are you talking about? You look fabulous. You're still the size six you've always been. How many women can wear the kind of skirt you have on today, even women half your age? And don't talk to me about your hair. People would kill to have your curls."

"You mean the hair I pay a fortune to color so I don't have to look at the grays?"

Fern cocked her head to the side. "When did you start feeling sorry for yourself?"

Her key in hand, Tootsie unlocked her door and

pushed in. "At 12:01 a.m. this morning."

Fern pushed in right behind her and headed for the chair Tootsie kept in the corner of her office nearest the windows that looked out onto the alleyway separating the radio station from the building next door. "I swear I've never known you to be like this, even when that miserable husband of yours left you. I'd hate to think turning fifty means you're going to start having a daily pity party for yourself." She gave Tootsie a glare, which wasn't much of a glare, good-natured as Fern was.

Tootsie sighed. "You're right. I apologize for whining. It's just that turning fifty feels like something dire is waiting for me on the other side."

"That's crazy. There are plenty of good things you get once you hit fifty. Like half-price tickets on public transportation, discounts at the movies. You know Agrigento's on Route 3? You can get half off on their potato salad and coleslaw on Sundays when you buy a sub."

Tootsie's mood lightened. "I think I'll pass. Too much mayonnaise and sugar."

Fern made a face. "And that's why you're still a size six and I'm…well, I'm not going to mention what size I am."

Tootsie gave Fern an arch look. "Now who's feeling sorry for herself?"

Hanging her coat on the hook behind her door, Tootsie scooted around to the front of her desk and glanced at her phone. "I can't believe it. No messages this morning, which is curious knowing Robert—"

Fern held up a finger. "Speaking of our boss from hell—"

"Yeah, him. He usually has five or six things he's frantic for me to take care of, first thing. And by the way, when we were coming in, I couldn't help but notice that none of the salespeople were at their desks. Is there a meeting offsite again?"

Fern angled her head toward the other end of the hallway. "No. The entire coven has been in the breakroom for the last fifteen minutes. I have no idea what's up, but they're doing a lot of whispering. And about Robert, I need to tell you—"

"Maybe between the four of them, they've come up with a brilliant new sales campaign they stole from another radio station?" Tootsie interrupted Fern, while rummaging through her desk looking for her purchase order pad.

Fern giggled. "Are you saying our sales staff are not original thinkers?"

Tootsie picked up the pad. "I'm saying they're too light for heavy work and too heavy for light work." She looked up. "Did I send you a purchase order on Friday?"

"I don't remember seeing one. What did you need?"

"More swag for next month's promotions."

"I'll look for it when I get back to my desk. Oh, and speaking of missing something, I'm bummed I missed the battle in Robert's office on Friday afternoon. I heard a chair almost got thrown through the window."

Tootsie twitched, remembering. "Can you tell me why people at this radio station think having temper tantrums should be standard operation procedure? And yes, a chair almost did go through the window."

Fern giggled. "I wish I'd been a fly on the wall at that meeting."

Tootsie rolled her eyes. "There for a moment I was afraid I'd gotten in the way of the chair."

Fern cringed. "Yikes."

"It makes me crazy that Robert hasn't figured out how to manage his program director and his sales manager, who—"

"Who hate each other," said Fern, finishing her sentence.

"Stan would never have let the two of them carry on that way."

"Yes, well. Stan died eight months ago, and now his darling son is in charge, and everything has changed."

Fern leaned an elbow on Tootsie's desk. "I miss Stan."

"I miss him, too." She did. Stan Hillman had taken a chance, hired her, and given her, a woman who hadn't worked outside the house since she'd gotten married, a job she'd needed if she'd wanted to maintain her sanity...and pay the bills, since Arlo wasn't so good at that...until he won the lottery.

She peeled the edge of her turtleneck away from

her neck. "Who turned up the heat?"

Fern jumped up. "I'm glad I'm not the only one." She took a step toward the thermostat on the wall next to the door and stopped. "Oh, listen, I have to tell you—"

"What?"

"Robert needs to see you."

"What for? Oh, right. He didn't leave me any messages because he wants to lay them on me face to face."

"He said I should tell you to join him as soon as you arrive."

"I better do what the man says." Tootsie closed the drawer where she'd stashed her purse. "Where is he? In his office?"

Fern shook her head.

"Then where? The on-air studio?"

"Actually not there, either. He's in the promotions closet."

In the process of rising, Tootsie sat again and just resisted laying her head down on her desk blotter. "Again?"

Fern made a face. "Maybe this time he's hiding out from staff members who want to throw things at his head."

Tootsie had been right about premonitions. Robert went into the promotions closet when there was something he couldn't face. She laid both hands, palms down, on her desk and levered herself up. Grabbing her to-do list—so it shouldn't be a total waste of time while she was in the closet — she'd check her inventory to see if there was anything else she needed Fern to order. "I better head in that direction."

"I'll walk with you."

"No need." If there was a problem, even a minor one, it would take until next week for Tootsie to calm Fern. "Once I find out what's got his tighty whities in a twist, I'll let you know."

Tootsie power-walked past the program department, so distracted thinking what could be up with Robert, she didn't respond to the hellos from two just-out-of-college young women who were interning at the station.

Right now, they were of no concern to her. Robert was. The first time he'd gone into the closet was the day he'd taken over as head of the station right after his dad's death and she'd had to talk him off the proverbial ledge. She took a fortifying breath, rapped a staccato knock on the door, turned the knob, and entered.

Hunched over, head in hands, Robert had planted himself on the step stool Tootsie's promotional staff used to grab swag from the highest shelves in the closet. He shot to his feet when Tootsie stepped in. He must have jostled one of the shelves on the way up, because some of the mini-flashlights—for reading concert programs in the dark—fell to the floor. Robert didn't look down or say oops. Instead, eyes wide, his pasty-white complexion grew more pasty-white. "How did you know I was here?"

"The general manager's assistant told me."

He looked confused.

"Fern. Your father's assistant before he died and now yours? You told her I should come find you. In here." She tilted her head toward the door. "Can we go someplace less stuffy where we can both sit while we discuss whatever problem drove you in here?"

Robert was already shaking his head, his too-long black hair flopping onto his forehead. He shoved it back with a shaking hand. "I just couldn't do it anymore."

Not for the first time in the eight months since she got stuck with Robert, did Tootsie wonder where he came from. Stan and his wife, Mary, traveled a lot. Maybe they'd found him on a carousel at Newark Airport, going 'round and 'round, like a piece of unclaimed luggage?

Father and son couldn't have been more different. Stan had loved radio. Robert loved discussions about the works of Immanuel Kant and the sad state of South Sudanese independence. He obsessed over chess, and had been to European tournaments dozens of times. Radio? Not so much. "What couldn't you do, Robert?"

He screwed his face up into something that looked like shame, which sent a cold chill up Tootsie's spine.

"You'll find out." He looked at his watch. "In

about a half hour."

Tootsie folded her arms across her chest. "I'm not waiting a half hour. Tell me now, please."

He began to rub his hand across him mouth as if he were trying to wipe out a Lady Macbeth stain. "I couldn't take it anymore, Tootsie. That scene in my office on Friday. You saw."

Yes, the scene with the almost airborne chair. She'd been witness to lots of scenes in that office of late, most without chairs, thank God. "That was acting out."

"It's not that simple. There's something evil about it, the constant wrangling, everyone taking sides and defending their positions and for what reason? I don't see any humor, like you do, in how they carry on."

She started to object to his assessment of how station personalities chose to make themselves ridiculous, but stopped when Robert threw his hands into the air. "That fight on Friday told me I did the right thing."

Had the real estate in the promotions closet allowed, Tootsie would have paced, because that was the only way she could release her building frustration. "Like I keep telling you, to handle your senior staff, you need to give each something they want. It allows them to walk away, egos intact. You didn't, so you got a hot mess."

"It doesn't matter anymore. Not after this." He slid a sheaf of papers off the shelf where the remainder of the flashlights lay. "They wanted what we have and I decided to give it to them." The papers crackled when he held them out to her.

Tootsie snatched them up without looking at them. "Who's they, Robert?"

He shook his head back and forth, back and forth. "Now I don't need to worry about my sales manager's agenda, and don't try to tell me he doesn't have one. I don't have to worry about my program director's dramatics and his temper, either. Now I can do exactly what I want with the rest of my life, because the money I'm going to be paid is so good, I'll never have to worry about anything unexpected happening to me ever again."

"What do you mean?" Heat blossomed under her collar.

He sighed as if he was shedding the last part of an unbearable burden. "The station, Tootsie. I'm selling the radio station to Jim and Chuck Petrocelli."

Tootsie thought she might have gasped. But how could she have heard it for the sound of her head exploding? She opened her mouth once, twice, before she found her voice. "You sold WCLS? To the Petrocellis? You sold our radio station to the Slasher Twins?"

# CHAPTER TWO

Tootsie had met Jim Petrocelli when she first began to work at WCLS. Stan had sent her, his brand new marketing director as his representative, to the annual Tri-State Media Award Dinner. She'd been seated at Petrocelli's table. To make conversation, she'd introduced herself.

He'd looked her up and down and said, "You work for Stan Hillman, do you? A word of advice? Don't bother thinking this is a good time to hit me up for a better job. I don't hire women managers."

After that, for the rest of the evening, she was stunned into submission and silence. Because after all, what was there to say? She didn't have the juice and definitely not the guts to challenge a bully. Not like she'd had when she was a kid.

*Sold to the Petrocellis.* She swallowed hard. The Petrocellis owned a crap load of radio stations of every size. They kept on buying and 'reorganizing' them in the name of profit. Just like at every other station they bought, WCLS staff would be 'scaled back', meaning pretty much all 35 of the men and women who had poured their hearts and souls into their work at the radio station would be fired.

Tootsie stared down at the papers Robert had thrown at her. They were still clutched in her hand. In the other, her to-do list. She exhaled a humorless laugh. "Well, Toots. There's no need to check inventory."

She stepped out of the promotions closet into the hallway. The red light, mounted above the door to the on-air studio across the hall from the promotions closet, flicked on, a warning for quiet in the hallways. Voices had been known to carry even with the door closed. Tootsie eyed the light, knowing Lauren Peralta, morning drive personality, had potted up her mic and was reminding listeners what they'd just heard. Next she'd pimp the four commercials, scheduled for this stop-set, and cue up whatever concerto, symphony, or overture came next.

The red light above the studio door popped off. "So." Tootsie whispered. She wound her arms around her waist and squeezed. "So," she repeated. "What's to be done?" Nothing. Because no one could stop the disaster coming their way. Not anyone. Certainly not her.

She pushed away from the wall on which she'd been leaning and paced down the hallway to the ladies' room. Good. It was empty. She threw Robert's pages down onto the counter next to one of the sinks along with her worthless to-do list.

What a strange thing Robert had said about never having to worry about unexpected things and that being a reason for selling to the Petrocellis. That made no sense. But when had Robert ever made sense?

She braced her hands on the counter next to the sink. Dropping her head down, a feeling of helplessness swamped her.

*Be a girl who does the right thing.*

She picked up her head to stare at herself. What the hell? First the thought of that day and cops popped into her mind and now this...Grandma Hannah's words from that letter? Thinking about those cops from thirty years ago and doing what was right? It brought back memories of deep pain. And grief. And loss. She'd spent thirty years running away from the memories. Why had it all surfaced, today when she could do absolutely nothing? Even if she wanted to. Which she wouldn't.

The door opened. "Tootsie, what's taking so long?" Fern took a step in.

"Robert's sent out an email. He's called a meeting in the big conference room. The email said it's about the future of WCLS. I'm nervous. You need to come. Right now."

"I'll be there in a minute."

"Hurry. I'll save you a seat." The door closed with a snick.

Oh, yeah. She definitely wanted to hurry just so she could watch the Petrocelli train come barreling into the station. The people she'd worked with all these years were about to be run down by a pair of heartless rich men, whose goal in life was to become richer. All she'd be able to do is watch.

She squinted some more. All she saw in the mirror was herself, she of the pointy-chinned, too-thin face, small nose and small mouth, large, dark brown eyes that were a match for her short, brown, newly-colored curls, peri-menopausal thinning eyelashes, and those damn upper lip and chin hairs she now had to pluck every other day to keep from looking like she needed a shave.

She turned and let herself out of the ladies' room. After one last look, she whispered, "Happy birthday, Tootsie Goldberg."

"That was longer than a minute," Fern patted the seat of the chair she'd saved for Tootsie.

The conference room was filling up. Tootsie looked around as most of WCLS's employees filed in.

"I stopped by my office to drop off some papers." The ones she didn't need, and the ones she didn't want to look at.

Fern took out a small, pink, battery-powered fan from her skirt pocket and turned it on. Its whirring, plastic blades set wisps of her red hair dancing around her cheeks. "Will you please tell me why they call it the Change? It's more like after a lifetime of service to men and children, God decides to set you on fire from the inside out."

"And ignores you when you ask why." Tootsie's mouth shaped the words of an 'I'm burning up script' she and Fern had developed over the last month in comradeship and sympathy, when her hot flashes had started in earnest.

Murmurs behind her had her turning. Here came Robert, walking alone to the front where a long, narrow table stood with three chairs behind it and three glasses of water on it. He slunk into the middle seat.

"What's this crap about, Toots?" whispered Lenny Tolliver, easing into a seat behind her, his headset slung around his neck. "I've got commercials to edit for our asshole sales manager and wouldn't you know it? The jerk needs them on the air yesterday."

There was no love lost between Michael and Lenny. There was no love lost between everyone and Lenny. Tootsie half-turned toward him. "You'll find out."

Lenny snorted. "Pull the other one. You know and don't want to say."

Too true. But it would do no good to say anything that would fast track Lenny. Lenny liked nothing better than to heckle.

She leaned toward him. "Here's a suggestion. Whatever is about to happen, keep your opinions to yourself."

He curled his lip. "I don't like the sound of that."

As people settled in, there was an undercurrent of whispers that ebbed and flowed with the scraping of chair legs against the tile floor.

Fern turned off her fan, reached into her purse, and pulled out a tissue. Blotting her forehead, where her copious red curls had plastered themselves to her skin despite the fan's best efforts, she said, "Do you want to make a bet that our dear program director isn't going to show?"

Tootsie glanced at her watch. "When did Marc Antonio ever come in before noon? If he showed now, he'd be two hours early."

"You have a point. About Marc Antonio... is Michael going to press charges against him for the chair incident on Friday?"

"I doubt he will, but if I know Michael, he'll whine that he's being forced to toil away in a hostile work environment."

"Excuse me."

Speaking of...here was the bane of Marc Antonio's existence. Michael Le Boff, the perfect model of a modern general sales manager, taking a seat at the end of Tootsie's row. His three henchpersons—sales staff—slunk in at the same time and took seats behind Michael. Each one was more smarmy, silver-tongued, and shallow than the other.

As for Michael, if the man blinked, Tootsie had never seen it. Though she knew nothing about his private life, she'd had the occasional thought that the bed he slept in was shaped like a coffin.

There was a flurry of activity at the back of the room. Tootsie stiffened. The men those glasses of water had been set out for had arrived. She came around in her seat to see if she was right, and yes, she was.

There they were, the Slasher Twins, Jim and Chuck Petrocelli. In fifteen years, Jim hadn't changed. He was still an ugly little troll. As was his brother Chuck, who she'd never met.

*Don't bother thinking this is a good time to hit me up for a better job. I don't hire women managers.*

Should she worry that he would remember her? She wiggled in her chair, nerves jangling.

Looking neither right nor left, the Slasher Twins marched to the front of the room as if they owned it. Which they did. Or would. At any moment. They were both short and fat. It amazed Tootsie that two men who resembled bowling balls with five appendages—head, arms, legs—could wield as much power as they did in the industry, and could cause as much havoc. Each flanked Robert and sat.

Robert came to his feet. "Thanks for coming, everyone."

"You're welcome." Lenny, of course.

Robert gave Lenny an anxious glance, and cleared his throat. "As you know, these last months have been tough for WCLS."

"That's because your father had the nerve to die and leave you in charge." Again Lenny. This time slightly louder.

There was a snicker somewhere in the back of the room.

Robert plowed on. "The whole radio industry has been under siege. What I found out, after my father passed, is there aren't as many people listening to WCLS as there used to be. Our listeners, our seventy and eighty-somethings, now have Spotify accounts. That's bad for WCLS's bottom line."

Lenny tapped Tootsie on the shoulder as Robert went on with his so sad story-telling. "What's he talking about? Plenty of people listen to the station."

"Zip it for once!" Tootsie hissed through clenched teeth. If Lenny would just stifle it, maybe he could keep his job while the Petrocellis fired everyone else. Every station needed someone to produce commercials, no matter what format.

Robert scoured the room, looking, no doubt, for a friendly face. "Expenses were high. You all know that."

"Robert. A question." Vito Marconi came to his feet from a chair he'd been sitting in against the wall at the back of the room, "Did you discuss this with the Committee?"

Robert looked away.

Tootsie frowned because she'd forgotten. As Robert droned on about music testing, she leaned toward Fern and whispered, "Aren't you on the Committee?"

Fern shook her head. "I used to be. Before Stan died. The last discussion I remember we had was about how someone brought his cat into the studio and Lauren broke out in hives so bad she had to go to the hospital." She turned and glared at Lenny.

Lenny glared back. "How would I know she was allergic to cats?"

Tootsie ignored Lenny. To Fern, she whispered, "Is there something about the Committee I don't remember that I should? Why would Vito bring it up, now?"

Before Fern could answer, the bowling ball to Robert's right lumbered to his feet. He put his meaty hand on Robert's shoulder and forced him to sit. "Okay, enough. I'm Jim Petrocelli. My brother and I are taking over this radio station."

The murmuring in the room came to a dead stop, as if someone had topped it with a lid on a cast iron skillet.

Petrocelli scanned the room. "WCLS is an out-of-the-mainstream radio station. Your market share sucks when compared to the real classical radio station in this market, WQXR."

With a contemptuous smile on his lips, he added, "But none of that matters." Nodding like a malign bobble-head doll, he continued to scan the room, starting and ending with Lenny. Lenny wilted under Petrocelli's glare.

"As of today, everything here at this radio station, from business model to format to personnel, will change," continued Petrocelli. "You're the first to know." Petrocelli chuckled. Like that was funny.

Loud whispers cascaded through the room. Fern took out her fan.

"When we buy a station, we try to make the switchover easy on the former employees," Petrocelli went on.

Somewhere behind Tootsie, there was a loud humph. Lenny.

"Some of you, who can prove to me you can make the transition, may keep your jobs. For example, I've met with your sales manager, and he seems like someone who can adapt." He nodded once in Michael's direction. Michael nodded back, all smug graciousness. His three sales hussies formed their lips upward in the same oily smile.

Tootsie and Fern eyed each other. That explained the early morning meeting in the break room.

The features on Petrocelli's face tightened. "I hope you'll show me and my brother the kind of gratitude we deserve for being as generous as we plan to be."

To this, a snicker and more whispering. Someone, Tootsie thought it might be Jolisa, one of the admins in the continuity department where they scheduled commercials, said, "Could you explain what you mean?"

Petrocelli cut his eyes in her direction. "I'm talking about your health insurance and severance."

The murmurings stopped. Petrocelli nodded.

"I had in my mind whoever would not be in our employ after today, I would give a fair severance package. I'd pay for your health insurance for a month, and give you all a month's salary. Although, when I look around the room at most of you…"

"Oh, no," Fern whimpered.

Tootsie took Fern's hand as Lenny jumped to his feet. "Who are you kidding? You're going to fire all of us, just like you do at every station you take over." He glared at Michael. "Except him and his useless people."

Petrocelli leaned his considerable bulk across the table and planted his hands on the edge. Raging Bull-like, he aimed his chin, blood-red with anger, toward Lenny and sneered. "You don't know jack about my plans."

Her hand still grasping Fern's, Tootsie turned to look over her shoulder. Everyone in the back row had risen to their feet. Arms folded across their chests, animosity was stamped on every face. Her heartbeat ratcheted up. Sweat broke out on the back of her neck. It had nothing to do with menopause.

Without taking his eyes off Lenny, Petrocelli said, "Everyone in this room can thank your friend here. Because of him, there'll be no severance. There'll be no health insurance. You guys are on your own."

A groan rocketed through the room. Tootsie's heart began to beat a sharp tattoo and her stomach went into quasi-upchuck mode. This was disaster. Her friends needed that severance. None of them could afford to be without their health insurance.

Someone had to say something.

She waited. But no one stood. No one called out. She shifted in her chair. Tried to make eye contact with Vito. Or even with Lenny. To see if she could urge them with a look to speak up. But no. They were both silent.

She turned back around and looked at Petrocelli, standing there with a satisfied grin on his face and she began to burn.

*Don't bother thinking this is a good time to hit me up for a better job. I don't hire women managers.*

It was fifteen years late, but who was counting reaction time…he'd had some pair saying that to her. Had she asked him for a job? Given what everyone said about him, none of it good, even if he'd fallen all over himself and pleaded with her, pretty please with sugar on top, to take a job with him as his very first woman manager, would she have?

Rat. Jerk. Turd. She should have called him all those names to his face fifteen years ago. Or told him what she thought of his chauvinism. Yeah, she'd let it pass, shame on her. But now? She was *not* going to let this one pass.

She dropped Fern's hand and shot to her feet. Cupping her hands around her mouth, she yelled into the tumult that had risen in the room. "Mr. Petrocelli! Mr. Petrocelli!"

Chuck Petrocelli shot her a startled glance. Robert slapped both hands onto the top of his head. Scowling, Jim Petrocelli swiveled toward her. Everyone else in the room did, too.

"Did you want to speak?" Petrocelli slitted his eyes at her.

Tootsie caught her breath. *What was she doing?* If she hadn't been able to face the man's glare, and his insulting way all those years ago, why did she think she could do it, now?

The urge to slink down in her seat had her knees bending. Until she glanced at Fern, and the plea in her eyes. Fern, who Tootsie knew needed every bit of that severance and every bit of the money that would pay for her health insurance. Fern, who though she, Tootsie, had the money to pay for it all and would, was too proud to take the first penny.

She turned her gaze back on Petrocelli, the miserable human being, and his sneer, and his attitude that the men and women of WCLS...mere ants that he could stomp on at will. And that last thought gave her what she needed.

Courage.

She stood straight. "I do want to speak."

Petrocelli shrugged, the look of contempt still curling his mouth in a perversion of a smile. "Whatever. The floor's yours."

She took a breath. And dove in. "Perhaps we've gotten off on the wrong foot today." Be gracious, she told herself. Start there.

Petrocelli raised one eyebrow. "I'd agree with that."

"We were all a little startled. We would have reacted more calmly had we known in advance so we could have prepared ourselves for today."

Behind her, Lenny said, "How, exactly, could we have prepared ourselves for this?"

Tootsie ignored Lenny. To Petrocelli, she said, "We all know change of ownership happens in our industry."

Petrocelli eyed Lenny before returning his attention to Tootsie. "Go on."

"We love this radio station."

"You tell him," murmured Fern to a chorus of yeses and mm-hmms.

"We understand it won't be classical anymore."

Petrocelli nodded. "That's right. It'll be talk like no one's ever heard before."

Lenny snorted. "Just what people need. Another blowhard talk station."

A trickle of perspiration snaked down Tootsie's spine. "I'm sure it'll be successful," she said raising her voice, hoping to draw Petrocelli's attention away from Lenny...and have her words do some good. "I hope my colleagues will be able to find new jobs soon."

The room stilled.

"What you offered us might not be all we would want." She could sense, without looking, the vigorous nods behind her. "But we'll take what we can get." She swallowed, hoping she didn't choke on her next words. "And thank you for your generosity."

Tootsie let go the breath she'd been holding. Maybe she'd done it, found the guts to save a small part of the day.

"Now, that's the kind of thing I like to hear." Petrocelli smiled that non-smile. "Thank you for acting like a professional."

"Says the man who's no professional."

She sighed and closed her eyes. Lenny just couldn't help himself.

Pointing at Lenny, Petrocelli jeered, "You should learn how to keep your mouth shut."

Before she could stop him, Lenny jumped up. "You think your lousy one month's worth of health insurance will give us more than one moment's worth of help?"

"Lenny," Tootsie groaned.

"I guess you'll have to figure it out," Petrocelli shot back.

Petrocelli fixed Tootsie with a black glare. "You've done your thing, and now it's time for you to shut up."

Shut up? *Shut up?*

Before she could think how to answer *that*, Lenny went into full Lenny mode. "You scumbag! Drop dead, you piece of shit!"

Now, everyone came to their feet, roaring, and Tootsie sat. The air went out of her. She'd failed.

Petrocelli pounded on the table. The water glasses sloshed over. "I've heard enough. Within the next hour you will all have your desks and work stations empty of personal belongings and—"

Shouts coursed through the room.

"—And you will take your personal belongings, nothing that belongs to the company, including anything in the music library. Then you will vacate the premises."

There was a momentary hush, like the leaded stillness at the onset of a tornado over Arkansas and then chaos reigned. A couple of people eased out of the room, but most stayed, waving fists and making colorful death threats.

Her face flushed and shiny with perspiration, Fern tugged on Tootsie's hand. "Oh, this is terrible. Who will hire me at my age? I'm going to be on the street," she wailed. "Do something!"

# CHAPTER THREE

Tootsie had done as much as she knew how. What more did Fern think she could do?

*Be a girl who does the right thing.*

She looked around the room. Rosa Zuccotti was sobbing into a wad of tissue. Rosa's 65-year-old husband was confined to a wheelchair. He needed constant home care. With her job at the radio station, Rosa had barely been able to afford it. Now? How on earth would she be able to pay for his round-the-clock nursing?

Alan Fishbein was slumped over. Years ago, he'd gone bankrupt. He'd struggled all this time to get back to normal where he wasn't petrified each month that he wouldn't be able to pay his bills.

Buddy Zoeller looked like he was going to throw up. Buddy was on the spectrum. Stan had hired him to keep track of all the CDs in the library and know how to find them among the thousands the moment someone needed them. He'd done an excellent job. Now, he'd be lucky to get a job in a supermarket as a bagger.

Rosa was 59. Alan was 63. Buddy was the youngster of the bunch. He was 54. Maybe Petrocelli told himself it was okay because they could all just retire. They couldn't. Stan had never set up a pension fund. Most everyone hadn't saved enough to retire on. Now they needed to find other good paying jobs. But who would hire them?

Because they were older.

The young ones would find jobs. But Rosa, Alan, Buddy, and yes, Fern, and the others who weren't quite old enough for Medicare and Social Security? They were out on a limb and the Slasher Twins had just sawed it off.

"Damn Petrocellis," she said under her breath. "Heartless assholes." A hot flash to end all hot flashes lit her body on fire. It exploded all along her nerve endings.

*Be a girl who does the right thing… be a girl who does the right thing… be a girl who does the right thing.*

"This," she said… "Is," she said louder… "So wrong!" She yelled.

Tootsie bolted to her feet. Fern did, too. She took Fern by her shoulders and turned her in the direction of the door. "Go get Vito. The two of you go to the studio."

Fern stood. "Why? And why Vito?"

Tootsie had no idea why today of all days, Vito had decided to hang around after his shift but she wouldn't question it. He was the voice behind the mic during the overnight. Insomniacs talked about how listening to him murmur about Mozart and Mahler put them into a deep and dreamless sleep.

"Because Vito's got a following, that's why. If listeners hear Vito during a time when he's not supposed to be on-air, they'll know there's something off."

Fern's face brightened.

"Tell Vito he has to push Lauren aside like he's taking over the mic with breaking news. It will most definitely be breaking for our listeners. Tell him to say WCLS is under siege and will go off the air unless somehow they can stop it from happening."

Fern nodded with vigor.

"Tell him they have to do what they think will help. They need to call attorneys, call judges, call their state legislators, even their congress people and senators."

Fern's eyes had gone wide. "The president?"

"Maybe not the president." She gave Fern a push, eyeing Chuck Petrocelli who was yelling into his phone.

"Go," she said. "I'm going to hold off the Petrocellis for as long as I can and give you time to get in there."

Fern made her way through the back of the room where Vito was standing, arms across his chest, mouth pressed shut in an angry line. She grabbed one of his arms, cupped a hand around her mouth, and leaned close to his ear.

Vito threw up his head and stared at Tootsie. Then with the smallest of nods, he ushered Fern out in front of him, and together they left the room.

Tootsie slipped off her shoes and turned to Lenny, who was muttering under his breath. "Take my hand."

Bracing her, he said, "Why?"

She hoisted up her skirt and climbed onto her chair. "After you crapped all over what I was trying to do to fix things, now you ask?" She put her thumb and index finger into her mouth and let fly with a piercing whistle.

Everyone stopped cold. Tootsie grinned. She hadn't done that since she was a kid. It was good to know she still could.

Jim Petrocelli straightened, his face flushed purple. "What do you think you're doing?"

And wasn't that the question of the day? What *was* she doing? Whatever it was, it felt great. She slapped a hand to her hip. "Robert forgot one teensy little detail when he made his deal with you."

Petrocelli exhaled an impatient breath. "Forgot? No, he didn't." He swiveled in Robert's direction. Robert gave him a tepid smile. Petrocelli turned back toward Tootsie. "He didn't forget anything."

"Oh, yes he did." Tootsie dug her toes into the chair's cushioning to keep her balance, and the words just bubbled up. "He forgot the Committee."

Petrocelli glanced at Robert who was busy studying his glass of water. "Whatever it is, it doesn't matter."

"It does matter. The Committee makes all decisions for WCLS." She sent a hostile glare Robert's way. "*All* decisions."

"Good job, Toots," said Lenny. "Good job!"

Not hardly. The words that were coming out of her mouth were a whole lot of BS. She was making it up as she went along, the delaying tactic she'd told Fern she'd use until Vito could get into the studio and do his thing.

Petrocelli stuck both hands in his pockets and rocked back and forth on his heels, like he was enjoying the scene and just waiting for it to come to an end. "Why don't you stop while you're ahead, Ms. Goldberg. Maybe for a woman your age standing on a chair might not be the smartest thing."

*A woman her age?* Really? First he tells her to shut up and now this? That was the red flag he wanted to wave in her face? "I'm not stopping until you hear what I have to say," she shouted. "Whether you want to give him credit for it or not, Stan Hillman knew his success at WCLS came because he made his employees, through The Committee, part of his decision-making process."

"Who the hell does something like that except a crazy idealist like Stan Hillman?" Jim said with a dismissive wave of one hand. His diamond pinky ring glinted in the overhead fluorescent light. "A radio station should not be run like a commune."

"Says the piggish corporate thief," Tootsie snapped, letting it all rip. "He was successful because of that very mechanism he created."

"What's your point?"

"The Committee matters," she yelled. Cheers followed her words.

Petrocelli's face darkened.

"Tootsie." She looked down to see Michael had stepped up to her chair and was staring up at her. "You know The Committee is internal to WCLS."

Now that he no longer needed to keep it hidden, the extra-terrestrial being let his smirk show. His clutch of sales streetwalkers stood behind him sporting identical smirks.

"You two-faced jerk," Tootsie seethed at him.

Michael's eyes widened.

"You knew about this." She waved an arm around to encompass the room. "And you kept it to yourself. You sold us out. Someone should write 'Benedict Arnold' across the front and back of your jacket with a red Sharpie so people are forewarned about you, both coming and going."

He prissed up his lips. "That's not helpful."

"Step down from the chair, Ms. Goldberg," Petrocelli raised his voice over the renewing crescendo of noise. "Or, I'll have someone take you down."

Tootsie stamped her foot. The chair wobbled.

Lenny tightened his hand on her skirt. "'You don't get it, do you? You are not the owner of this radio station. This meeting is moot."

There was a roar. Instead of heading for the door, any one left in the room—and that was most everyone—surged toward the front.

"Get back," bellowed Petrocelli. He got in his brother's face. "Where the hell is that fucker and his crew? Get them in here. Now!"

Chuck nodded and grabbed his cellphone.

Lenny put his hands on Tootsie's waist to brace her as the crowd surged around her chair to get to the Petrocellis.

Eyes wide, looking like he was barely breathing, Robert sat like a stone as Jim danced from one foot to the other, backing away from the people who leaned over the table to get to him.

Tootsie grinned and then she laughed. This was what it felt like when you did the right thing. When you stood up on a chair to do what needed to be done to stop bullies and bad guys in their tracks. How had she let herself forget what it was like?

She kept grinning. Until she felt a tap on her wrist. It was Fern, back from the studio. She didn't look happy.

"We were too late. Petrocelli's people were there and they wouldn't let Vito and me in. I think we're screwed."

Were they? The fire burned bright in Tootsie's belly. Who knew if they could engage enough of their listening audience to make a difference? Who knew if The Committee had any pull or if it even existed anymore? Who knew if it wasn't all going to hell in a hand basket? Except there was this amazing exhilaration, knowing that she was once more doing the right thing.

She let fly her whistle again. "Listen everyone," she yelled. "The Committee hasn't spoken. Our listeners haven't spoken. The Petrocellis are not in charge. We are." She motioned to Vito. "Take a couple of the men with you, get back to the studio and throw Petrocelli's people out. Retake our mic."

As Vito gathered his posse, Tootsie turned to everyone else. "Don't let anybody in your offices or cubicles. Guard all station property."

"Tell it like it is, Toots," Lenny sang out.

Tootsie pointed at Marc Antonio's two interns who were staring up at her like they'd never seen somebody speak truth to power. Which they no doubt hadn't. "You two. Get into the music library. If the Petrocellis send someone in there to try to take all our old CDs, don't let them." She thought about that for a second. "They can have anything written by Schoenberg after 'Verklärte Nacht.'"

From her vantage point, she could see Petrocelli glaring at her, hate searing his eyes. "I'm going to have you arrested, lady. You're going to pay." A trail of spit trickled down his chin.

"Maybe I will," she sang out, all but dancing on top of her chair. "And maybe I won't!" It had been a long time since she'd felt this free. She'd forgotten how much she liked it. No, wrong. She *loved* it. She threw back her head and crowed.

Which was when the chair went out from under her and her crow of exultation ended on a shriek of dismay. At the same time, a big, hard hand grabbed her around the waist before she could go ass over teakettle.

"Lenny! What are you doing? You need to stop—" But that was as far as she got because when she turned, it wasn't Lenny who had not just a big hard hand, but a big, muscled arm around her waist.

It was the man from the couch. The man in the black windbreaker. She glanced around. There were two other black-wearing, beefed-up hulks with him.

And didn't that make it all clear. Black Windbreaker had been waiting for the Petrocellis to call him in from the couch in the lobby, him and his pals for just this, to make sure everyone left. Some went without resistance. Not Lenny.

As Tootsie watched in shock, Lenny took Black Windbreaker on. There at first, it seemed Lenny might win. He dodged, he feinted, and floated like a butterfly, until he was so spent, he didn't have the stinging like a bee in him, anymore. Which was when Black Windbreaker went for the takedown.

But Lenny wasn't done. He threw himself at the man. Black Windbreaker sighed, and grabbed Lenny's arm.

"Hey," Tootsie yelled. "Do you have to be so

physical?"

Black Windbreaker ignored her.

"Asshole," Lenny squeaked. "Leave me alone."

"Mr. Petrocelli wants you gone." Black Windbreaker didn't bother to raise his voice. Then, in a quick maneuver, he twisted Lenny's arm behind his back.

Lenny screamed.

"Stop it!" Tootsie scrabbled around the chair to get closer. "You're hurting him!"

Black Windbreaker gave her the cop look, the one she'd *always* hated.

"You bully!" Adrenalin rushing, Tootsie began to shake all over. "Didn't you hear him shriek?"

"I did. It was a good one."

"What?!" She slapped a hand to her forehead. "You think this is funny?"

Inscrutable stare. "No."

"You're going to break his arm!"

Lenny staggered and writhed, and did his best to wriggle himself out of Black Windbreaker's grip.

"Trust me, ma'am. I won't."

"Are you crazy…trust you?" With a sick feeling she remembered how she'd made the mistake of trusting the cops *that* day on the bank of the Ligonier River and it had all gone south. "Have you been drinking your own Kool-Aid?"

Lenny took that moment to make a massive effort to get out of Black Windbreaker's grip. Hair obscuring his face, his free arm flopping around like it wasn't attached to his body, he gargled once, and went limp.

Which was when Tootsie stopped thinking and reacted, like she'd reacted that last time, thirty years ago. "You cretin, you jerk!" she shrieked and threw herself at Black Windbreaker. She clamped down on his forearm, which could have been a slab of cement for all it gave. She shoved him as hard as she could. He didn't budge. She changed direction and yanked. The result, even less successful.

Panting, she managed, "Let him go!"

Black Windbreaker looked down at her from under his pitch black eyebrows. "Ma'am, all I'm doing is making sure he doesn't hurt me or himself. Your friend is fine."

"Fine?" Tootsie's voice kept climbing higher, more mad cow hysterical, in contrast to Black Windbreaker's quiet voice in the din around them, his measured words, delivered in uninflected tones.

"You think he's fine?" On a growl, she bunched up her muscles, took a running start, and kicked the man. In the shin.

Tootsie had forgotten she'd ditched her shoes. She'd forgotten if his arm was a slab of cement, his shin—if she'd been thinking anatomy she'd remember it was a bone—would be harder than cement. Pain shot up from her toes to her hip. She staggered backward into the chair, coming down hard. Somehow, she landed on the seat.

She stared up into Black Windbreaker's eyes.

They were so dense she couldn't tell what was iris and what was pupil. His eyebrows came down to meet over the bridge of his nose. "What the hell?"

Lenny moaned. Tearing his icy stare away from her, Black Windbreaker eased Lenny's arm out of the grip he'd had him in and helped him to stand upright. "You good, man?" He slapped him on the back like they were friends. "Are we all right, now? No more crazy stuff?"

Yanking his T-shirt into place, Lenny answered him with a death glare.

Rubbing her leg to ease the ache, and watching Lenny stomp out of the room, it came to Tootsie that maybe Black Windbreaker had been right. Though that grip he'd had on Lenny looked painful, it must not have been. Not that she'd admit it and give the beast any satisfaction.

She got to her feet. She wanted to curse him out. She wanted to tell him where to go. She wanted to...whatever the worst thing was, that's what she wanted to do.

Before she could do any of it, Fern tapped on her shoulder. "C'mon with me, sweetie. Let's get out of here."

Tootsie reached into the faux wood-design metal tissue holder that sat on the corner of her desk and ripped a single tissue out. Her hand shook so, she all but knocked the box to the floor. "You need this."

Fern took it and wiped her forehead. "You could tell?"

"It was the color of your skin. It matches your hair."

Fern patted her fire-engine red curls and sighed.

The two women had made a tactical retreat from the conference room to Tootsie's office. Once inside, Tootsie locked the door. Not that she thought a lock would keep anyone out if they wanted to get in. Especially if it was Black Windbreaker. The marauder.

Fern reached into the bodice of her dress and blotted her chest.

"A bad one, huh?" Tootsie asked to be polite.

"Nah. It would be a bad one if flames came out of my rear." Fern took her fan out, pointed it at her face, and flipped it on. The wisps of hair that surrounded her face puffed out in the fan's mini-breeze. "Do you think we should maybe pack some of your things?"

Tootsie powered up her computer. Half paying attention to Fern—because the other half was focused on what she was looking for—she said, "Yeah. In a moment. I think there are some boxes I broke down stashed in the bottom drawer of my file cabinet."

Fern made no move to get them. Fan still whirring, she said, "This is insane. Do you hear what's going on out there in the hallway? People are running around out of control."

Yeah, they were. But Tootsie wasn't thinking

about that. She was thinking about what she'd done back in the conference room, how the warrior in her, buried deep for thirty years, had come out in spades, and how back there at C&K Chemicals, there by the Ligonier River she'd attacked a cop. Because he'd pushed her grandmother and her grandmother fell. And then she died.

She had no plans to talk about that with Fern.

Fern turned off her fan, and laid it down on the desk. "Well, I guess that's that. It seems like I'm in the job market."

"Maybe you don't have to be." As Tootsie's computer powered up, and as she forced herself to stop thinking about that day when her life turned upside down, she clicked through to the radio station's common drive. Eyes on her screen, she said, "There aren't many executive assistants who are as good at their jobs as you are. Maybe the Petrocellis will ask you to stay."

Fern snorted a humorless laugh. "I'm not sure I could work for them after everything that just happened."

Tootsie scrolled down to what she was looking for. "I understand." Because it wasn't like she could, either.

"It's going to be hard to find a job that pays what this one pays me." There was a plaintive tone in Fern's voice. "You know, a living wage."

"In another year, you can get social security."

"That will be nice. I'll tell myself I don't need to

pay my rent and eat for another twelve months. No biggie."

Tootsie snorted while continuing to search for one particular folder. She slowed and stopped as she came to it. It had the names of every single promotional company she'd ever done business with. It had information about advertisers Jim Petrocelli would no doubt sneer at because they advertised on a classical radio station. Should she delete it? He'd no doubt say he didn't need it. But he would be wrong. He just didn't know it yet.

She sat back and folded her hands in her lap. Turning to Fern, she said, "Let's not look on the dark side. I know in my heart you're going to find a great job soon."

"You have a lot of faith in me." Fern leaned an elbow on Tootsie's desk and sighed.

"I do. I always have."

Fern made a face. "I just hope it's justified."

"Justified, hmm." Tootsie looked once again at her keyboard. "So, what do you think? The Petrocellis know the radio business well. Would you say that's right?"

Fern gave her a 'where-is-this-coming-from' look. "I would."

Tootsie wiggled her toes in her shoes, which thank goodness she'd recovered from the conference room, and placed both hands on her keyboard. "They can call on the many contacts they've developed over the years to do the business part of radio. Is that right, too?"

Fern stared at Tootsie's hands where they rested on the keyboard and a slow smile turned her lips upward. "I'd agree with that."

"And it's a known fact that you don't miss what you don't know you had."

Fern's smile turned sly. "Uh-huh."

"Well, then." With a flourish, Tootsie hit delete. The whole folder disappeared into her trash, which she then emptied to make sure no one would find what she didn't want them to find.

Tootsie was way more pleased with that piece of sabotage than she ought to have been. "All right. Let's you and I think next steps. First thing, we need to get you on unemployment."

"Yeah, unemployment." Fern's lips turned down. "You know what unemployment will cover? A pepperoni pizza and a Lean Cuisine or two." She sighed. "I do have to lose weight. Maybe this will be the diet of all diets."

"The way I'm thinking, you're not going to be on unemployment long enough to do too much dieting. Nope. We're going to put together a killer resume for you and you'll be hired in no time."

Fern slapped a hand over her face. "Resumes are hard to write."

Tootsie pulled out a pad and pen. "I'm jotting down a couple of thoughts I have about where exactly you can start looking."

"Tootsie, how great is it that you know how to

do this stuff? Did you ever think you could help people with their resumes and do job placement for a living?"

Tootsie stopped writing.

*Be a girl who does the right thing.*

Was helping Fern, maybe others, find jobs the right thing? She tested the feeling and came up with...a blank.

"Let's not worry about me because—"

Outside the door there was a sudden thud. The pens in Tootsie's *For Tchaikovsky, Heads will Roll...Off* coffee mug, gave a little skip, and then settled.

"No, no, noooooo!"

Fern's eyes widened. "Who was that?"

All thoughts of helping Fern search for a job flew out of Tootsie's head. "I'm not sure."

Tootsie stared at the door. One part of her wanted to snatch it open and watch whatever the partisans were doing to turn the Petrocellis' world upside down. The Tootsie Goldberg who'd told herself for years to be smart and not get involved didn't move. She'd already done way too much, today. "I don't think I've ever heard anyone on our staff scream."

"That was definitely a scream."

The desire to get up and look growing stronger, Tootsie forced herself not to move. "It was a maddened animal scream."

They could hear more running, more shouting. But now an addition: someone was taking a hammer to a wall. Tootsie's pen cup jumped in rhythm with the banging.

Fern kept glancing at the door. "You know how we talked about packing? I'm not sure we should even take the time to do it. Maybe we should get out of here."

Tootsie eyed a couple of pictures on her desk, of her sons, Sam and Josh. Distracted, she thought about them, off on their own, working jobs that made them so busy they had no time to gift her with anything...including a phone call on her birthday.

She blinked herself back to the reality of now. She'd think about that later. When she wasn't worried about what would come next beyond her office door.

"Maybe I should pack one box with my stuff." Tootsie pointed at it. "They'll probably let me back in to get the rest. Don't you think?"

Fern lifted the third picture Tootsie had on her desk: the tiny picture in its tiny, blue, fake jeweled-encrusted frame that sat right next to her phone. "What about this one of your grandmother? This you definitely don't want to forget."

Like she'd ever leave it. No. It was her talisman.

Outside things had gone silent. Tootsie straightened. "What do you suppose is going on, now?"

"I don't know."

A frown skittered across Fern's forehead. "That thing Petrocelli said...can he have you arrested?"

He could. He might. Getting arrested again...a

chill ran across Tootsie's shoulders. "I don't know." But she did know because her ridiculous brain had decided today was the day to remember. "I was arrested once. When I was twenty."

Fern's eyebrows quirked upward. "Really? You're the last person I'd think would get arrested. You're so law abiding. Well, except for all those parking tickets you get."

"My personal form of protest against the predations of the State." There, a joke. To ward off any other questions Fern might ask to probe into a part of Tootsie's life she'd forgotten…on purpose. Until today.

"The…what?" Fern looked confused. But then she said, "The thought of having anything to do with cops…" Fern shivered. "Not my idea of a good time."

It had never been for Tootsie either. Not since that day after they hauled her into the police station and they charged her with entering a restricted area, disorderly conduct, disruptive conduct…and the big one about assaulting an officer of the law. And the last time she saw her grandmother alive.

Fern leaned both elbows on Tootsie's desk. "You don't think the Committee has the final say on whether Robert can sell the station?"

Tootsie sighed. "No, I don't. I just riffed on it. I told you. It was a delaying tactic for you and Vito to get to the studio."

Fern opened her mouth to respond but never got

to say a word because of the sudden pounding on the door.

"Lady. If you don't unlock this door, I'm going to break it down."

And then he did, anyway.

# CHAPTER FOUR

Fern let out a shriek. Tootsie grabbed the edge of her desk.

The man in the doorway was wearing the uniform of the day: black jacket, shirt, cargo pants, and boots. The name embroidered on his shirt pocket was A. Snedeker. "You heard Mr. Petrocelli. Get your shit and your ass out of here."

As he placed his fat fists on her desk and leaned over her, Tootsie was stunned by the narrow meanness glowing in his muddy, brown eyes.

"Charming language. Thank you so much for the advice." Keeping her voice from trembling—and proud of herself because she had—Tootsie pointed toward the door. "Now that you've shared, you can turn around and get out."

"I don't think so." Snatching the pictures of her boys from her desk," he bared his teeth. "You need help packing."

Fern surged to her feet. "You better put those pictures down," she yelled.

He jerked around. "What did you say?"

Fern stumbled backward and came up against the wall with a thud.

Tootsie shot up out of her chair, which rocked backward and slammed into the wall behind her desk. "You better not touch her!"

A human tyrannosaurus rex, Snedeker swung his head back toward her. "You giving me orders?" He dropped both pictures he was holding onto the floor, and stamped on one and then the other. The frames cracked. The glass shattered.

Tootsie's heart jumped. It was as if he were stomping on her beloved sons, not just their pictures.

"What about this one?" He snatched up the picture of her grandmother. "This thing is so big, it might not fit in a box. Oh well." He dropped it. The frame separated in pieces. He smashed it like he had the others.

Tootsie's entire body filled with a fierce rage. He'd gone far when he'd smashed the pictures of her boys. But now he'd gone beyond far, destroying not just the picture of her grandma Hannah, but the smile in her sparkling, blue eyes...the eyes that said I love you, my wonderful Tootsie. And with the stamp of one big boot, that special smile was gone. An enormous grief rose up inside her bigger than the world. "You...you rotter!"

"We're calling the police," screamed Fern, pressing herself against the wall.

He turned on her. "Shut up, you fat bitch."

Tootsie's vision blurred. There was no thought. Just reaction. She hurtled around to the front of her desk, grabbed her tissue box and slammed it against his back.

He roared, swerved around, and reached for her. With his thickset hands, he flung her to the floor, her head clunking up against the chair where Fern had been sitting.

It was strange. Her world went upside down and silent, except for the sound of her blood pulsing in her ears. She was an observer of her own self, her gaze following with a strange objectivity as Snedeker squatted in front of her. Was he going to hit her? That would hurt, right? She should raise an arm to keep him from hitting her in the face.

She was trying to go through the motions when Black Windbreaker hurtled into the room and time snapped back into place. He hauled Snedeker up, and pushed him toward the door. There was a lot of effing and s-h-ing, and words muttered so low and deadly, the observer in Tootsie wished she could've heard.

And then Black Windbreaker was there, in front of her, stooped down on his haunches. "You okay? Where does it hurt?"

"I don't know," she wheezed.

"Can you move?"

Her head throbbed. One hand stung. Lifting it, she squinted at the trail of blood snaking across her palm. "Look at that, will you? I cut myself."

"Yeah, you did. On a piece of glass. It's everywhere." He reached into the tissue holder lying on its side on the floor, grabbed a handful of tissue, which he pressed against the cut. "Anything else I should know about?"

"My tailbone." She shifted her legs and tried to sit up. "It hurts. Maybe it's broken."

Reaching around with one hand, he felt said tailbone. He pressed here, there, and a lot of everywhere. His hands on her tush brought her world into stark focus. "It's okay," she said with haste as his fingers kept up with the exploring. "I'm good."

"Yeah, you are. If it was broken you would be screaming your head off." He slid his hand out from under her, took her hands in his and squeezed. Not a lot. Just a little. It was a reassuring squeeze, like he was saying, with the warmth of his big, callused paws, that he cared that she was going to be okay.

Except why would he? He was the Petrocelli's muscle. "I guess you're happy you don't have to call a hearse."

He shook his head and sighed. "Lady, why am I not surprised *you'd* say something like that?" He slid his hands up her arms. "Let's get you standing." Lifting her to her feet, he steadied her until she got her balance. "See if you can get yourself out of here without more drama. Okay?"

And then he was gone. Fern was fluttering around her, over the edge into hysteria. Vito came into her office and put a hand on her shoulder. "What can I do?"

"If I keel over, call an ambulance."

As it was, she wouldn't let them. Fern and Vito, who were already in her office, and Jolisa, who came in after to pick up the pieces of the broken picture frames, convinced her driving home by herself, which she wanted to do, was a non-starter. She needed to go to the hospital to make sure she didn't have any broken bones or other injuries that couldn't be seen.

On the way, Vito, who elected himself her chauffeur, kept singing the police brutality song. Tootsie told him they were probably cops but working as private security, which meant the brutality thing might not hold. Truth was, she would have made a complaint, had it just been Snedeker. For some reason that escaped her, she didn't want Black Windbreaker to be caught up in such a mess.

By the time they got to the hospital, whatever little adrenalin had bolstered her up was gone, and she was relieved to collapse onto one of the gurneys that passed for a bed in the emergency room.

After a CT scan, and a couple of other tests, they determined she'd not gotten a concussion and though she'd have some serious black and blue marks, all her bones were intact. They let her go with her hand bandaged—thank goodness no stitches were needed—and a prescription for the pain. Vito took her home, warning that he planned on waiting until she got to the front door. She shuffled as fast as she could up her front steps, not wanting him to wait.

As he drove off, she bent gingerly to pick up the piece of paper stuck halfway under the door. Was it just this morning that Brian had asked her to sponsor some fundraiser Tim was taking part in at their church? Here it was...the form for her to sign. How weird. The rest of the world had gone on while hers had turned sideways, upside down, and inside out.

Sighing, she stuck her key in the lock and opened her door. She trudged across her foyer's dark gray slate floor, past her curio cabinet, and dragged herself up the steps to her bedroom, eased out of her clothing, dropping it all on the floor. With careful maneuvers, she positioned herself on her bed and onto her side. As she fell into a dark sleep, she mumbled, "Happy half-century, Toots."

She slept, off and on, for two days. Now, awake, if not refreshed, she was sitting at her kitchen table, nursing a cup of coffee, a pillow cushioning her sore coccyx, when the grandfather clock in the foyer struck twelve bongs. It echoed through the snug Tudor she and Arlo had bought when the boys were little.

She checked her phone, which she hadn't since she'd been sleeping, to see if she'd gotten any calls. Surprise, surprise...Josh and Sam *had* called her with their birthday wishes after all. Josh had left a message. When her fingers could manage to hit the keys on her cell, she'd call him back. Sam, in far off Singapore, had What's App'ed her. She sighed. Sam…her tough son. She'd reach back out to him, but the conversation would be as stilted as it always was.

Next to her coffee cup was Tim's form. She needed to sign it, put it in an envelope, and drop it off at the Stoddard's down the street. She was trying to decide where to find a pen when her phone rang. She stared at it, wondering if it was either of the two boys trying her again. But that wasn't what caller ID told her. It said…

Her mother, the woman she referred to by her first name, Francine.

Because Tootsie refused to call her mom.

Tootsie sagged in her chair, leaned her forearms onto the table, laid her head down on them, and waited for voicemail to pick up. Ding. There she was. Mommy dearest.

"Darling, I'm so sorry I forgot to call you the other day. Happy belated birthday."

"Thanks," Tootsie mumbled, mashing her nose into the crook of her inner elbow.

Her mother made a little giggling sound. "Frankly, I look so good these days, I don't understand how I could possibly have a daughter your age."

"That's weird." Tootsie gusted a breath. "Considering you were there when I was born."

"Any who…" Her mother trilled… "I know you're at work and you always tell me not to call you there, so I'm leaving this message because I wouldn't ever want you to think I forgot your birthday, even though I did. So call me." She giggled again. "I hope you won't be too tired to spend a few seconds talking to your mother. Anyway, toodles."

Tootsie took a sip of her coffee, which had gone cold. She stared at her toast, which had petrified into a rock. "What do you think? Should I call her back?"

The toast kept its opinion to itself.

"Maybe you should try to make things better with her. You're fifty. She's seventy-two. Wouldn't it be the right thing to do after all these years?"

But the memory of that day by the Ligonier River, and what her mother had done after, had kept her from ever trying to make things better between them.

Tootsie stared out through her sliding doors at her deck that stretched the width of the house. It was bare, now, empty of the flowerpots she'd placed all around the edges, pots full of bright orange Nasturtiums, red Dahlias, bright blue Ageratum, and white Petunias.

"Wouldn't it be the—" Everything in her came to a halt.

*Be a girl who does the right thing.*

Again with that sentence. "Grandma," she whispered. "Are you speaking to me from the grave? Is trying to fix what's wrong between me and

Francine the right thing?"

She snorted. "What does it say that you're sitting in your kitchen all by your lonesome and talking to yourself? Worse, you're expecting an answer for how to fix what's unfixable?"

Before she could answer herself—and that would have made her certifiable—her phone rang. It was a safe call. Fern.

"Hello?"

"Where have you been?"

"Right here. In my house." Asking questions of the dead.

"Are you up for a little excursion?"

Tootsie's brain curled around the word, excursion. That meant going somewhere. She didn't know how she felt about that. "What kind of excursion?"

"Some of us are getting together at the Starbucks across from the radio station this afternoon. Meet us there?"

"What about? I hope not a rehash of the big brawl."

"It won't be. Well, maybe a little. We might want to talk about suing someone, although we don't know who."

Tootsie leaned on her side, and with great care levered herself back into a sitting position. "I'm not sure who we would sue other than ourselves since we were the instigators of the big battle."

"But the Petrocellis were the ones who hired

those terrible men."

*They* weren't the instigators, either. She winced, remembering how she'd climbed up on that chair, what she said—no screamed like a banshee—she'd always wondered what a banshee was. She'd have to google it sometime soon. Or maybe never.

"Anyway, I told Vito and a couple of others about how you're helping me find a job. They want to ask your opinion in case the radio station sale is final, and need to start looking, too. You don't have to, obviously, because Arlo won the lottery, which is great. But we all want your advice on how we should go about it, considering none of us have been in the job market since before the turn of the century."

Tootsie wished she could offer Fern and her friends some financial support until they got themselves set again. But just like Fern would, she knew everyone would turn her down out of pride. She'd offer help, anyway. She doubted anything would change.

She hated as well to punch a hole in Fern's enthusiasm. Over the past 48 hours, when she hadn't been fully asleep, Tootsie had thought about it and come to a conclusion. "The radio station sale *is* final. We may not like it, but we have to get on with our lives as best we can."

"And that's what we're trying to do: figure that out," Fern sighed.

Tootsie sighed, too. "Here's the advice I can offer. Start with an employment agency."

"But Toots, you always come up with something important no one else would think of. Besides, Elwood is coming."

Elwood hadn't been at the Petrocelli meeting. Of all the people who should have been there, Elwood Robinson, WCLS's business manager should have been. She stood. "What time are we meeting?"

The group, all except Elwood, was there before Tootsie arrived: Fern, Vito, Jolisa, Taryn, who was one of Marc Antonio's assistants, and Lenny. Concern on all their faces—except Lenny's—they asked how she was doing and if she felt better. Assuring them she would live, they let the subject go. Tootsie was grateful.

They had already pushed three of Starbucks' miniature tables together. The ladies looked as if they were headed across the street to work. Vito, too, was all professional in his button-down baby blue shirt and chinos. Tootsie was glad she'd thrown on a pair of presentable trousers and a nice, cotton-knit, full turtleneck sweater to hide some of the bruises.

Lenny, however, looked like he'd dressed from a rag bag. He had on a faded, black, long-sleeved tee with what looked like a mustard stain on one sleeve. His jeans were splotched with dirt, as if he'd rolled in a dust bin. His hair hung uncombed around his ears, and he sported a livid black eye and red, puffy bruise that covered the right side of his face. On his feet were flip-flops. Flip-flops in January? Was he crazy? Well, yes. He was and always had been.

Tootsie wanted to blame Black Windbreaker for Lenny's black eye. Looking back, she recognized that Black Windbreaker had restrained Lenny, not tortured him. Plus, he'd been kind to her there in her office when he rescued her from whatever Snedeker had planned for her next.

He'd held her hand so gently. Said hand twitched. She'd felt the power of his gaze, warm, black, and of all things concerned. She could cut him some slack, couldn't she?

Uh…no. He didn't deserve *any* slack.

She pulled off her gloves. "Where's Elwood?"

Fern scooted over, making room. "On his way."

"Remind me again." Tootsie shoved her gloves into her purse. "Why exactly is Elwood coming?"

"We want to ask him about The Committee," said Vito.

"Vito, let's not talk about the Committee." Tootsie sat, careful not to come down too hard on her tailbone.

"Don't start the conversation yet," Fern said, rising. "I'm going up to get the drink I ordered. Want me to get you something?"

"Yes, a plain, ordinary decaf will do, nothing fancy. And hold the sugar and cream." Tootsie said, handing Fern some money.

As Fern made her way toward the counter, Tootsie laid the truth out. "The Committee's a lost cause. It's a waste of time thinking it might save our jobs."

The look Jolisa gave Tootsie said she was confused. "Why did you throw The Committee in Petrocelli's face?"

And wasn't that the question of record? Wincing at the memory, Tootsie said, "I didn't know what else to say, and things had already gone sideways."

"I think you're wrong, Toots," Vito said. "I sat on The Committee a few years ago and Stan listened to us. He followed our advice any number of times."

"About what?" Tootsie unbuttoned her coat and draped it over the back of her chair.

"Remember I told you I sat on it too?" said Fern, coming back to the table. She handed Tootsie her coffee, slipped into her seat, and plunked down a tall drink with a dash of whipped cream decorated with caramel. "When Lenny set the microwave on fire because he left his popcorn in for ten minutes instead of three, Stan backed The Committee when we told Lenny he had to buy us a new one."

Lenny slouched further into his seat and stuck out his lower lip. "I don't want to talk about The Committee. I want to talk about police brutality."

"Len." Tootsie leaned toward him. "They *were* cops, but they weren't acting as cops. They were hired security. So, you might as well sue the Petrocellis because they were the ones who hired them. And that will be a waste of time because the Petrocellis have a lot of big-time lawyers. You know what that means."

Folding his arms tightly across his chest, Lenny stuck out his lower lip even further. "I don't care. It was police brutality."

Everyone sighed and stared into their own memories.

After the silence became less freighted, Vito said, "I still think we should investigate if The Committee had more juice than we remember."

Each person at the nest of tables looked at Tootsie. Like she knew something. Which she didn't. She drummed her fingers on the table, trying to decide what to say…if there was anything to say and came up with, "What if it did? How do we find out? It's not like we have access to any records that might tell us what part it played."

Jolisa folded her hands on the table in front of her. "That's one of the reasons we asked Elwood to join us. We hope he can fill in the blanks."

With a careful shifting, Tootsie sat back. "He certainly knew all about station business."

"We'd like to know what he knows, me especially," Taryn said, tossing her long, blond, Gen Z hair back over one shoulder. "Marc Antonio never said anything to me about any committee."

Lenny roused himself, scratching his head like he needed to excavate something. "That's because Marc Antonio is a lousy manager."

Taryn eyed him with distaste before bending toward Tootsie, her hair shifting with her. "The way you're moving, Tootsie, it looks like things still hurt."

Tootsie twitched. "I'll live."

"You scared the wits out of me when you jumped on that man," Fern said.

"Okay." Tootsie exhaled a breath. "We're not talking about this." Because she didn't want to be reminded of what she did on Monday. Or thirty years ago, either.

Lenny made a sound of disgust. "I do want to talk about it and why we didn't do some real damage to those guys."

Damage…Lenny had no idea. Tootsie adjusted the cover on her coffee cup. "We couldn't. We shouldn't have tried."

Lenny's wounded eye began to twitch. "We didn't have to go like sheep."

"As I remember, *you* didn't," Jolisa gave him a narrow-eyed glare.

Lenny shrugged, not too worried, it seemed, about Jolisa's opinion. Then, eyes flashing with anger, he said, "Why are we trying to make like it was nothing? That guy who tortured me was a tool. They were all tools. We should definitely sue."

Everyone stared at their hands, took a sip of coffee, or looked outside at the traffic on the street.

Tootsie laid a hand on Lenny's arm. Beneath her fingers the muscle twitched. "Len. Get a grip."

He snatched his arm away. "We should do something big."

Through gritted teeth, Tootsie said, "Do us all a favor, Lenny. Take your we-need-to-start-the-revolution talk somewhere else."

Lenny folded his arms across his chest and frowned into his coffee.

A cold shot of air blew into the already cool room, and here came Elwood, carrying a bowed-out leather briefcase, no doubt in use before Taryn was born.

"Oh, good." Fern got up to pull over another chair.

Bustling across the room, breathing like he'd been running—not a good thing in a man who had an off-the-scales BMI—Elwood said, "I never thought I'd get here. They've started the repaving project on LeMoyne Avenue and one lane alone is open going both ways. The traffic is terrible." Settling his generous bulk into the chair, he propped the briefcase on his knees and unsnapped the latches.

Lenny sat up, interest brightening his eyes. "We don't care about how long it took you to cross the street. We want to know about The Committee and that the members needed to be consulted before Robert sold the radio station."

Everyone looked at him with disgust, although why any of them thought Lenny would pretend to manners he didn't have was ridiculous. Not that Elwood noticed. He was too busy pulling out a sheaf of papers from his briefcase. "I took the liberty of putting together a history of The Committee. Here it is." He laid it down on the table.

As he did, a small scrap of paper separated itself,

floated to the floor, and landed at Tootsie's feet. She bent to pick it up, just as Elwood jostled the table and all the coffee cups threatened to go over.

Startled, she sat up and grabbed hers, as did everyone else, moments before they sloshed hot coffee all over the table.

Oblivious to the almost disaster, Elwood said, "Stan formed The Committee so the employees could feel they were part of his decision-making process."

"See? I told you so," crowed Lenny. "The Committee had a say in the sale of WCLS."

His ponderous jaws jiggling, Elwood shook his head. "That's not what I said. The decisions Stan let The Committee make concerned housekeeping-type, day-to-day activities. He never intended for anyone but himself to make decisions that concerned the business part of the radio station."

Pointing to the papers, Tootsie said, "Do you mind if I look?"

Elwood pushed them toward her. "Not at all. That's why I brought them."

While everyone talked over everyone else, and asked Elwood questions, Tootsie looked through the year-by-year overview of what decisions had been made by The Committee.

Like the popcorn incident. Or when Marc Antonio's programming staff held a Halloween party for listeners, complete with a string quartet playing Mussorgsky's *Night on Bald Mountain*, they decorated the room with pumpkins, which they left to rot, and

The Committee made them clean it up.

As she skimmed on, nothing Tootsie read rose to the level of The Committee having a say in the station being sold. Although, as she looked, something did occur to her. She put the pages down. "Four pages, printed back and front, is a little thin for 35 years' worth of activity, don't you think, Elwood?"

"I said I'd bring all I found and that's what I've done," Elwood grunted. And then, strangely, he looked away.

Tootsie blinked. On Elwood's always nerdy face for a flash of that one second had been something Tootsie had never seen before. Irritation.

Unsettled, she said, "It was just a question. No need to get upset."

"I'm not." But nothing said that was a lie more than the tone of his voice and his gaze looking everywhere except at her.

Len snatched up the papers and flipped through. Looking at Elwood, he said, "This is all bullshit stuff."

Elwood eyed Lenny with disdain. "Like I already said. The Committee is a big nothing burger."

On Lenny's face, disbelief.

Elwood whined, "Do you think I don't know what I'm talking about?"

Tootsie leaned forward. "Gee, Elwood. Why are you so upset?" But Tootsie had already gotten a vibe she couldn't put a name to, an Elwood she didn't recognize though she'd known him for years. "So, why weren't you at the meeting the other day?"

"I had the flu."

Tootsie folded her arms across her chest. "And just look at how fast you've recovered."

Elwood ignored that. "As for Robert selling the station, it was all done on the up and up. Sorry if anyone thinks otherwise." As he jammed everything but the envelope with the papers back into his briefcase, Elwood's body language screamed the need to get away from their little coffee klatch A-SAP.

Tootsie wanted the opposite. "Why don't you visit with us for a while. You look like you need a—" She improvised "—a moment."

On a forced laugh, he stood. "Why would you think that?"

*Because there's something you're not telling us.* "Hang out with us for a little."

"I don't have time. The Petrocellis asked me to stay on, and I need to get to the office."

*Was this it? Was he embarrassed?*

Vito folded his arms across his chest and gave Elwood a considering stare. "Good for you. You've got a job."

"Thanks," Elwood mumbled and gazed at his hands where they were draped across his briefcase. But then whatever, he seemed to shake off. Hefting up the briefcase, he stood. "Well that's that. I'm going now." And he did. Hot-footing it out of the café, he stepped to the curb, rushed across LeMoyne, and into the station.

In her memory Elwood was not someone Tootsie had ever seen rush for anything. "Well, that was weird. Or is the way he acted just me and my rich imagination?"

Vito stood up. "Elwood didn't mention he still had his job until he got pushed to say so. That was why he acted weird."

Okay, so at least two of them thought so. "But why? It's not as if keeping a job while everyone else got fired is a crime against nature."

"He's got survivor's guilt." Vito grabbed his jacket. "If Elwood says the sale was legit because The Committee had no standing, I have to believe him. After all, Elwood was Stan's right-hand man. Which I think means he knew about the sale. It also means there's nothing more we can do. So, I'm going back home. I've got a resume to write."

Jolisa stood, too. "If Vito thinks Elwood told us everything, I'm going to start a job search, as well."

"I'm going to catch a bus into the city and do some shopping," said Taryn. "There's nothing like a little retail therapy when you're worried about whether you'll have enough money to pay your bills."

As the three left, Tootsie gazed out Starbucks' glass front to the radio station on the other side of the street.

"If you ask me," Lenny said, "he's hiding something."

And that was what Tootsie thought. Alarm bells that had begun a faint ringing inside her head began to sound a little louder.

Scratching his arm, Lenny muttered, "he's a rat. Maybe he sold us out."

"Because he took the job the Petrocellis offered him?" Tootsie was half-listening to Lenny while she tried to figure out what it was Elwood had done that made her think he'd lied. "He needs the job. You can't blame him for taking care of himself."

"Who's going to take care of me?" Lenny whined.

"You are."

"With what?"

Tootsie tapped the table in front of where Lenny was slouched down. "With your talent. You're going to call in favors and find yourself a job so quickly you won't have time to get all exercised."

Lenny made a face. "I can't call in favors. Nobody likes me enough to do me a favor."

Tootsie softened toward the man in spite of all his annoying qualities. "Forget the talk about favors. You're an amazing creative director. There's not more than one or two in the entire Metro area who can do the kind of magic in the studio that you can."

"You're such a great cheerleader, Toots." Lenny wiped his nose on his sleeve. "It's what you always do, even for me and I know how I'm not your favorite person."

What could she say to that?

Lenny lifted his head and Tootsie saw the shards of pain etched deep in his eyes. "That job was my life.

Without it, I don't have a life."

Tootsie wilted with sympathy. "Please don't take this so hard." She would have given him a pat on the arm but she didn't want to touch any part of his T-shirt. She settled for saying, "You'll figure it out."

"I did figure it out. Just now when Elwood left." He rose and headed out the door, his flip-flops slapping against the sidewalk. He stood at the curb and waited. And then he stepped off into the path of an oncoming bus.

# CHAPTER FIVE

The bus's forward motion and shrieking brakes carried it to within a hair of Lenny's chest. Tootsie screamed along with the brakes. As the bus rocked back on its chassis and came to a sharp stop, she jumped to her feet, and rushed outside, Fern right behind her. They got to Lenny at the same time the bus driver burst through the bus's door, lunged at Lenny, and bellowed, "What the hell!"

"I...I..." Lenny stuttered, and ran a hand across the top of his head.

The driver, who was a head taller than Lenny, and three times his girth, got down in Lenny's face. "Were you using my bus to kill your ass?" The driver poked Lenny in the chest. You better be glad I got no passengers on board." He pointed off in the direction of some vague distance. "Get out of my sight before I do something I'll get fired for."

Lenny ducked his head and, this time looking both ways, scurried across the street as fast as his flip-flops could flap.

The driver, hands on hips, shook his head in disgust. "Man is batshit crazy."

Tootsie had been saying some variation of that statement for years.

Muttering something under his breath, the driver kicked the front tire, boarded his bus, and drove off.

"To my dying day," whispered Fern, "I'll never get that vision out of my mind."

Shivering, Tootsie held the door to the café so Fern could scoot inside in front of her. "Me, neither."

Fern rubbed her right ear. "I won't forget your scream, either. I think I'm deaf on this side."

Letting the door close behind her, Tootsie kept her eyes on Lenny. "I hope Len isn't following Elwood into the station."

Fern fanned herself. "That would be a disaster."

For a moment, Tootsie had thought about going after Lenny. But then he turned on a heel—not that flip flops had heels—and rushed into the parking lot, got into his car and, tires squealing, drove off. Making a mental note to call him later, Tootsie hoped, in the meantime, he didn't try to drive off a bridge somewhere. "It would be."

Around them, the café was returning to normal. Customers who'd been busy working on their laptops, before all the excitement, returned to their work. The baristas went back to prepping their frappemochaccinos-with-ten-pumps-of-whipped-cream drinks. The whir of blenders filled the room.

But Tootsie was no longer thinking about the blenders. Or Lenny. She was focused on that scrap of paper from Elwood's briefcase that had floated to the floor. There it was against a base of one of the three tables still shoved together.

"I'm going to get one of the cake pops." Fern pointed to the counter. "Which one do you want?"

Eyes on the paper, Tootsie said, "Whatever they have."

While Fern sailed across the room, Tootsie slid into the seat she'd vacated, bent, and grabbed up the paper that had dropped. It was the size of a large Post-It note. Penned across it, in Elwood's crabbed handwriting, appeared a series of nine numbers: 646-823-313 and one word underneath: Comstock.

"What have you got there?"

Paper in hand, Tootsie looked up at Fern, back again. "Elwood dropped this."

Fern sat and peered at the paper. "Is that a phone number?"

"Not enough digits."

"And it's not a social security number for the same reason." Fern took a bite out of her pop. "What's that word he wrote?"

"It's Comstock. Did you ever hear of a Comstock associated with the station?" Although, as she thought about it, it could be a town or street name.

Fern held out the pop she'd gotten for Tootsie. "It rings a bell. I'm not sure why."

"That's not helpful." Tootsie held the pop in one hand and turned the note over with the other, thinking there might be something on the other side. "The number, though, what do you think it is?"

Fern munched on her pop. "Maybe it's an algorithm."

"Maybe we don't know what an algorithm is."

"Also true." Fern chomped on the now empty stick. "We should call John Grisham and tell him we've found the answer to the Da Vinci Code."

"It's Dan Brown, not John Grisham. Somehow I don't think Elwood would be hauling around the solution to Brown's story in his briefcase. Especially since Brown wrote the ending to that book a long time ago."

Fern sighed. "Well, my inquiring mind would like to know why Elwood wrote Comstock and those numbers on the same piece of paper and what one has to do with the other."

"Maybe nothing. Maybe he wanted to remind himself of something and this piece of paper was handy."

Fern pointed her naked cake pop stick at Tootsie. "Maybe it's the code to the back door."

Tootsie sat back with a thump. The chair creaked in protest. "Fern, that's brilliant."

Eyes wide, Fern said, "It is?"

"Think about it. By now, the Petrocellis have

changed everything. Remote access to the server, and keycards to get into the building. But if you didn't have your new card yet, you'd have to memorize the code to put it into the keypad until your new one came, and if you're like me, you'd have to write it down because..." She made a face... "memory fades with age."

With a disgusted huff of breath, Fern said, "That could be. But not in your case no matter what your age is. You remember everything."

Tootsie ignored what she knew Fern meant as a way to make her feel better about her birthday, and tapped her finger on the paper with the numbers and the name. "My spidey sense tells me Elwood doesn't want us to know something."

Fern took out her fan and turned it on. "Because he acted a little hinky just now? Aren't you letting your imagination run wild?"

She might be. She probably was. "Have you ever seen Elwood lose his cool or raise his voice? He did both just now."

Tootsie came to her feet and pushed her arms into her coat. "You could say I haven't recovered from the other day and my brain has hunted over into paranoia mode. But I don't think so. That little scene was off. I have to know why and then..."

*Be a girl who does the right thing.*

"I'm going across the street to confront Elwood and see if he'll come clean."

Because this...*this* was the right thing.

\*\*\*

As she waited for the Walk/Don't Walk sign to change in her favor, Tootsie had second thoughts. Maybe Elwood was nervous because he was late for work and he didn't want to start off on the wrong foot with the new boss. She could understand that. But there was something about those four pages. How could there be so few when WCLS had been around for 35 years?

Maybe there was some kind of charter for The Committee that Stan had set up? If Elwood would show her a copy of that or something like it, and it said what he'd told them, then she'd be happy to go away and leave him to his job with the Petrocellis.

The light turned. She hurried across the street to the radio station, noting a black car parked in front. Could the idiot driver not read? It clearly said No Parking on this side of the street. Where was Brian when you needed him?

Once inside the station lobby, the changes were starkly apparent. It no longer looked like WCLS's lobby, although the couch where Black Windbreaker had been sitting remained. A stray thought jumped into her mind and had her wondering what Black Windbreaker's real name was. Not that she wanted to know.

*Liar, liar, pants on fire.*

The lobby walls had been painted a startling scarlet red with diagonal, black stripes. Down had come WCLS's call letters and up had gone the new station's calls, WXRN-FM. If Tootsie hadn't thought there'd been a format flip, all she had to do was listen to the indignant bickering—the signature sound of talk radio—pouring out of the lobby speakers.

Plastering on a smile, she stepped up to the plexiglass wall behind which sat Petrocelli's new receptionist. "Good afternoon." Even before Tootsie said another word, the skinny-as-a-wood-plank woman telegraphed that Tootsie's 'good afternoon' had ruined the rest of her day.

"I'd like to see Elwood Robinson, please."

The receptionist raised one penciled-on eyebrow almost to her so-last-century-blonde beehive do. "Have you got an appointment?"

"I'm a colleague of his."

"A colleague?" The woman's eyebrows came all the way down. "From…?"

As if Blondie had no idea. "From WCLS," Tootsie said. "The station that was in this very space just two days ago."

One side of the receptionist's mouth curled up so far that Tootsie could see she needed serious periodontal work. "Elwood is busy. Write your message down." With a twenty-five-inch French-manicured talon, the receptionist pushed a note pad through the slot at the base of the plexiglass. "Somebody will give it to him."

The implication was it wouldn't be her…and probably never. With a very broad, very fake smile, and in her sweetest voice, Tootsie said, "Would you mind seeing if he could come up to the front right now?"

Birdie gave her a hard-ass smile. "I'm sorry. Was I stuttering when I said he's busy? Leave the note. When he's ready, he'll get back to you. Until then…?" She raised one of those eyebrows, the color of which didn't match her hair.

Tootsie slammed her mouth shut before she could say one thing more that would give—she glanced at the name plate to the right of the desk—Audrey McDaniel—another opportunity to be obnoxious. Not bothering to say buh-bye, it was nice to know you—which it was not—she pivoted around and exited the building.

Once on the street, she was enveloped in the roar of construction on LeMoyne Avenue. Buffeted by the wind coming off the Hudson River, she turned up her coat collar and headed for the parking lot where the wind might be less fierce. Sliding one glove off, she took her phone from her pocket. Finding Elwood in her contact list, she hit CALL.

The phone went right into voicemail.

*This is Elwood Robinson…*

She rolled her eyes as he went on about the new radio station and thanked her for calling him, yada, yada, and have a nice day. Finally the beep.

"Elwood, thank you so much for meeting with us, just now. I know you're busy with the new station."

At least according to Talon Lady he was.

"I'm kind of jealous that you didn't have to pack up your stuff. What a pain packing is, right?"

Tootsie paused and then got to it. "You didn't have to put that report together for us about The Committee, but we appreciate that you did."

As a gust of icy wind found her, she hunched into her coat. "But there's something that will be amazingly helpful and I'm asking you as a colleague. We're still colleagues, aren't we?" She forced a laugh.

"There must have been a charter for The Committee. Or notes from Stan setting out what it was responsible for. If you'd be willing to show me whatever that was, then I can tell everyone that the sale of the radio station to the Petrocellis was totally kosher."

Kosher, as in the way it was supposed to be.

"Would you do that, Elwood? Give me a buzz. We'll make it quick. Thanks."

She pressed END without adding 'have a nice day'. Five minutes later, after hopping from foot to foot in the cold, it occurred to her that he might not call back. And that was when she remembered the numbers on the scrap of paper Elwood had dropped. She reached into her pocket, but she'd left the paper on the table in Starbucks. "Crap," she whispered and thought about going back across the street to retrieve it.

Except she still had her keycard on her key chain. And maybe, just maybe the Petrocelli's had changed the code on the front door but had forgotten about the back door.

Before she could tell herself what she was doing could get her in a world of trouble, she headed around the building to its other side. If her keycard still worked, she'd slip inside and march down the hallway like she belonged there. She'd knock on Elwood's door, ignore his startled look, and get right to the point. She'd say what gives? And maybe she'd get the answer she was looking for.

Picking up her pace, she strode into the alley, the echo of her heels ricocheting off the walls. The gray metal door still sported the call letters, WCLS-FM, and the warning painted beneath, *Employee Entrance Only*. Maybe she was right. If the old calls were still up, maybe they hadn't changed the code back here.

She glanced around. No one in sight. Stepping up to the keypad to the right of the door, she slid her card in, and waited for it to flash green. Nope, red. She stared for a moment, and tried again. No go. Once more. No go again. Which was when she concluded no matter how many times she tried, her card wasn't going to work. And was proof the Petrocellis had changed all the access codes.

Behind her, someone cleared their throat.

Tootsie whirled around. Black Windbreaker.

The last time she'd seen him, he'd held her upright. Today he looked like he wanted to hold her for questioning.

# CHAPTER SIX

A sudden hot flash saturated her system. "What are you doing here?"

On his long, olive-skinned face, not one sign gave her a hint what he was thinking. He was a still life in black, from his close-cropped hair to his shit-kicker boots. "I think that's my question."

Giving in to her nerves…bad idea. Besides, how could she explain the keycard in her hand, and why she was trying to get into a building which she no longer had any business being in? Honesty…always a good choice. "I wanted to see if my keycard still worked."

He came toward her. "Yeah. That makes sense. Why didn't I think of that?"

She opened her mouth. Nothing came out.

He looked at her out of those fathomless, black eyes. "You should have turned it in."

A zing of temper loosened her tongue. "You have some chutzpah. When exactly was I supposed to do that? After that bozo friend of yours threw me to the floor? Or later, when another one of your buddies hounded me outside before I could even put on my coat?"

"Yeah. None of that should've happened. I'm sorry."

Crazy as it was to say, she believed he was. But it didn't get him any points. She folded her arms across her chest and tapped the toe of one shoe on the alley's cracked pavement. "That's lovely. Now, if you don't mind can you move aside? I have things to do. I can't stand here all day."

His eyebrows met over the bridge of his nose in one big unibrow. Even that didn't ruin his to-die-for looks. Grrr.

He took one hand out of his pocket and held it out to her, palm up.

She widened her eyes at him. "What? You want to dance?"

His expression altered. Got hard. "Hand it over."

"Hand what over?" Like she didn't know and wasn't playing dumb.

Gaze now locked with hers, he said, "This isn't a game. The keycard. Now."

"Why should I give it to you? Oh, I know." She brandished the card in his face. "You've elected yourself the Petrocelli's enforcer."

The way his lips disappeared into a thin line,

Tootsie knew she was pushing the envelope. Thinking that was enough bull on her part, she slapped the card onto his upturned palm.

Which might have been a mistake.

Because as her cold fingers met his hot skin, her internal pilot light flared into overdrive. She wanted to tear her coat right off, forget the unbuttoning part, and throw it to the ground.

All because she'd touched him.

"Can I go now?" she said, turning on a heel, and throwing the words over her shoulder, desperate to get away.

No answer. She didn't plan to wait around for one. Bolting out of the alley, she rushed to the corner, where she pressed the traffic light's walk/don't walk button multiple times. Like *that* had ever helped.

A quick glance behind her said Black Windbreaker was standing at the mouth of the alley, watching her. She shivered with... God, she hoped it wasn't with pleasure. Because that would be just too screwed up. The second the light turned, she sprinted across the street and away from him. The man was dangerous to her in ways too numerous to count.

"What were you just doing?"

Tootsie jumped and faced Fern. "I thought you were waiting for me inside so we can check out the job scene for you."

"I was." Fern's grin grew cagy. "Until you walked down the alley and that hot guy from the other day followed you. I wanted to see what would happen.

How about sharing?"

Tootsie turned them both toward the café. Stepping inside, she steered Fern to their tables and sat. Rather than go through every detail of her visit to WCLS, she gave Fern the SparkNotes version. She left out anything about the disturbing reaction she'd had to Black Windbreaker.

"Why did you try the back door? You were the one who said they'd change the code."

"Hope against hope?"

Fern squinted at Tootsie's forehead. "Are you having a hot flash?"

"What gave it away?" Tootsie reached under her coat collar and swiped at rivulets of sweat still running down the back of her neck.

"The fact that you've turned a shade of red that I once saw in a crayon box."

"Awesome," Tootsie groaned.

"Take off your coat. That'll help. Meanwhile, I need something to eat. The cake pops didn't do it. I'll be right back."

"And I'll be right here," Tootsie said, but Fern was already on her way to the counter. Tootsie threw her coat on one of the chairs still pulled up to the tables where their little group had sat. She stared out the window, and there he was, again. Black Windbreaker was getting into that black car parked in a No Parking zone. Of course he was parked there. *She*—and everyone else—couldn't without risking a ticket. But cops? There'd be a problem with that? Uh, no.

"Okay, I'm back." Fern spread napkins on the table and placed a scone in the middle. She lifted an envelope from her purse, extracted a page. "Check out these listings. They're the ones I thought I should respond to."

Tootsie pulled the page toward her. "You got these off the online job sites, right?"

Fern nodded. "Copied and pasted."

Running her finger down the page, Tootsie paused at each one Fern had highlighted. After a minute she glanced up. "I wonder how many people are looking at these listings at the same time we are."

About to bite into her scone, Fern paused and placed it back on the napkin. "A couple dozen?"

"Maybe. Maybe more." Tootsie tapped the page. "These job openings aren't what you should be looking at. You should go after the ones not being advertised."

"How do you go after a job no one's telling you they have?"

"You take advantage of your network."

"That's easy for you to say because you talk to everybody everywhere. I talk to people who phone Robert. And then it's just a quick transfer to the boss."

Tootsie got it. Fern wasn't loaded with self-confidence. "Let's figure out the people you know and the people I know, give them a call, and see who's hiring."

Fern slumped. "I wish there was another way."

Tootsie hated to see her friend so despondent. "Chin up. You've got more talent in your little finger than 99% of the people looking for executive assistant positions any day of the week."

"Thanks, but—" Fern gasped. "Can you believe this?"

Puzzled by the conversational switch, Tootsie said, "Believe what?"

"Turn around and look at who's going into the radio station."

Tootsie sighed. "Please tell me it's not Lenny. If it is, I'm going across the street to take him home." Or to a therapist.

"It's not Lenny. It's Marc Antonio. What's he doing? Is he checking to see why he's not hearing Mozart coming out of his speakers but a rant on the latest Washington scandal?"

Tootsie swiveled in her seat to catch the tail end of Marc Antonio's black cloak wafting through the radio station's front door. "That wouldn't surprise me. He says once he's put together the play list, he doesn't have to listen to the station."

"Yeah." Fern took a bite of her scone and chewed. "That sounds like him."

Three minutes later, Marc Antonio made his exit.

"That didn't take long." Tootsie rose and hastened to the door. "Let's see if he'll come over and talk to us."

Peeking her head into the cold, she waved. He

saw her, nodded, and stepped into the street. As if synchronized, each and every vehicle on LeMoyne Avenue paid Marc Antonio heed. Without the first sound of a horn, each came to a halt as he moved in a stately fashion across the road, looking neither right nor left.

As he opened the door to the coffee shop, and glided over to where Tootsie and Fern were seated, the baristas froze in place and the blenders seized up.

All hail the king.

Tootsie held up a hand to him. What was the point of waiting when she knew what was coming?

He bent, took that hand, and brought it to his lips. He made a soft, kissing sound in the air, a quarter inch above her knuckles. "My darling, Tootsie. How are you? You are well?"

She took her hand back. "As well as can be expected, considering I lost a job I've held for a zillion years."

Marc Antonio removed the broad-brimmed black fedora he wore winter and summer, and his unruly black locks sprang forth around his ears, in one lobe of which he sported an extravagant diamond stud.

He placed the hat on the chair most recently occupied by Elwood and focused his eyes, glistening and black, on Fern. "Fern, my treasure. You, too, are well?" Marc Antonio threw his lean-as-a-whippet body into another of the little Starbucks chairs. It protested. "It seems we are all out of a job." He waved his long-fingered, pianist's hands in the air. "*C'est la vie, n'est ce pas?*"

Tootsie eyed him with shock. "Why aren't you ranting about what happened to our radio station?"

He raised one perfectly arched, and probably tweezed eyebrow. "What would that gain me?"

"Relief?"

He straightened. "I'll miss WCLS, but since Stan is gone, it hasn't been the same. Robert doesn't understand the business of radio. He's all but destroyed what his father built up all these many years. He's a carbuncle on the ass of an elephant."

Tootsie raised an eyebrow. "So, it would be safe to say that WCLS going away won't be a blight on your life."

"I'm producing a concert series about the life and music of Clara Wieck Schumann that will air on NPR starting in April. Yesterday, I worried that I wouldn't have time to complete it by deadline, considering all the responsibilities programming the station that I have…oh, pardon…that's past tense. And…" He held up one long finger. "I've been asked to take the directorship at the Sedona Early Music Festival in Arizona, to which I thought I would have had to say no. But now I think I can say yes. So, my dear, WCLS going away is the opposite of a blight on my life."

"Well, I'm glad somebody's got what to do," muttered Fern.

Marc Antonio came out of his slouch. "May I

assume this comment means you, one of the most organized and competent people I know, have not already found other employment?"

It was Fern's turn to raise an eyebrow. "Thanks for the vote of confidence. But when I do start looking for a job..." She waved at the list of jobs on the page in front of Tootsie... "There's the business of my age."

He held out both hands, palms up, two smooth, pink expanses of skin. "Why would your age matter?"

Tootsie and Fern looked at each other.

"In fact, my dear Fern," Marc Antonio continued, oblivious to their non-verbal what-are-you-drinking communication. "I love your age. Yours is the age of intelligence, of steadfastness, of loyalty."

"That's true," said Tootsie, one eye on Fern, who was beginning to smile.

"Why do I say this?" Marc Antonio continued. "I'll tell you. Until this moment, I was preoccupied with thoughts of failure. I was most distressingly desolated."

Tootsie rolled her eyes. "Your point, Marc Antonio...could you make it? The sun's going down in another four hours."

Ignoring Tootsie and her mouth, he turned to Fern and fixed the intensity of his deep, black eyes on her. "Little did I realize my worry was unfounded, that the solution to my problems could be found here in your very person."

Yup. She'd had a thought that was where he was

going. Tootsie let a grin fly. "Cut to the chase, already."

With a little nod in Tootsie's direction, Marc Antonio reached across the table to take Fern's hand. Lifting it to his mouth, he repeated his gallantry with a well-placed air kiss. "Oh, my queen of efficiency whom I have only been able to admire from afar, tell me you will say yes. Make me the happiest man on the face of the earth."

Eyes big, Fern said, "Wow. That was an amazing boost to my ego. The thing is, I'm not sure whether you want to hire me or marry me."

He flicked his fingers in the air. "Darling, I was asking you to work for me. As adorable as you are, marriage is not on my mind. I'm married to the one person who can meet my standards: myself."

Once more, Fern looked blank-faced. "Toots?" Fern, it seemed, was amazed and maybe a little in denial.

Tootsie was neither. She knew if Marc Antonio said he wanted Fern to work for him, that's what he wanted. "Go for it. Here's why."

She raised one hand and held up an index finger. "You know him." She held up a second finger. "He knows you." She held up a third finger. "You know classical music. He won't have to explain it to you. That will make both of you happy."

Tootsie gave Marc Antonio a pointed look. "It doesn't mean she'll give in to every one of your harebrained ideas—like the one where you thought it would be a great idea to have a tug of war across the George Washington Bridge between lovers of Beethoven and Bach."

Once again, Marc Antonio held up his hands in protest of innocence for that crack-brained idea.

"What you need to do is," said Tootsie to Fern, "Make sure you buy a pair of ear plugs, so you can deafen yourself when he has one of his hissy-fit breakdowns."

Marc Antonio put his wounded look on. "How can you suggest I would ever—"

"You're a brilliant musician," Tootsie interrupted, before he could go down the 'you've insulted me' path. "Everyone knows about those three amazing works on the history of classical music that you wrote."

Chin in the air, he said, "I did write them."

"Well, good for you, and I mean that. I also know that at heart, you're a kind man. You'll treat Fern with respect."

His cheeks turned a faint pink.

Tootsie wagged a finger at him. "Just keep the cray-cray stuff to a minimum, okay?"

He gave Tootsie a rueful grin. "I promise I will control myself. Now that I have this gem...?" He eyed Fern with a questioning look. "I do have you, don't I?"

Fern nodded. "You have me."

Marc Antonio rubbed his hands together. "That's settled and—"

"Hold up." Tootsie interrupted because she knew better than most that they hadn't finished their negotiations. "As long as you pay Fern a fabulous salary, which I know you can afford, it's settled."

A splayed hand pressed against his chest, Marc Antonio said, "You think I would not pay this pearl, this woman without equal, the recompense to which she is entitled?"

Tootsie sighed. "Marc Antonio, you are the cheapest man I've ever met."

Marc Antonio reached into the inside pocket of his cloak, and pulled out a checkbook. "I will show you how wrong you are." He scribbled some figures, signed his name with a flourish, and laid the check on the table between the two women. "There. How's that for a signing bonus?"

Tootsie thought she was seeing double. Fern fumbled for the tissue she'd laid in her lap. "Dear God.' She pressed it to her throat. "This is the equal of three months of my salary at WCLS."

Marc Antonio gave Tootsie a keen look. "And proves to certain people I am not cheap. Besides, I got my bonus from the radio station. It was quite large, as it should have been, so I can certainly afford to share the bounty."

Tootsie wondered if there'd been some kind of seven-second delay between when Marc Antonio said the words, 'bonus' and 'quite large'. Had the Petrocellis given Marc Antonio severance when they wouldn't give it to anyone else? "You got a bonus?"

"Actually, no. It was a figure of speech."

Some figure of speech.

"I haven't been at the station for the last two months," Marc Antonio continued. "Elwood was holding my checks for me."

Fern narrowed her eyes at him. "You never heard of direct deposit?"

He twisted his mouth in confusion. "What's direct deposit?"

Fern sighed. "Oh boy. Have I got my work cut out for me."

Seeming to weigh and then ignoring that one, he said, "Elwood and I shook hands and then I left." About to get up from the table, Marc Antonio paused. "He told me he's very busy with the new station, though he didn't seem to be busy."

*He didn't seem busy? So why couldn't he answer his phone?*

Rising from his chair and retrieving his hat, Marc Antonio held out his hand to Fern. "My dear, I wonder if you would walk with me to my car to discuss how we must proceed. I'm parked in the lot."

As he helped Fern with her coat, she said, "I want to say a word to Tootsie. I'll be with you in a minute."

"Of course. I'll wait by the door."

Fern leaned toward Tootsie, excitement making her quiver. "Thank you, Toots. I know I have this job because of you."

But Tootsie was half-listening to Fern. She was

staring across the street at the radio station where a man in sweatshirt and jeans came outside. He was carrying a huge-ass saw. "I didn't do anything. I encouraged him to pay you well, that's all."

The man stepped into the ground cover that filled the beds around the building and turned the saw on. Bending to the base of the just over six-foot marquee sign with the name WCLS, Tri-State's Classical Radio Station emblazoned on it, he began to saw at the post.

Fern turned at the sound. "Huh?"

Tootsie's heart sank. "That guy there." She pointed. "…He's replacing the sign with our station name on it with the new one."

"That sucks," whispered Fern.

More than the sign on the wall inside, more than the raucous sound of talk coming out of the speakers, for Tootsie, this was the final nail.

She slapped one hand on the table. "I'm done."

Fern narrowed her eyes. "What do you mean, done?"

"I'm taking another crack at the back door."

On a curl of her lip, Fern said, "May I remind you that you don't have your keycard, anymore?"

Tootsie didn't need reminding as she retrieved the memory of Black Windbreaker holding out his hand for her to give it to him.

And how that meant she'd touched him.

She pushed the memory down and tapped Elwood's paper where she'd left it on the table.

"Remember this? You said it. These numbers are the code for the back door."

"You *hope* they're the numbers."

Tootsie crossed her fingers. "I'm sure."

Fern got in Tootsie's face. "I think you should leave it alone."

Tootsie thought for a half second. "Nope. I've made up my mind."

Mouth dropped open, Fern said, "What do you think is going to happen if you march back up to that door and the code works? What will happen once you're inside? Are the new employees going to say hi how are you, what's up? Or are they going to call the police?"

"Fern?"

Both women looked up as Marc Antonio called out. He pointed to his watch. Fern ignored him, which Tootsie thought was a good start to their relationship.

"I'm not going in the middle of the day," Tootsie said. "I was thinking more like after midnight when the one person who will be there is the jock and maybe another person he can argue with."

Fern just shook her head. "You're crazy."

Tootsie huffed a sharp breath. "I may be. But it feels like someone doesn't want us to know something. It feels…" She floundered for the right word. Not finding it, and giving up, she added, "…like all the puzzle pieces don't fit together."

"I get it, Toots, but—"

"You don't get it." She was at a loss as to how to explain this feeling she had. "There've been too many times in my life when I walked away from something I knew was wrong. I'm not going to walk away from this."

Fern brandished a finger at her. "You could get hurt."

"I won't." Tootsie crossed her fingers again. "I'm going tonight."

Fern sighed. "That's what I was afraid you'd say. That's why I'm going with you."

# CHAPTER SEVEN

Over the years, Tootsie had been at WCLS late more times than she cared to remember. Being at her desk, no chatting all around to distract her, it was a good time to get lots of work done. Before this, it had never felt eerie or lonely. That was then and this was now. And she didn't feel lonely, not with Fern who was right behind her, clutching a fold of her coat. She also wasn't inside.

*Yet.*

Stan had never bothered to put security lights in or an alarm, so she stood, safe, in the dark, for now. With her glove off her right hand, she began to punch in the sequence of numbers from Elwood's sticky note. With Fern dancing from one foot to the other and jostling her, her finger slipped onto a number not in Elwood's sequence. The light flashed red.

"Will you relax?" Tootsie hissed. "I can't do this

with you breathing down my neck."

"Hurry. I'm freezing."

Tootsie cast an exasperated look behind her. "Then go wait in the car."

"No way. I'm not leaving you to do this by yourself. You could get caught."

Tootsie's finger slipped on another number. The light turned red, again. "Didn't we talk about this? We're not getting caught."

"You're so sure," Fern intoned.

Tootsie swung around. "Will you please?"

Fern's hand still wound up in Tootsie's coat, the wool was so twisted, her belt was in danger of becoming a tourniquet around her rib cage. She was about to be cinched to death by her own clothing. "Let. Go!" She wrenched herself out of Fern's grip. "Relax."

"I can't relax just because you say relax." Fern's face screwed up. "Because once you do this, once we get into the building—if those numbers really are the new code—there's no going back. Life as we know it, changes forever."

"You think maybe that's a little dramatic?"

"Maybe yes, maybe no, but…"

Tootsie didn't need Fern to finish that sentence. She knew what her friend's point was. If she didn't punch in the last number, she could step away from the precipice. Forget about WCLS. Not worry about what happened that shouldn't have. Move on. Get in her car and go home.

Maybe later she'd think about it. Right now, she needed to focus all her psychic powers on the last of the nine little numbers in her cold little hand.

Once more, she punched in the first eight, and then paused. She stared at the keypad as if it could speak. Which, as it happened, was not one of its features. On a slow exhale, she pressed the last number.

Green light.

Fern gasped. "Ohmigod, ohmigod!"

"Ssh!" Tootsie pulled the door open.

"Okay, okay." Fern patted her chest, hand encased in a heavy winter glove. "I'm cool, I'm chill. No, I'm not. I'm burning up." Fern shoved Tootsie into the building and closed the door behind her.

It was dark inside, except for the soft glow of the Exit sign above the door, the silence total.

After a long minute of listening, Tootsie looked down the hallway to the on-air studio. The light above the door came on and glowed red, which told her whoever was in there would be staying put. Things were good. For the moment.

"Take off your shoes," Tootsie murmured.

"I can't." Fern's whisper was as loud as some normal-toned voices. "I put special knots in my sneaker laces so they wouldn't untie and trip me up while I was breaking and entering with you."

"Then stay here. Don't move." Tootsie gripped Fern's arm. "Follow me if someone comes out of the studio." Which was a ridiculous thing to say because then it would be too late to prevent all hell from breaking loose. "And don't whisper." She added, "I'm going now." And then she scurried down the hall to the line of executive offices. In the narrow, carpeted space, bathed in the eerie light from the nighttime lights above, she paused.

No light seeped from underneath any of the closed doors ahead. No one was sitting at any of the desks in front of the offices, no random producer, no new staffer popping up because they were proving to the new boss that they'd work all hours. Unless they were sitting in the dark.

She tip-toed past her office, or more accurately said, what used to be her office, to the next one which was Robert's. Or what used to be Robert's. And stopped. Logic told her to backtrack to Elwood's. That's where she needed to start.

She reversed direction, and tiptoed back three doors. She tried the doorknob, turned it in one direction and then the other. Locked. Unless she was willing to break Elwood's door down, she wasn't getting inside. Which left one place for her to search. If that door wasn't locked, too.

Starting back in the direction she'd come from, Tootsie passed by her door and tiptoed on to Robert's, which had the name of the new guy on it. It would be a guy. Jim Petrocelli had told her way back when, hadn't he? He didn't hire women managers.

*Asshat.*

Flattening her ear against the new guy's door, she

heard nothing but more silence. She jiggled the doorknob. It gave. Which had her heart doing a little loop-di-loo. She pressed her hand against the door's cool, wood surface, and pushed. Poking her head around it, she stepped inside and closed the door behind her.

She stood in pitch black dark. Weird thing…it sounded like the darkness could breathe. "Get over yourself, Tootsie," she whispered. "And get down to business."

This office had once been a mirror-image of hers, same size, same shape. Her office and Robert's were back-to-back. But when Robert took over, he decided what had suited his father for 35 years wasn't a grand enough space for him. So, he'd put in custom-made cabinets and drawers on the wall that separated his office from Tootsie's, bought a designer desk to replace his father's utilitarian model, and knocked down the wall between his and the office on the opposite wall that he shared with Tootsie.

With its couch and two chairs and a little table nestled between them, Robert called it his conversation area. Tootsie had sat in one of the deep-cushioned chairs too many times to count while Robert completed one of his many allegedly important phone calls before he could "make time" for her. Passive aggressive twit that he was, he loved making people wait.

The shades over the three windows that looked out onto the office building next door were drawn.

Tootsie fumbled in her coat pocket for the miniature flashlight she'd brought with her. It had been a joke gift from her Secret Santa at last month's holiday party, a miniature black and white cow with a keychain substituting for its tail. The cow made a mooing sound when you pressed the button on its back, which also turned on its beam. The mechanism that controlled the moo had stopped working after a dozen moos, which made Tootsie's inner child sad.

Turning on the beam she played it over the desk Robert had bought, a cherry wood behemoth with curlicues for handles and a useless but beautiful Tiffany lamp sitting on one corner. She tip-toed across the office, skirted around the desk, and headed for the bank of drawers behind.

She pulled the topmost drawer open and started her search. Neat hanging files marched, left to right, in alphabetical order. Each file was stuffed with paper. Laying one hand on the plastic, multi-colored tabs, she shined the cow on the A's, the B's until she came to the Cs and found nothing that said Committee.

Frustrated, she glanced around. And there! On the shelf that ran along the top of the cabinet, a big pile of folders rubber-banded together. She grabbed them and removed the rubber band. Then, turning, she placed them on Robert's designer desk, and fanned them out. She went directly to the C's. *Carnegie Hall, CDs no longer of use, Committee—*

Committee!

She flung open the file on a crow of triumph. Which died when she realized the file was empty.

"So new guy," she said to herself, not bothering to lower her voice to a whisper because who was there to hear? "Did you get rid of what was in this folder because it was of no use to you, just like all the rest in this pile are of no use? You definitely didn't know I was coming and decided to get rid of what was in here, right? Which is a completely crazy thing to say, because you don't know me, do you?" Tootsie amended.

Playing the cow light over the other folders in the stack, she thought she might have been right, because all the others were empty, too.

"Nothing here that's a puzzle piece that could fit," she muttered.

As she began to wind the rubber band back around the folders, she realized there was another skinny folder right under the Committee one. She juggled the cow and peered at the tab: *Comstock*, the word on Elwood's sticky note. "Hmm."

She laid that folder on the desk and opened it. Unlike the other folders, this one held a 5x8 note card. "New guy didn't see this. Otherwise he would have gotten rid of it, too," she murmured. On the card was scribbled a paragraph in Stan's cramped handwriting. Tootsie lifted it out of its folder and read the top line. Elizabeth Comstock. All right then. Comstock wasn't a company name or a street name. it was a person.

She fumbled her phone out of her pocket, juggled her cow and the folder and took a picture of the card. Stowing the phone back in her pocket, she studied the card and the scrawl of Stan's handwriting. "So, what's the deal, Stan? What about Elizabeth Comstock justified her having her own folder?" Reading on, she added, "And what's this about an award?"

She turned the card one way and then the other, focusing on the first letter, one of Stan's big, looping Ts. She'd prided herself on being able to read Stan's writing, but truth was she couldn't always, and the rest of what he'd written was illegible. "What is this word? Is it thanks? Or maybe it's three, or—oh, I don't know—something ridiculous, like thrice?"

"I doubt it's thrice," said a deep voice behind her.

Ditching the cow and the folder, she stumbled back against the cabinets, and let her scream rip.

He might not have been more than a shadow, but she recognized the shape of the man she'd met in the alley that afternoon. As for the voice...she had a feeling it would be stuck in her aural memory forever.

Tootsie groaned. "What is it with you? Have you moved in here, now?"

"I'm working."

Sensing him coming closer to her, she said, "Why didn't you warn me? Why didn't you let me know you were in the building?"

Black Windbreaker came around to the side of

the desk where she'd plastered herself up against the wall of cabinets. "You're kidding."

"I am not kidding." Yet one more hot flash accompanied an adrenalin-induced headache. "Were you in here the whole time?"

"I was sitting on the couch out in the lobby. Reading."

"In the dark?"

"I don't need a light to read on my e-reader, not that you need to know about my reading habits. And then I saw you coming down the hallway. I slipped in here because I was sure it was where you were headed."

Tootsie's eyes, growing accustomed to what had been pitch black but was now gradients of black, she could see he was holding a hand out to her.

"How about I help you up," he said. "Let's forget about where I was, and you talk to me about what you're doing here in the middle of the night."

She itched to shine her cow beam in his face. But after this afternoon she knew better than to provoke this man. "Why exactly do you think I should?"

Which once said, she knew was almost as provoking as if she'd beamed him with her cow.

He moved not one inch. "I'm waiting."

She held up her hand. He pulled her upright as if she weighed no more than a couple of the CDs they'd used before everything became automated. The moment she was upright, she pulled her hand from his. Like she'd been scalded.

He was too close. The heat of his body, the soft in and out of his breathing. The urge to run was overwhelming. Except she had nowhere to go.

"You do know that up until the beginning of the week there wouldn't have been a problem for me to be here at any time, including the middle of the night," she managed.

"But that's not now." As he reminded her of the obvious, he moved toward the door. "I'm turning on the light." Which he did.

Tootsie winced at the sudden brightness. There he was, standing in the doorway, wearing what she was beginning to think of as his costume: T-shirt, trousers, boots, all black. No windbreaker. Even the watch on his left wrist had a black band.

He'd folded his arms across his way too nice, way too manly chest. "I'm waiting."

He didn't yell. He didn't threaten. He didn't have to. His quiet presence said danger ahead, girlfriend. Pay attention and fly upright.

Which was why she opted for a straight-up explanation. "I'm here because I'm looking for something important."

With quiet steps—how did a man his size walk so softly—he came back across the room, skirted around the desk to stand between it and where she had plastered herself against Robert's—whoops, new guy's—fancy file cabinets.

There was a strange hiccup of silence while her brain zig-zagged through every possible next thing to

114

say. And came up with nada.

Leaning back on the desk, Black Windbreaker ran his gaze over her, not in an undressing kind of way, more like a curiosity way. For a second she wondered what he saw.

"You've surprised me."

*This* was what he was thinking? "I have?"

A twitch of his lips. "Except for that bullshit answer you gave me about having a right to be here tonight, what you just said about breaking into this place makes sense. Don't ask me why I think so, but there it is."

"I hope you don't expect me to pat myself on the back for winning your approval."

"I didn't say I approve. And I'm waiting for your answer. What are you doing here?"

Righteous indignation boiled up. Until she remembered. She had no right for righteousness. And she had no way to bluster through, so she swallowed the snide comment that was about to come out of her mouth. "Whatever I'm doing, you've already made a case against me for breaking and entering."

He raised one eyebrow.

"That's what you call it, right?"

"More like criminal trespass." He shrugged. "And burglary."

Cherry bombs exploded inside her head. Beads of perspiration bloomed behind her ears. Sneaking into the station...she hadn't thought of it as burglary. Burglary was a *crime*.

She glanced down at the card with Stan's scrawl on it, still in her hand. Her mouth dry, she attempted, "But I'm not taking anything." And that was true. She wasn't. *Except you did snap a picture of what you're not taking,* her honest self reminded her. She shut her honest self down.

"That's a pretty damn weak explanation. We both know you plan on gathering information."

"Yes. Information." Naturally, he knew. "Okay. Burglary. Look, I'm sorry. For everything, including kicking you the other day."

"That little tap? It was no big deal."

Into the charged silence, she wondered why she shouldn't kick him again, the patronizing oaf. She kept her feet on the carpet and settled for, "I shouldn't have."

His slow blink was the sole acknowledgement that he'd heard her.

She, who never let silence get on her nerves, rushed on. "I guess you could charge me with assault, maybe even battery on top of the breaking and entering and burglary."

When he still didn't move a muscle or seem to take a breath, she said, "I'm going to ask you for a favor."

He stared.

"If I promise I won't do any of it again will you think about forgetting tonight? I came here with my friend, Fern." She squeezed her hands together. "Whatever you do to me…" Visions of being thrown into the equivalent of a third-world hellhole flashed through her mind... "Please let her go. She's innocent."

At last his face lost the cop look. "Innocent?"

To think her impetuosity was going to affect Fern, maybe cause her to lose the job she hadn't started yet, it hurt. "Okay, not innocent. You've seen me, but you haven't seen her so you can pretend she's not here."

"I can't do that."

"Why not?"

"Because you just told me she is."

While she'd been busy not letting anything stand in the way of her finding out about The Committee, she'd forgotten about that thing called consequences. "Still," she went on, "You could forget I told you. Maybe your ears got clogged up and..."

He raised both eyebrows. "My ears got...?" His voice trailed off, too, no doubt too stunned to finish whatever it was he was going to say.

Which was when the camel's back broke. All the frustration she'd been feeling since the Petrocellis marched into the building—was it days or years ago—boiled over. "Yes. You can. If you wanted to."

She jabbed a finger up into his face. "What happened the other day was terrible. I'm talking about how the sale of the station went down. That's why I'm here. To see if I can find something that tells me it shouldn't have taken place. You ought to be sympathetic. If whoever you work for suddenly decided to fire you, you'd be pretty ticked off. You'd wonder what you were going to do to replace your salary, wouldn't you?"

"That's not about to happen. I'm in a union."

"You're in a—" Hitting him right here and now was probably not a good idea because... "Will you finally just say it? Are you a cop or not!"

"Yeah, I'm a cop. I work here in Fort Lee. Didn't you know?"

She'd been right. He was a cop. And she reminded herself for the hundredth time these last few days that she did *not* like cops. Except there was this thing about *this* cop... She slapped a hand against her forehead...maybe to jar her brain out of its brainlessness... "Idiot me. I should have known. Because of the attitude." She pointed at his hip. "And that big bad gun you wear like it's a piece of jewelry."

"It's not jewelry."

She ignored him and rushed on. "The Petrocellis are the kind of useless human beings who set out every day to destroy businesses and the people who work at them, all in the name of profit."

He shrugged. "Not my concern. Unless they break the law."

With her hip, Tootsie slammed shut the drawer, the one in which she'd found nothing to help her. She stomped out from behind the desk. He followed. She whirled on him and held up a hand to stop him from spouting more of his I-don't-do-gray-area cop talk. "Maybe there's no law against what the Petrocellis did to us, but there should be. And you!" She pointed at him again. "I can't keep calling you Black Windbreaker inside my head. What is your name, anyway?"

"Inside your...?" He rubbed a hand across his. "You call me Black Windbreaker?"

She gazed at him from the top of said head down to his black boots. "What else should I call you? It's your color palette."

A look of confusion remained on his face. "My name might be a good place to start."

She wanted to scream. She could. The sound would tear walls down, break glass. Maybe even break his head. "Is this you being your typical dense cop self that you won't tell me just so you can keep me twirling in the wind?"

His face lightened to something that looked like—could it be, considering what she knew of him—humor? "It's DiLorenzo. Steve."

"Well, DiLorenzo, Steve." Her chest heaved with the pace of her racing heart. "I want to see if there's something here that happened wrong and if the gods are on my side, get back the jobs for everyone who worked at WCLS. That's why you should let Fern go. Me, too."

He rubbed the top of his scalp. "I'm sure there's somebody out there who can follow your logic."

"So...?" She took a couple of breaths to keep from combusting on the spot. Or from having a heart attack.

"I wasn't supposed to be here tonight," he said. "Except my guy called in sick. I shouldn't be doing this but I'm going to let you go."

"You will?" She canted her head to one side, as if that would help her look inside his denseness and see if he meant it.

"Yeah, because I'm tired of standing here arguing with a drama queen."

One teensy part of her wanted to call him on that. But no. She was getting away scot-free. And so was Fern. She gave him a smile. Some might have said it was genuine. Maybe even she would have said it was genuine. "Thank you. Thank you so very much."

He got a disgusted look on his face. "Don't thank me. Just do me a favor. Stay out of this building. You need to make a case against the Petrocellis? Do it some other way that doesn't involve me. And let's hope we don't run into each other anytime soon."

"Don't worry. There's no way I want to see you ever again," she snapped and knew. That wasn't a hot flash in her pants. Nope. Her pants were on fire. Because…well, yeah. She was one awesome liar.

# CHAPTER EIGHT

By the time Tootsie depressed the ignition button and the engine turned over, her hands had stopped trembling. Now, if she could control the nervous, post-danger giggles that threatened to erupt every time she thought of the weird back and forth between her and Black Windbreaker...Steve. "Well, that was special."

"You were so sure tonight was going to be a piece of cake," Fern accused.

Tootsie maneuvered out of the space she'd parked in two blocks down from the radio station. In case someone was watching. Hah! What a joke.

"At least the Petrocellis didn't install an alarm on the door." Which if they'd changed the code, they might have. She shivered. What a dunce she was that it hadn't occurred to her. Her breath puffed out in the frigid air inside the car. "Still, tonight was a good night."

One corner of Fern's mouth curled up in a sly smile. "What made it a good night for me was watching you come down the hallway with that hunky man. That is once I got over wanting to pee myself. He looked yummy hot tonight."

That man kept showing up where she didn't want him to, and stopping her from getting to the bottom of what had gone down with the sale of WCLS. And every time after, he left her in a farklempt state. "His name is Steve."

Tootsie proceeded to tell Fern about the empty folder with the word, Committee, on the tab, and the other with the name Comstock on it and its 5x8 card.

"So?"

Tootsie slowed to a stop at a traffic light just turning red. "Look, I could be wrong. It occurred to me that those two folders were empty because the new guy started to go through them to get rid of content he doesn't need."

"Maybe." Fern adjusted her seatbelt around her middle. "So did you take that card with you? All the years I worked for Stan, I got good at reading his scribble."

"Black Windbreaker made me put the card back." As Marge's engine hummed, she added, "But he didn't confiscate my phone and I took a picture. My phone's in my coat pocket."

After slipping the phone out, Fern scrolled to the picture. There was a prolonged silence while she turned the phone sideways and then back again. "When you took the picture, you shined some light on it so I can't read a thing."

Damn cow and its flashlight on steroids.

Fern sighed. Tootsie did, too.

They sat in silence until the light turned green and Tootsie accelerated. "I still want to know who Elizabeth Comstock is or was. Is that too much to ask?"

"Wait." Fern did some more tapping. "I'm googling her." Another silence, and then she said, "There are a lot of Elizabeth Comstocks, but most of them just have a Facebook page."

"How do we find out who Stan's Elizabeth Comstock is?"

"You know who might know?"

"Who?" Tootsie maneuvered around a car parked too far away from the curb.

"Angie."

Though her nerves had still not settled, Tootsie couldn't help a little grin. "You mean our very own Angie of the Seven Veils?"

Fern snorted a laugh. "I'll never forget the look on peoples' faces when she began to shuck those big, long scarves. I thought Robert would have a conniption fit."

Tootsie shook her head. "He was the one who said to celebrate Richard Strauss' birthday we should all come in dressed as characters from one of his operas. Then, when Angie decided to strip off her scarves…veils…like she was Salome dancing for Herod –in the opera—and was about to get naked, it suddenly wasn't okay?"

Fern snickered. "I mean, she was wearing clothes underneath."

Tootsie made a sound of scorn. "What a big prude, Robert is."

"I think he was freaked because Angie is 80 and he was afraid he'd go blind if he saw her you-know-whats and her other you-know-whats."

"I should call her."

"If she'll take your call, I'll be surprised," retorted Fern.

"Yes. Considering how I didn't say Robert, don't do it, don't fire her, and worse, don't have her escorted from the building like she was a thief. Angie has every reason to think I'm as bad as Robert."

"Speaking of people who have thoughts about you, I wonder what the Petrocellis think."

"Hah. If they thought I was in their new manager's office tonight, they would like me less than they liked me the other day. But they're not going to find out. Remember, Black Windbreaker—did I tell you his name is Steve—said he wouldn't tell."

"I hope you're right."

"I am right. In fact—"

"In fact, what?"

"Nothing."

But it was not nothing, and she saw it in her dreams. It was the partially open door to the on-air studio she'd noticed as the two of them, escorted by Black Windbreaker, walked past it on their way out of the building. And her mind, filled with Black Windbreaker, hadn't noticed. Until later, when her mind was clear of him and she realized that open door could mean the jock had heard or worse, seen them. It was the "could" that had her not able to sleep…until her phone rang at 7:01 a.m. Bleary-eyed, she stared at it, because of course she'd just fallen asleep. "Hello?"

"You're home? I was going to leave a message but now I don't have to."

"You have such keen powers of observation, Arlo." She put the phone on speaker, laid it on her pillow, pulled the covers up to her neck, and closed her eyes. "What's up?"

"I wanted to tell you we're leaving for Marbella. That's in Spain."

"Thanks for confirming it didn't move to France."

"No need for sarcasm. We made a last-minute decision to go. Because of the snowstorm coming."

"Are you taking the jet?" One of the first things Arlo had done when he collected his lottery money was buy a fractional ownership of a jet that was based at Teterboro. One wouldn't want to go to an actual commercial airport, like Newark, would one? "Silly me. Of course you are."

"Yeah, um…"

Tootsie was running out of patience. "You called me for a reason and it wasn't about Marbella."

"I did. I wanted to confess. I was a rat to you the other day. Making like you're old or something. Fifty is not that old."

"That's good. Because you're over fifty and I'm sure you don't want Raquel to think of *you* as old."

He ignored the shot. "And I wanted to tell you something I should have said, instead. Our marriage, it wasn't that bad."

"It wasn't that good, either."

She bit her lip. She could have left that unsaid. In his clumsy way, Arlo was trying to be nice.

He cleared his throat. "If I had to do it over again, I might not have asked you for the divorce. We might still be married."

"C'mon Arlo," she said, voice gentled. "You know you wanted to get as far away as you could from me and my managing ways."

"Hmm. You know I think you're right. I forgot how you were always pushing me to do one thing or another. I hated that."

She rolled over and planted her face in her pillow. The phone jiggled. She reached one hand out from beneath the covers and steadied it. "That's true," she said, her voice muffled. Arlo, she remembered too clearly, wasn't into doing things. Unless they were for him.

"So I guess I'm not going to be sorry I said you

were old the other day." He laughed.

Tootsie rolled onto her back. Her eyes flipped open and she stared up at the ceiling. That *there*. That was one of the many reasons why she was glad Raquel was the current Mrs. Goldberg.

Arlo must have realized her silence wasn't an invitation to continue. "Um, and I just wanted to let you know what we're doing."

"Nice of you," she grumbled. "Oh, and a word of advice when you pack?"

"Yes?" The caution in his voice said Arlo knew she was about to say something he wasn't going to like.

"Take cotton briefs. It's hot in Marbella. You know you get chafed. You don't want to be on vacation with a heat rash. Bye." And she cut the call before he could say another, single thing she did *not* want to hear.

She threw herself out of bed and marched back and forth around her bedroom, now fully awake...and mad. *What if we were still married?* "Oh, like I want to consider that," she gritted.

Stomping downstairs, she drew up to plonk herself down on the second step from the bottom. She could have predicted that their marriage would end in divorce if she'd been thinking straight when she said 'I do' at their big, fat Jewish wedding.

She'd married Arlo on a rebound of pain, two months to the day after her grandmother died. It took her mere moments in time after that to know it was a mistake. They were oil and water. She was the energizer bunny. He waited around for ships that would never sail. She told it like it was. He spoke in passive aggressive tongues. Worst of all, he loved acting the man of the house, a la 1950, and insisted things go his way…and after a while she had no energy to argue with him. So she swallowed…and let things pass…and didn't divorce him when she should have. And then *he* divorced *her*.

She pressed both hands to her head. Like that would keep her brains inside her skull. "Why, why, why? I wasted half a lifetime with that man." She spun around to stare at her curio cabinet and all the collectibles in it…and especially the blue vase that sat on the top shelf. It wasn't fine porcelain. It didn't measure up to her Royal Doulton princesses, or her Meissen monkeys, or her Limoges hand-painted boxes. But it was the most beautiful thing in the curio cabinet…because it had been her grandmother's.

Her lips tightened. And hadn't Arlo made fun of the vase? Hadn't he said she should get rid of it? Compared to all the rest of the so-called nice things in the cabinet, the vase was common, nothing more than trash.

Her blood heated. "Arlo Goldberg, I need you out of my life and I'm not waiting another moment!"

She jumped to her feet and headed toward the mudroom where she'd placed her boots on a rubber mat, her knock-around jacket on a hook, and a rake against a wall. She'd used It a couple of months ago, and never stowed it back in the garage. She threw on the jacket, slipped her bare feet into the boots, hefted the rake, and threw open the back door.

A gust of frigid air tore into her. She looked up at the sky, where the sun was showing its anemic winter face. She sniffed. There was the smell of snow in the air. Okay, so it was going to snow. Even Arlo could be right now and then. She looked out at the yard where she was about to put an end to one of his wrongs.

Rake clutched in her hand, she stepped outside and looked around at the sculpted beds that formed the perimeter of their property. She'd wanted lots of flowers in those beds. Arlo had said no. He was allergic to gardening and sweat, so his solution had been Pachysandra, a wonderful ground cover. It would take care of itself. So he didn't have to.

She tramped up to the nearest bed, her feet sliding around in her boots. For a fleeting second, she thought maybe she should go back inside and get dressed. But no. She was on a mission and there'd be no pausing for any reason, including frostbitten toes. She raised the rake over her head and brought it down with as much violence as she could manage on the nearest Pachysandra clump. The soil resisted her efforts. Well, yeah. It was frozen. But that didn't matter to her. The Pachysandra had to go.

She went at it, clump by clump. She began to sweat. She was hot, not temperature hot. She was hot, she was mad, and she wasn't going to take Arlo anymore. She chopped like she was removing heads, obstructions, and the fury she felt having wasted all those years with that worm of a man.

"Vengeance is mine," she ground out, between her teeth. "Die, die," she panted, screaming Arlo's name inside her head. She paused and then attacked a larger than most clump. "And you too, Robert. You too, Slasher Twins. You too, Elwood." For good measure she added, "You too, Lenny, for scaring ten years out of my life."

The mutilated fruits of her labor were piling up all around her, when she paused because she'd heard something besides the sound of the Sanger kids' laughter from the other side of the palisade fence, the one Arlo had insisted they put up once the money from the lottery came in. For privacy and protection.

"Hello?"

"Toots? Where are you?"

Fern.

Tootsie stood. "I'm in the back."

"I'm coming."

In a second, Fern appeared with a large, square packing box in her arms. She was leaning back for balance, the box, either heavy, unwieldy, or both. She was dressed for the day in a menopause blue, three-quarter length Michelin Man style jacket, with navy sweats belling out beneath. She stepped her way in white sneakers through the clumps and dropped her box at Tootsie's feet. It landed with a whomp.

Gazing around, Fern said, "Don't you think it's a

little early to prepare the back forty for spring planting?"

Tootsie leaned on the rake. "Nah. You can never plant rutabaga too early."

Fern made a sound of irritation. "I hate rutabaga."

"I've never had one." Tootsie pointed the rake at the box. "What's in there?"

"You remember all those questions you had about those two folders you found in Robert's office?" She touched the toe of her white shoe to the box. "I think I found some of the answers right in here."

Tootsie wanted to see what was in that box, but before she did, her first order of business was bringing her body temperature up above the hypothermia line by taking a very hot shower, getting dressed, and drying her hair to reduce her chances of dying of exposure to the elements. Coming back into the kitchen where she'd left Fern, she said, "Before we get started looking, do you need a cup of coffee?"

"Nah. I'm spreading out my caffeine intake."

As the brewer spit and coughed and coffee trickled into her cup, Tootsie said, "Okay, what's the scoop?"

Fern had set the box down on the table between them. "I had this at home. It's stuff I made copies of over the years. I've got some of Stan's obituaries here.

Don't ask me why."

"I know why. You admired him."

"The thing is the obits made me remember him talking about how he got into radio."

"By making so much money in the real estate business that he could afford to indulge himself and buy a radio station? Yeah, *that* story."

Fern nodded. "And that's when I remembered this."

She reached in and pulled out a sheaf of papers that had been clipped together. She handed it to Tootsie. "Check this out."

Tootsie removed the paper clip. At the top of the first sheet in the pile was the word, **Minutes**. She began to read.

*Stan introduced his son Robert to The Committee. Angie objected to Stan bringing Robert to a meeting without informing them first. Stan said he hoped the members could make an exception since Robert was home for just a couple of weeks before he returned to Bhutan, where he'd been living for the last year.*

Tootsie made a face. "This sounds like Angie, objecting to nonsense."

"And here." Holding out another sheaf of papers, Fern slid them across the table. "It's some kind of document that says The Committee's purpose was to handle employee activity and relations, kind of like the human resource department we never had."

Tootsie read the first paragraph and looked up. "Here it is in black and white. The Committee has no jurisdiction over the business of the radio station."

"Like you said yesterday when we were talking in Starbucks." Fern's lips turned down in disappointment. "Dead end."

"Yeah, I guess so." Tootsie got up to freshen her coffee. "Are you sure I can't get you anything?"

"No. We have to let everyone else know."

"Except..." Tootsie held up one finger. "What's the thing with Elizabeth Comstock?"

Fern put everything back in the box. "Tootsie, seriously. Leave it alone."

Tootsie wanted to, but something in her rebelled. Things still felt...what was the word...unsettled. Yeah, that was it. Unsettled. Like there was a piece of popcorn lodged in between her back teeth and dental floss couldn't quite get it. Rising, she took her cup to the sink. "Don't worry about letting everyone know. I'll do that."

As she washed her cup out and set it in the dishwasher, she came to a conclusion. "I'm calling Elwood and asking him if he knows who Elizabeth Comstock is."

Fern rolled her eyes. "You just won't give up, will you?"

Tootsie keyed in Elwood's number and waited for him to answer or for voicemail to kick in. When it did, she began. "Hey, it's me, Tootsie. Again. I have a question. Who's Elizabeth Comstock?"

Putting her hand over the speaker, Tootsie leaned toward Fern and whispered, "An innocent question, right?"

While Fern shook her head in disgust, Tootsie continued. "Anyway, Elwood, if you can just tell me who she is, that will be awesome. Well, that's it. Have a good day."

Tootsie came back to the table to sit. "Do you think Elwood will call me back? My sense is he won't."

"There are a whole bunch of things you've been doing these last few days that don't make sense. Calling him is one of them, and oh by the way, you do know that curiosity has killed more than one cat."

Tootsie made a scoffing sound. "Don't be ridiculous. Making a phone call won't kill me. Besides, if I was a cat I'd be entitled to eight more."

Except a shiver that stood up the hair follicles on her scalp said she'd given herself a ayinhora. She tamped them down because no way were her follicles going to keep her from doing what she still believed needed doing.

"Instead of looking for something you probably won't find, why don't you figure out what's next for you. You know, the next chapter in your life."

"Well, I could look for another job, but the thought of working for someone else, who might be like Robert, doesn't appeal to me."

"Do something else, then. Something different."

"Like what?"

"You could form your own company."

"Doing what?"

"I don't know, maybe helping people find jobs, kind of like you helped me find mine."

Tootsie made a face. "We talked about this already. It doesn't speak to me."

"Well, if you're not going into business, how about just enjoying yourself? You could learn how to play mah-jongg."

Mah-jongg… She forced a laugh. Francine played mah-jongg. She'd been playing mah-jongg the night Grandma Hannah died. "I don't think so."

"Okay, so no mah-jongg. What about becoming a volunteer? You know…do good deeds. In Judaism, don't you guys call that tikkun olam?"

"Tikkun olam doesn't mean good deeds, exactly. It's more repairing the world."

"There you go. Find some good organization, where you can volunteer, and start repairing. Or how about working on repairing your relationship with Francine?"

"You want me to hug it out with Francine?" Tootsie had never forgiven her mother for not getting up from her game that night because all the little mah-jongg tiles, the bams, the cracks, and the dragons were more important to her than checking to see if her own mother was okay that night because Tootsie was still stuck in jail and couldn't. "That's not going to happen."

"All right, then. None of the above." Fern stood.

"I came over for two things. To bring you the box, and tell you I'm flying to Arizona with Marc Antonio later on today to scout the location for the music festival."

"As long as you get out before the big snowstorm that's supposed to be coming."

Fern dismissed the storm with a wave of one hand. "One of those models the weather people are always spouting about has us getting 1-3 inches, which stops nothing from moving, to another model that says 12-18. Truth is no one knows what we're going to get. Unless the airline calls and tells us the flight is canceled, I'm on my way to the airport."

Tootsie walked outside with Fern, waved, and watched her drive off to her new and improved life working with Marc Antonio. "Good for you," she murmured, feeling a little melancholy because she was stuck, and she didn't know what she was stuck on.

She started back in the house, wandered in to the kitchen. Reaching into the refrigerator, she checked the contents for a snack. There were no snacks. There wasn't anything else, either. She closed the doors and folded her arms across her chest.

Fern had brought it up, the business of fixing the long-standing rift she had with her mother. This time her brain didn't laugh. But it did raise its hand and point out that with time moving on—as it had a habit of doing—if her mother kicked the bucket before they could straighten things out between them, Tootsie would feel guilty that she hadn't tried.

Of all the things she thought about doing, this was not it. "Maybe another day," she muttered. She looked at Fern's box. "Maybe another day for you, too," she added. Glancing outside at the yard, with its piles of Pachysandra, she had a thought that she should go back outside and finish the job she'd started. Or not.

What to do… No matter what she decided, she wasn't about to stay in her house. She'd had enough of her own company. With a sudden spurt of energy, she put on her coat, and just like that, she and Marge were driving into town. Because at last she knew what she could do. Pay her parking ticket the old-fashioned way. In person. And she'd make it a two-fer. Pay the ticket and give Neal Morgan, Glen Allyn's mayor, a piece of her mind about the lack of convenient parking in town. At least she could say that would be fun.

After that, she'd hit the Stop & Shop. Since the threat of snow was real, she'd have to hope the shelves hadn't been cleared out because everyone in town was expecting the zombie apocalypse.

Just as she found a parking spot by the courthouse—a legal one—a couple of snowflakes lazed to the ground. She checked the weather app on her phone to see how many inches were expected. The model that had suggested they'd get 1 to 3 inches was now saying 8-10. She was definitely going to Stop & Shop after this.

Stepping inside the courtroom, the first thing she

noted was the crowd. Some people had seated themselves on folding chairs set up on one side of the room. Waiting for the clerk to make her appearance was a line of people on the other side, paying fines, or maybe getting an absentee ballot for the next election, or a permit to put an addition on a house.

Shunning the line, deciding she could afford to wait for it to thin out in spite of what snow was coming, Tootsie found herself a place to sit on one of the folding chairs. She sensed more than saw someone sit down next to her. She sighed and thought about getting up to find another place to sit. But it was too late.

"What are you here for, Toots?" Helene Benson leaned toward Tootsie on a wave of Calvin Klein's Eternity. "Don't tell me it's because you got another parking ticket."

How bad was it that Helene, an acquaintance and one whose presence Tootsie never sought, knew about her relationship with Glen Allyn's police. "I did. They give me so many tickets, I'm a line item in the town budget."

Helene pursed her lips. "That's terrible. I wouldn't want to be a line item."

"I was kidding."

"Oh." Helene didn't smile. Which was when Tootsie remembered Helene was not in possession of a keen sense of humor.

"Aren't you afraid they're going to take away your license?"

Tootsie couldn't tell Helene that at this point in the weird game she and Brian played that they were entertaining each other. It would take too much explaining.

Tootsie held up the ticket. "I pay them right away so they leave me alone."

"The cops in this town..." Helene shook her head. "I swear they've got some sixth sense thing going. They always know when your meter runs out."

There was a time when Tootsie thought about getting a non-descript blue or gray car to replace fire-engine red Marge. But then Brian might not have been able to spot her so easily.

"Speak of the devil. Here's Brian Stoddard, and he's with..."

"Who?" Tootsie swiveled in her seat to see Brian and whoever he was with. But she couldn't tell because Helene was blocking her line of sight.

Helene fanned herself. "He is...oh my God, there aren't words. I have never seen anyone so...oh damn, he just turned away, but girlfriend, that is one smokin' hot man."

Well, yeah. Now that Tootsie had come halfway out of her seat, she could see what Helene was all fatootsed about. Or at least she could see his back. Inside the black jacket worn by the man Brian was with were some amazing broad shoulders that tapered down to a narrow waist, nicely proportioned narrow hips, and to go with the package, a more than perfect tight ass. She savored the moment for a moment, admiring Mr. Ohmigod-let-me-salivate-all-over-you. Until he turned around and she had another kind of moment.

It was Black Windbreaker. *What was he doing here?* "Who?"

She must have said that out loud. "She cleared her throat hoping to get some saliva in her mouth so she could speak. "Just someone I met recently."

Helene leaned in and cupped a hand around her mouth. "That is one delicious man. If I were you, I'd take advantage of knowing him and put myself in a position of *really* knowing him." She poked Tootsie on the arm. "If you know what I mean."

Tootsie drew back "Are you crazy? He's a cop."

One eyebrow raised, Helene said, "And your point would be cops have different equipment?"

"My point is he would be the last man on the face of the earth whose equipment I would want to make use of." She flushed. "That's not what I meant…about equipment."Helene shrugged. "If you don't have dibs on him, do you mind introducing us? I'm pretty sure his equipment meets my standards."

Tootsie bristled. "I don't plan on having a conversation with him anytime soon."

"If that's the story you're sticking to…" The up and down look Helene gave Tootsie said it all…as far as Helene was concerned, Tootsie was being territorial. Standing, Helene moved a couple of rows back.

Tootsie was not sorry to see her go because she

needed to be alone to think. Had she just reacted like she was…ohmigod…jealous? Possessive? Of all men, Black Windbreaker? "You are losing it, Toots," she gritted, and unbuttoned her coat.

Somewhere, someone laughed. From across the crowded room her gaze met Brian's. She squeaked. Big mistake. Because now that he knew she was here, uber-friendly Brian would come across the room to say hello. Could she hope he'd leave the guy she didn't want to say hello to behind?

No such luck. Not when Brian leaned toward her nemesis, said something, and Black Windbreaker looked her way. Which was when she knew. All the prep in the world couldn't have helped her for what came next. When he turned toward her, he brought the smile he'd hit Brian with. And she saw what Helene saw: a man whose bones she wanted to jump.

Before she could gasp into her turtleneck collar, the smile went away, he went deadpan, and he became the cop, again. That was reassuring. Because the thought that had careened into her mind, the one about jumping his bones, had scared her half to death. Because why would she want to find out what the man who'd been driving her nuts, looked like under all that black clothing?

Brian started in her direction. He motioned for Black Windbreaker to come with him. She groaned and then began a prayer that she'd be able to make it through the next few minutes. She lifted one hand in a half-assed wave, and smiled in an equally half-assed way. Curling her fingers in on the palm of her hand, she rested it on her knee and waited for their arrival.

"What's this, Tootsie?" Brian's cheeks were wreathed in smiles. "You decided paying your ticket online wouldn't be as good as paying it in person? How old-fashioned."

Black Windbreaker's gaze hadn't left her face, not from the moment he and Brian had started toward her. "Tootsie, huh. Nice name your mom gave you."

"Thank you." She gave him the death glare. "I was named after the movie. Or the candy. Take your pick."

She flicked her attention back to Brian. "You don't have to introduce us. We've met."

On a raised eyebrow, Brian said, "Sheesh, Toots. Steve's a cop and you acknowledge him? Where exactly did this amazing meeting happen?"

Before Steve could say something she most definitely didn't want Brian to know, Tootsie said, "Your friend, Steve and I met in a place where you would never think we would meet." She fixed Black Windbreaker…Steve…with a look that said if you have anything else to say, keep it to yourself.

He raised one eyebrow.

Brian looked at one and then the other. "What am I missing?" He held up a hand and backed away. "Don't bother answering. I need to see the judge."

As Brian made himself scarce, and as Tootsie felt her inner pilot light come on, Black Windbreaker—

she had to stop calling him that—Steve angled his chin toward the chair Helene had just vacated. "Do you mind?"

He'd already upended her day by showing up where she hadn't expected him. What difference would it make if he stood or sat. "Knock yourself out."

"Thanks." He turned the chair around so they were knee to knee. Straddling it and sitting, he gave her a considering look. Not that she knew what he was considering.

What was with this man and his faces? And yeah, his silences. There he sat, looking at her, forcing her to look at him. The Tootsie who had spent 30 years walking away from challenges that could be painful thought it was best to get up and leave. But that would mean not manning up to his stare. Newly-awakened Tootsie—at least the newly-awakened Tootsie from Monday and the brawl at the radio station—was not about to walk away. "What's up with you?!"

"Nothing." He gazed around the room. "Maybe nothing."

She cast her eyes upward, as if seeking an answer from a higher authority than the one sitting in front of her. "Choices, choices…What's the best way to answer that? Should I roll my eyes? Should I shake my head *while* rolling my eyes? Should I ask you if English is your first language?"

She leaned forward and fixed him with a stare

filled with every bit of the frustration she'd dealt with since he'd shown up in her life and seemed set on making her crazy. "It's either nothing or not nothing. There is no such thing as maybe nothing."

He pursed his lips. "I'm not sure about that."

"What are you?" Little sparks flowered inside her head. "The arbiter of all things grammar?"

He gave her a one shoulder shrug. "What are you here for?"

"Like Brian said. To pay a parking ticket."

*I do not have the hots for this man... I do not have the hots for him...*

She willed away that horrendous thought her brain cooked up. But ignoring how her panties were melting and her nipples cutting through the lace of her bra? Not so easy. Hurriedly, she said, "No breaking and entering, no burglary. And since I saw you, I haven't graduated to manslaughter or serial murder, which is no doubt a disappointment to you since then your dream could come true and you could arrest me."

"You'd be wrong about that."

The unreadable look he gave her sent a shiver snaking down her spine. It told her not to ask him what he meant. "Well then, let's leave it how we left it last night."

"This morning. It was after midnight when you broke into the building."

She closed her eyes. Slowly. And then opened them again. "Idiot me. What could I have been thinking? Here I was imagining the earth had rotated and we were living in Central Time."

Again, with a little inscrutable smile. "So you're paying it?" He pointed at the ticket which she held folded in her hand.

She rounded on him. "Didn't I just say so? And, anyway, I don't think I want to have a conversation with you about this parking ticket."

"I wasn't thinking about this one." Again, he pointed at the ticket.

Tootsie had no idea what he meant by 'this' one. With him and his mysterious smile up in her face, she couldn't remember what made her think it was a good idea to pay her ticket in person. She brandished the ticket at him. "I was going to plead guilty but now I think I won't. There are too few legal parking places in this town and the cops are just waiting to pounce on you. It's their quota."

He ignored the quota thing and took the ticket from her hand. "You're going to plead not guilty to this when from what I see here it's obvious you're guilty?"

She snatched the ticket from his hand. "Who are you? Inspector Javert?"

A frown knit his brow. "Who?"

"Oh, for Pete's sake." She jumped up and stormed over to where the clerk was, for the moment all alone, having dispensed with judgment against the most recently guilty. She grabbed her checkbook—how lucky she was to find it since she'd been paying everything online for years—slapped it open, and began to write. She pushed the check toward the clerk, and said, "I think that's all I need to give you." The woman thanked her, and Tootsie turned to exit the building.

And walked right into Steve.

She took a quick step back before they could touch. Which would be a bad thing considering her current state of mind. "What! Can't you bear to be away from me?"

A rueful smile crossed his lips. "It's unfortunate."

Words caught in her throat. What did *that* mean?

Since they'd met—mere days ago that felt like eons—he'd been speaking in cryptic soundbites. Now *this*. Though she didn't want to give him credit for it, it meant something…something a little too unsettling for her to consider.

"I'm going now, Javert. If you have anything to say to me, tell Brian. Better yet, keep it to yourself."

Almost at once, he did this thing where his two eyebrows come together like a unibrow. Ick.

She slapped her hands on her hips. "Have you ever heard of wax?"

The unibrow went away. "Yeah. Candles."

*Blockhead.* "Forget it." She charged for the door, and then whirled around. He stood where she'd left him. "Are we done? Are you ready to stop showing up in my life?"

She gave him a mock salute. "This is where I tell you to have a nice day. And sayonara!"

# CHAPTER NINE

Stepping outside the courthouse, Tootsie took a breath. There was something about this man… All she had to do was look at him, and her blood pressure climbed through the roof. Why? He was just a man. Oh yeah, right. He was just a man like Hurricane Sandy had just been a little rain and wind.

She stared out at the town's quadrangle, its paths, old-time lamps, with gazebo in the center. She felt a presence behind her. She wheeled around, sure of who she was going to see. And was right. The man of her dreams. Or nightmares. "What now?"

He stood there in his parka, which he hadn't bothered to zip up. Probably because neither cold, wind, nor snow kept him from showing up for the purpose of tormenting her. He watched her with a strange intensity which she couldn't compute.

He looked like he was about to say something.

But never did because Genene Cohen rushed out of the courthouse and around him. "Tootsie, oh, good. I caught you."

And good, though she didn't know it, that she caught the situation before Black Windbreaker could say whatever was on his mind that would send Tootsie's heat index soaring again. "Hey, Genene."

"I just wanted to say how sorry I am that your radio station got taken over. I guess now you'll have time to do other things with your life. It would be great if you'd get involved with something in town."

Tootsie resisted rolling her eyes. Genene was a nice woman. She happened to be the assistant mayor and worked in the same sphere with Neal. Which Tootsie would never hold against her. Besides which, right now she didn't need to be caught up in the backwash Black Windbreaker seemed to create anytime Tootsie saw him.

Giving him the side eye—where he stood practically touching her—to Genene she said, "You've been trying to get me on one town committee or another since our boys had their bar-mitzvahs together all those years ago. By now you should know that isn't my thing."

Though when her grandmother had been alive, it might have been.

"You'd be such an asset, though." Hunching her shoulders, Genene rubbed her long-sleeved-sweatered arms. "Well, you can't say I don't keep on trying."

A fierce gust of wind blew in Tootsie's face. She

shivered and pointed at the courthouse door. "I appreciate the fact that you do. Right now it would be a good idea for you to go back inside before you freeze to death."

"We're closing up. Because of the snowstorm." Genene hopped from one foot to the other.

"How much are we supposed to get?"

"They're saying 20-24 inches, maybe more. The Nor'easter took a turn…toward us. And you know what that means."

"Yeah, more than the one to three inches and definitely more than eight to ten inches."

Genene made a face. "I hate Nor'easters. They're saying we should all take precautions because it'll be quite the storm."

So, now Tootsie had to worry not only about the storm named Black Windbreaker wreaking havoc on her insides, but she also had to worry about the storm about to wreak havoc outside. How awesome was her day?

Waving to Genene, trying to slough off her tension as she did, Tootsie started down the steps. Meanwhile no wave to Black Windbreaker was needed as he'd decided to retreat into the courthouse, for which she was grateful.

She tried, but couldn't get rid of his presence in her mind. More flakes spotted her windshield as she drove toward the supermarket and then found a parking space. And she thought of him. As she snagged a cart before some other harried shopper could…she thought of him…and growled her frustration.

Inside the store, it was bedlam. She wheeled her cart down one aisle and then the other, barely avoided getting run over by more than one person rushing about. Everyone seemed intent on filling up on supplies before the new ice age enveloped Glen Allyn and its immediate environs.

Many shelves were empty. In the bread section a couple of loaves of spelt, and a package of non-gluten rolls, stood up all alone in the corner of the lowest shelf. "I don't need bread, anyway," Tootsie muttered.

By the time she exited the store with what she'd bought—a couple of apples, a steak to grill, some veggies, and some flanken—what the Jewish world called short ribs—there was a good half inch of snow on the ground and the wind was blowing swirls of it around the street.

One of the boys who bagged at the store came loping toward her, slipping and sliding, before he righted himself. "You need help cleaning off your car?"

"Take it easy," she cautioned him. "I can get this by myself."

But he was already there. "If you give me your brush, I'll do the roof."

Which he did. After he brushed off the worst of the snow—and she'd given him a tip and a big thank you—she allowed herself a tight smile. No way Brian could give her a ticket for not having removed the snow from her roof. Or Black Windbreaker, either. And then she warned herself to stop thinking about Black Windbreaker.

Later, her groceries stowed in the fridge and pantry, Marge snug as a bug in her garage, she stood, cup of coffee in hand, and stared out the window, amazed. The wind was blowing the snow sideways, and the two cars parked across the street were just white shapes against a blinding white background.

As she stood there, the sky getting darker, a black, four-door sedan ventured up the street, idling for a minute near her driveway. And then it pulled in and parked under the limbs of her neighbor, Ben Hart's huge oak tree, which stood at the end of their side- by-side driveways, its stately, old branches over both.

Today of all days, someone decided to visit? She didn't recognize the car. But when the door opened, she had no problem recognizing the visitor…if she could call Black Windbreaker a visitor.

The hairs stood up on the back of her neck.

How did he know where she lived? No, wait! He was a cop. He knew everything. He probably knew her phone's ring tone was from the second movement of Beethoven's *Pathetique* Sonata.

She rushed into the kitchen and put her cup down on the counter. And then she rushed back into the front hallway to wait. Her eyes landed on the old curio cabinet where she kept all her porcelain memories and fixed on her grandmother's turquoise-blue vase, with its amateur-like bird design. For luck.

*Luck?*

When the doorbell rang, she took a deep breath and opened the door. A fierce swirl of snow blew in to settle on the gray slate floor of her foyer.

He looked to his right and then to his left, which was strange, as if he didn't want anyone to notice him standing on her doorstep. Except *she* noticed him. No matter what he did, she *always* noticed him, and how bad was that?

Bad or good, whatever. She still stepped aside. "Do you want to come in? It's too cold to be standing out in this weather."

More snow came in with him. "I would have done this at the courthouse, but I thought it would be better if I came here to give it to you, instead." He reached inside his jacket and pulled out a paper. "Here."

It was folded vertically. She opened it flat. It didn't take more than a couple of blinks for her to figure out it was an arrest warrant. For her. For criminal trespass.

Folding it up again, she said, her voice all normal toned, "I thought you weren't going to arrest me."

"The jock saw you when you were walking back out of the radio station. He called his boss." He paused. "Who called his boss, Jim Petrocelli."

How amazing. A whole conversation. Almost normal. Odd, the way her head swung upwards while her body remained anchored in place. Odder too, how the papers she was holding made a snicking sound as they met the granite tile of her foyer at the same time she headed in the same direction.

"Hey." He was a quick-moving blur. "Don't you pass out on me." He nabbed her by her upper arms.

How weird and tinny his voice sounded.

"I'm not passing out."

"Uh huh."

He steered her into the living room and eased her down on the micro-suede cushions of her sofa. He sat down next to her and, with one big hand, gently—it was weird to imagine him doing anything gently—pushed her head down between her knees.

The spots that filled her vision receded, though her skin felt clammy. "You don't have to do this. Unless this is you having me assume the position."

The hand stopped for a beat. "Anybody ever tell you you've got a mouth?"

Arlo had. Her mother had. "No."

"People in your life must be deaf."

Ha ha. He'd made a funny. The hand began to soothe her again, and ohmigod, pure rapture. He told her not to close her eyes? Too bad. She was closing them for savoring purposes. But even savoring had to have a time limit. Which was when she flipped up her eyelids and saw what she had on her feet. Fuzzy socks. She couldn't go to jail in fuzzy socks. She pressed up against his hand. He shifted away, almost, but still hovered. In case she fell, she supposed. Her heart gave a little lurch at that small kindness.

She stood, taking care not to overbalance. "What should I do now?"

He stood, too, towering over her. She had this strange feeling that it would be oh so nice to wind her arms around his waist and lay her head on his chest.

"You need to come with me," he said.

Okay, so no winding her arms around his waist. Or any other kind of touching.

Outside her big bay window, she had a clear view of his police issue cop car crouched in her driveway, dark, solemn, seriously official, altogether threatening. It already had a dusting of snow on it. A heavy dusting.

She flicked a glance at him, the man who was going to put her in a cement room with a hard leather bench, a dirty toilet in the corner and metal bars on the door. Note to self, her brain opined. Take along a box of antiseptic wipes.

She headed for the kitchen. If she could stay in motion, he wouldn't be able to handcuff her. That made sense, right?

"I need a glass of water." Her mouth said, Gobi Desert dry. "Do you want one? A soda? Maybe a cup of coffee or tea?"

"Tootsie. We need to go."

He'd called her by her first name. She'd think about that later. When she was in jail. Grabbing two cups out of the cabinet, she stuck one under the sink's instant hot water spigot, filled it halfway, and stuck a teabag in to steep for herself. Then she shoved a coffee pod into her brewer. "Hot drinks are so important on days like this, aren't they? Do you take milk? Sugar?"

He shook his head and sighed. "Black is good."

She had a reprieve for however long it took the coffee maker to do its thing…and then for him to drink his drink.

When the brewer was finished brewing—too soon—she handed him the cup, their fingers brushing. She hadn't meant to touch him. It was startling. Just like last time. But she drew back because she wondered what it would feel like when those same fingers cinched handcuffs around her wrists. With a shudder, she said, "I knew you'd take your coffee black."

"You did?" He took a sip, keeping his deep, dark gaze on her.

"It's your color palette."

But then he'd stopped paying attention to her sartorial observations. He'd begun a slow turn-about, studying her kitchen, including the black and brown-striated, granite counter-topped island. He ran a hand across the surface.

"What? Are you testing for dust?"

She zipped up her lips, but it was too late. The smart-assedness was out there, and he was so right. She had a mouth.

She waited for him to tell her to step away from the cup and head out with him to his arrest mobile.

Instead, he stared upward at the rack above the island where her copper pots hung. She'd bought them after Arlo left. Because she could and because she'd wanted them. A beautiful display, she saw them through his eyes as if seeing them for the first time.

"I like a nice kitchen."

Not the words she'd expected to come out of his mouth… "You do?"

"Yeah." He stepped up to the windows, looked out past her deck to the back yard. "You might want to call your gardener. You have one, right? He left piles of weeds everywhere out there."

What was all this commentary from him…a way for him to pass the time until they could go? Her feelings about him being here in her kitchen…did she like it? She shouldn't. But she did. She was so confused. But she still wouldn't tell him about Arlo's Pachysandra and her useless attempt making like she was her own therapist.

Together, they sipped in silence.

"You know, you've got to decide what you're going to do. I can't wait forever."

He hadn't even finished his coffee and he was talking about her trip to the jailhouse. "I don't know what to do," she fretted.

"Why don't you discuss it with your husband?"

"I'm divorced."

"Call your attorney, then. Or go with me, and then call him. Either way, I can't afford to stand here much longer, not with this snow situation."

"Now, you're giving me options on how to get arrested? Because of the snow?"

He folded his arms across his chest and stared down at his feet. He stood without moving so long she thought he was praying. Probably for patience. But then he lifted his head and showed her his cop face. His jaw firmed, his mouth hardened. "Get your coat."

She opened her mouth on an objection when there was a tremor that shook the house, and an explosion of sound so loud that Tootsie felt it through to her bones.

Steve ducked and turned in the direction of the explosive sound.

"What the f—" He glanced once at Tootsie and then tore out of the kitchen to the front of the house. She tore after him.

By the time she caught up with him, he was standing in front of the bay window, staring out at her lawn and a solid white landscape. And then it registered.

Ben Hart's oak tree had given up the ghost and keeled over from root ball to crown, collapsing across her driveway where Steve's car was now a mass of metal and plastic parts, no longer connected, beneath a morass of broken tree limbs, branches, and twigs filled with thousands of dead, brown leaves.

They stood there, the two of them, contemplating the scene. Inside her chest, Tootsie's heart was doing cartwheels. Relief! Reprieve! The clarion call from inside the jail cell set aside for her had faded to nothing.

Tootsie glanced up at him. "What do you think? Change of plans?"

# CHAPTER TEN

He rubbed a hand across his mouth. "You have a car I can borrow?"

"To take me to jail?"

His gaze darkened.

"It's in my garage. Your car is in the driveway in front of my garage. What do you think?"

His cop face slipped, revealing an actual man who felt just the teensy, little bit of frustration...poor baby. "I need to make a call. Can I borrow a room?"

Tootsie didn't think it was a good idea to show how seriously pleased she was for the fingerprinting and mug shot business to have faded away into some indeterminate future and that it was him with the problem right now, not her. "A room?" she asked, instead. And without conscious intent, her brain leapt from innocent inquiry to double entendre about a room when why-oh-why would it occur to her since

Black Windbreaker was the last man she'd want to get a room with?

The gaping silence that followed told Tootsie she wasn't the only one whose imagination had just taken a flying leap. Seeing that touch of red crowning his cheekbones, she stuttered, "I mean I assume you need to make a phone call and you want some privacy."

He eased his cellphone out of one of those pockets men seemed to have a lot of in their jackets. He cleared his throat, like something had gotten stuck in it. "Uh, yeah. I have to call in."

She pointed toward the kitchen. "I'll stay out here while you talk to whoever you have to talk to."

He raised one eyebrow. "Yeah? And I'll have privacy with you not listening? You've got this open floor plan, no doors between any of the rooms."

A moment of wickedness rose, unbidden. "You could go upstairs to one of my bedrooms."

The red on his cheeks intensified, and he backed toward the kitchen. "That's okay. I'm good."

As he walked away, she braced one hand on the wall, her knees suddenly weak. What had just happened?

This man, *this cop*, should not be occupying so much of her head's bandwidth. But he had…since the moment she'd seen him, sitting on the couch in the radio station's lobby, and her body had gone into wicked mode. "Whatever it is," she muttered, "Remember." She pressed her forehead against the wall. "You do not like cops. This man is a cop. He is not your friend."

Within her ridiculous, secret self where she told herself truth instead of lies, she knew yeah, something had changed. Things were no longer so simple. Her body, it seemed, knew before her brain did. She wanted him. She wanted to stare into his riveting, black eyes. She wanted to touch his serious mouth with her fingers. She wanted to run her hand across his close-cropped black hair to see if it felt as silky smooth as it looked.

Yeah, like he was going to let her. And being the red-blooded male, she already knew. He'd want all of that to become something more.

"Get over yourself, you dope." She shuddered and began walking in circles like walking would clear everything up.

"Yeah, totaled," she heard him say.

Well, hoorah. He'd gotten hold of whoever he needed.

"Somebody needs to pick me up — me and a passenger."

Tootsie curled her sock-covered feet against the granite-tiled floor. At least he hadn't called her a prisoner.

"What?" There was a pause and then, "You serious?" A longer pause. "No way you're doing that. Find a way to get someone out here. If I have to, I'll come back to get her later this afternoon." Yet one more pause. "Shit. All right. Yeah."

Then there was silence followed by the sound of

him walking back into the foyer. His eyebrows hiked up. "You were listening, weren't you?"

"I was." She clasped her hands together. "You were talking about me."

"And you want me to tell you what the guy I was talking to said."

"Why not?"

He shook his head once. "Forget it." He pulled a pad from the inside pocket of his jacket. "You mind if I sit at your dining room table and work while I wait for my ride?"

She cocked her head to the side. "You want me to supply you with office space? If I give it to you, will it get me time off for good behavior?"

He frowned. "You're not taking this seriously, are you?"

"I'm taking this very seriously. I get a little strange when I'm feeling out of control and I'm feeling out of control because I'm headed to jail." *And because I want you, you big lug.*

A muscle worked overtime in his jaw. "You're not headed to jail. We go down to the courthouse, we do some paperwork. If a judge is available, he reads the complaint, listens to what you have to say, sets bail or lets you off on your own recognizance, and you go home to sleep in your own bed. Why are you making this into a federal case?"

"Maybe because one person's federal case is another person's civil disobedience?"

"I suggest you stop being cute. It's not earning

you any brownie points."

"You think I'm cute?" *Did he really? And what kind of brownie points were they talking about?* How on earth could she corral her wicked brain into giving up its thoughts and prayers? So far it wasn't working. It was stepping it up. "I'm not being cute. I'm nervous."

"Okay, enough."

That tone of voice told her nerves or not, cute or not, it might be a good idea to stop with her mouth before said mouth got her into more trouble.

He began to back away from her. "I'll be at your dining room table, working, until I get my situation sorted out."

As he stalked away, she took a shuddery breath, relieved he'd left her alone. To think. Because if she was a smart person, she'd have to take a couple of minutes…maybe more…to reason out how she was to deal with this very sudden and inconvenient situation. And no way could she rely on her old tried and true hostility toward law enforcement types.

Because no way could she square being arrested by this example of same who, every time she looked at him, the first word that jumped into her mind was sex.

She could start by keeping a safe distance. Except the tree draped over his car said they were together for the immediate future.

Meanwhile, though there was no manual telling her how to act while waiting to be taken to the Bastille, she could move on to the next, logical step.

She could, like he'd suggested, call a lawyer.

Retreating to the kitchen, she grabbed her cell and dialed Irwin Weingrad. Irwin had written Arlo's and her wills. Good she'd remembered to cut Arlo out. She'd hate it if she keeled over, while in jail, and Arlo, still a beneficiary, gave all her stuff to Raquel.

Irwin's assistant answered letting her know he was busy with other clients. It would be a while.

"But it's important. Life-changing," Tootsie said.

No doubt the assistant had heard that line before. So Tootsie left a message. She hoped by the time Irwin called her back, she wouldn't be in the cell Black Windbreaker might be reserving—in spite of him saying he wouldn't—for her from her dining room table.

The feeling of helplessness returned, swamping her, Tootsie knew she had to do something other than think about what she'd look like in an orange jumpsuit.

*Or what Black Windbreaker looked like without anything on at all.*

And didn't that fully-formed, unwelcome and distracting thought have her careening down a mental path that she couldn't afford to go.

Her eyes lit on the copper pots hanging above her island. She glanced outside. The snow was on a tear. And it was shivering cold out there, soup weather. There. That's what she would do. Make vegetable soup with beef. Hadn't that been her subconscious thought when she'd just bought everything she needed?

Yup, that was the ticket, and a perfect, if small way to corral herself back into what used to be the person that was calm, collected Tootsie Goldberg.

She threw herself into the job of cutting up her veggies while searing the flanken in some olive oil in the pot when she heard a sound behind her. She turned in its direction.

He'd taken off his parka. Its bulk had hidden the downward V of a perfectly proportioned male body, shoulders to waist to hips. Black Windbreaker...Steve...was one hot, 190 pounds or thereabouts gorgeous thing on a six foot and a couple inches frame of a too luscious man. And didn't the hits, she already couldn't deal with, keep on coming.

She swallowed and turned away as fast as she could. Her brain careened around from one safe haven to another. But with him in her kitchen there'd be no safe haven. Unsettled, refusing to let him see how he'd turned the world as she knew it inside out and upside down, she said, "Did you need something?"

Was that her voice up in the stratosphere?

"What are you cooking?"

She bayonetted a carrot with her knife. "You have to ask? I'm cooking a bomb, which I'm going to strap to myself and when I threaten to blow you and me up in shards of celery and carrots, you'll say, maybe arresting me was a bad idea. And then you'll leave."

The sleeves of his black knit shirt, pushed up to his elbows, revealed nicely muscled forearms dusted with black hair. His hands in his pockets, he ambled toward her. Looking down at the array of food, he said, "Nice bomb. Thing is, it looks like you're making soup."

"Soup. How smart are you," she snapped and waved her wooden spoon in his face.

He ignored her spoon as weapon. "I like soup. It's been a while since I had homemade soup."

"You don't have someone at home who can make soup for you?"

"Nope."

"Poor you." She flipped a piece of flanken onto its side so it would brown more evenly, her movements so sharp, she slopped some olive oil onto her stove. "Everyone should have someone to make soup for them."

"Why don't you ask me if I have someone?"

"Well, do you? Do you have someone like an old grandmother or your mother, who is still taking care of you after all these years?"

*What was the matter with her? Why couldn't she stop taking shots at him?*

"No."

"That's it? No explanation, like you're divorced, or because your wife ran off with another man, or you never got married because you've been too busy with your career, or you were always cleaning your gun and your wife hated the smell of the oil you use or—"

His expression altered, softened. "Or I was married and she died."

Tootsie's breath caught in her throat. Ears ringing, vision going wonky, she put a hand out to brace herself on the counter. "God. I'm sorry. I'm so sorry."

He gave her the briefest of nods.

She swallowed against the sudden need to throw up. She couldn't look at him. Not when she felt bitter shame for her callous mouth and deep regret. She felt—didn't see—him offer a tissue to her over her shoulder. She grabbed it and blew her nose. "That was unforgivable."

"It wasn't unforgivable." He paused before adding, "It was pretty stupid." And thoughtless. And cruel. If she looked at him this moment, she would shatter to pieces.

He grabbed a stool from in front of her island and pulled it up next to the counter where she was working. "You mind if I watch?"

She blinked and turned to look at him, anyway. Was that it? He wasn't going to take her apart, piece by piece? Or cuff her before her flanken was browned on all sides? With a catch in her voice, she said, "I don't mind."

Hefting the pot, taking it to the sink, she put the pot underneath the spigot to fill it with water. "I don't know what made me say that. I've never—"

"Forget it. You're stressed."

She skirted around him to get back to the stove

because he'd pulled the stool up so close. As she passed him by, she smelled his clean scent, sensed his body's warmth. She risked another glance. He was staring into her eyes. He wasn't wearing his cop face. Though his mouth wasn't smiling, his eyes were. "You want to know what she was like, right?"

How could he tell she wanted that? Black Windbreaker was a lot more perceptive than she'd given him credit for. He'd read her better than she'd read him. She gave him an abbreviated nod.

"Her name was Penny. She died five years ago. She was 33."

Tootsie shivered. "Way too young. Was it—?"

"Yeah, ovarian."

"That's so rotten."

"My daughters and I, we spent that last week together with Penny in hospice. Yeah, they were out of school all that time, but it was time with their mother they'd never have again. Their teachers understood."

He went silent.

The water in her pot began to heat to a boil. The pot hummed, the sound intimate in the quiet between them.

Grabbing a little kosher salt, she threw it in. "I didn't know you had kids."

He shrugged. "I didn't know you did, either. Until now."

"What gave it away?"

"I saw their pictures. On the sideboard in your

dining room."

"Why don't you tell me about your girls and I'll tell you about my boys."

"Stephanie and Carla are twins. They're 18. They're freshmen at Temple. I work security so I can afford to pay for it." He leaned his elbows on the counter. "Now, it's your turn."

"Sam is 27 and Josh is 24. Sam works for an accounting firm. He's in Singapore for the next couple of years. Josh is in marketing. He lives in Chicago. There's a woman in Sam's life and they're all but engaged." She made a face.

"Not good news?"

"I hope I'm going to like her." Tootsie lifted the lid to see how close the water was to a true boil. "When he gets married, I'll be the mother-in-law."

"I have confidence you'll figure it out."

His eyes began to sparkle.

*Was he teasing her?* "I will?"

"Yeah. You'll need to keep your opinions to yourself." He paused. "Start practicing."

She laughed. And he grinned. Not any grin. No, it was an all-out, don't-hold-the-mustard grin.

There in his broad smile, confirmation he wasn't going to hold her insensitivity against her. The tension went out of her shoulders. She felt almost snowflake light.

The water in her pot began to boil. "Everything will soften up. Then I'll add seasonings, some tomato paste. It'll be good," she babbled. Because that grin did things to her. Unmentionable things.

"It smells good in here." He sniffed and leaned forward a little in anticipation. She stiffened, as the clean scent of him overtook the smell of the soup and the war she was deep into with herself heated like she was the one on the stove, not the pot.

"Uh huh." She stared into his eyes that said things to her she didn't understand, at his gleaming, smooth skin, tight over high cheekbones. She stopped stirring and frowned. Something was not right with all that smooth skin. With the no wrinkles on his forehead, not even anywhere. "How old are you?" She blurted.

His eyebrows, which seemed to be the most expressive part of his face, hiked up. "Why do you want to know?"

She made a sound of exasperation. "Just answer the question."

"I'm 38."

She swallowed so loud, she was sure they heard it in town hall. "You're younger than I am. A lot younger."

"How much is a lot younger?"

She kept her mouth shut.

"C'mon. It won't take me a minute to find out. So, why make me work at it?" He paused. He cocked his head to the side. "Unless that's what you're trying to do."

She grimaced. "I'm thinking about the birthday I just celebrated—although I take that last word with a grain of salt. My fiftieth." Which was when something horrible occurred to her. "That's twelve years between us. I could have been your babysitter."

"Yeah, I know. I've been adding and subtracting for years." And then his lips turned up in a sly smile. "You would have been one hot babysitter."

Hot? He'd called her hot? And that meant...what...in the scheme of things? "What made you become a cop?" she asked, very much needing to not go down that new path.

"I was in the military. Army. In Iraq." He picked up the hem of his black shirt and exposed his taut belly. He pointed to a strange, whitened, small, slightly raised welt on his right side above the indentation of his waist. "This is why it was only one tour."

Her tongue froze on, "Oh." She'd never seen a bullet wound. As little as she knew about bullet wounds, she knew he was lucky to be alive after whatever made that hole whizzed through his body.

But luck and bullets weren't where her brain decided it should be, not when the part that was responsible for all image reproduction informed her that his belly was rock solid, all supple flesh over firm muscle. Saliva ran free in her mouth, her lungs went on hiatus, and her fingers lost all feeling. If she'd been holding the spoon, it would have dropped to the floor.

She swallowed. He was still holding his shirt up, exposing his belly. And, oh my...some fabulous abs.

"Can I put my shirt down?"

Did she want him to? She'd seen male bodies. Even naked male bodies. There was Arlo's, which was feh. Her boys, when they were little, thought it was hysterical to run through the house naked with their little shmeckels bobbing in the wind. So, no, she did *not* want him to drop his shirt in place. She wanted him to show her more. Still, maybe he was getting cold.

"Sure, drop your shirt," she managed. "So, um…" She steadied her breathing. "You exchanged one uniform for another?"

"That wasn't it. I wanted to be a cop when I was a kid. Some guys outgrow that. When I got out of the hospital, I realized I hadn't."

"And then you got the new uniform?"

"Yeah." He looked down and ran his hands up and down his thighs. "I'm not somebody who can stand by and watch when something's happening I know shouldn't happen."

Ah. And wasn't that an eye-opener. Did it mean she would once more have to re-evaluate what she thought about this man?

"So, what do you do with men like the Petrocellis? They cut some corners when they bought our radio station. I'm sure of it. I just need to find the evidence."

"I was thinking more like something I can see."

"You mean like if someone's lying on the ground and blood is pooling out beneath them, someone else is standing above the guy, while he's holding a gun, and smoke is coming from the barrel?"

"That would be one scenario."

She stared outside at the snow piling up in her backyard, at Arlo's Pachysandra, baby bumps in the gray and white landscape. She should know better, shouldn't she? He'd be all black and white because that's what cops were. So why did she feel let down?

"And about your scenario," he added.

Oh, great. He was about to treat her to another example of his limited vision of crime.

"Uh, huh." She went back to stirring the soup.

"When someone commits a white-collar crime...hey."

He took the spoon from her. "Stop being pissed off at me and listen."

She huffed a sigh. "Go on."

"Like I began to say when you decided to stir your soup so hard it was going to end up outside the pot..." He gave the spoon back. "...when someone commits a white- collar crime, where blood is not a factor, then yes, I'm concerned."

She stared, looking for what she hoped to find, but, as usual, his eyes were not a window into his soul. "What changed between the other day and today?"

"I thought about it."

"You did?"

"Pretty much, yeah."

"And?"

A series of looks passed across his face: hesitation, confusion, decision, before he reached out and smoothed the curls away from her forehead.

She almost leapt out of her skin. "What are you doing?" she yelped.

"Seeing if your hair is as soft as it looks," he said, his voice, wary. "Are you offended?"

"No. Just startled." She laced her fingers together to hide their sudden trembling. She opened her mouth to ask him why he wanted to touch her hair, but she wouldn't. Because she wasn't sure what she'd do with the answer.

"At the radio station, the other night. Crazy as you acted, you made sense."

"I did?" The feel of his warm hand as it had skimmed across her forehead, touching her there…for a moment she thought she'd faint. And it made her forget the thread of their conversation. "I–"

He silenced her with a finger across her lips. "Hush. I did a little research. Read some articles online."

"You did?" She canted toward him. If she was going to faint, wouldn't it be better if she fainted in his arms as opposed to the floor? "You read?"

"Shocking, but yeah."

She stared into his eyes, searching. Because the moment he'd touched her was the moment her world rotated another notch on its axis. "What did you find?"

"There was this thing in the *Daily Mouse*—"

"You read the *Daily Mouse*," she interrupted him. And smiled. "That left-wing rabble-rousing online rag? You, a right-wing, gun-toting, officer of the law?" She touched the cuff of his sweater where it grazed the skin at his elbow, shocking herself as she did.

His gaze lit on her fingers. "I googled the name, Petrocelli. The *Daily Mouse* came up in the search results. And yeah. It's too left wing for a cop." And he smiled, that elusive, so sparing smile.

The enormity of what was happening... she closed her eyes, kept them closed, hiding from this dizzying, fast-changing reality between them. Until he pressed one finger to a spot between her eyebrows.

That touch curled its way across her face and her neck to envelop her body to her toes. She forced her eyes open. "What was in the *Daily Mouse*?" she managed.

"This reporter got wind of a private meeting between the Petrocellis and some of their major stockholders."

He was telling her something important...she had to concentrate...concentrate. "What's the big deal about that?"

"If they're stockholder meetings? No big deal. If they're private? That might be a big deal, although I don't know enough about the rules to say."

"What did he or she find out?" And now she *was* concentrating.

"He. He'd been after the Petrocellis for a while.

He wanted to catch them out on a plan they had to buy a radio group with stations in Boston, New York, and Atlanta, but couldn't because they were strapped for cash."

"The Petrocellis have billions. How is that possible?"

"You're asking me a question I can't answer. I can tell you this reporter knew the restaurant they were going to and he was nearby, his equipment already set up."

"I imagine he used some kind of special microphone, and heard—?"

"What he didn't expect. Something about not screwing things up, not getting all the loose ends tied up."

Tootsie's brain got busy. "What didn't get tied up?"

"That I don't know. But there was something about separate accounts that would allow them to transfer liability, say, to avoid paying taxes. That should interest you."

How amazing and fabulous was it that the Petrocellis might be cooking their books? "Maybe there *is* a way to get WCLS back."

"You want to find the Petrocellis have committed or are about to commit a crime, don't you?" he asked.

The moment she got past the tedious business of being arrested, she was doing a detailed search of the Petrocelli's business practices. "Yes."

"Now you have a place to start."

Not that she was a forensic accountant, or would know how to do a detailed search of financial records. But there ought to be someone she knew who could. So deep in thought about who, she jumped when he took her by the shoulders and turned her toward the stove. "Your soup's boiling."

"Oh." She dialed down the flame under the pot, and, unseeing, stared into the pot. Though he'd been in the room all this time, and her awareness of him was already at some serious DefCon number now it increased tenfold along with her confusion. "So, you're helping me. Why?"

"When you broke into the radio station, you were doing something you shouldn't have. You didn't think of the consequences."

That was so true. "Okay."

"I didn't want to arrest you today at town hall. I had the warrant with me. I didn't want to embarrass you."

A fine tremble set up just beneath the surface of her skin. "I don't understand."

"You don't fit the profile of someone who would break into a place to steal something. Although I don't know what profile you do fit."

Though she was faced away from him, she could feel the bass vibration of his voice everywhere in her body, and her heart took up a fast beat. She licked her lips. "I thought you didn't do gray areas."

He took the spoon from her hand, and laid it

down on the counter.

An errant thought circled its way through her head. She would have to clean that spot in a moment.

"Then there's this." He reached out to pull her away from the stove, the pot of soup, and the hot burner on which it simmered. With hands at her waist, he pulled her the few inches left between them so her sweater and his shirt touched. And he kissed her, a bare touch of his lips to hers.

She told herself she should feel threatened. He was a big guy, an authority figure, and she was stuck in her house with him. With the snow raging outside, and his wreck of a car blocking hers, there was no way to escape. But she thought none of that. Because no matter what he looked like, or what he represented, she wanted more of what he'd just done, and finally, at last, she tumbled over into admitting it. "Did anyone tell you you're a really good kisser?"

He shook his head and took a step back. "I've wanted to do that for a while."

"So you did." She reached for his hand. "What now?"

He studied her, his serious eyes unblinking. "Now I want to do a whole lot more."

# CHAPTER ELEVEN

Tootsie froze. 'A whole lot more'? A little part of her raised its hand hearing those words, and said, 'hold up, girlfriend'.

"Um…"

He kept her hand in his, his thumb moving casually across the tips of her fingers. "Not your thing?"

It was so her thing. But while little bonfires raged in her heart and stomach, her brain zig-zagged between wanting to rip her clothes off and his too, the hell with soup, and the other part cautioning her against stepping into a scary unknown where someone could get hurt. Maybe her.

She took her hand from his and folded it against her stomach. "I don't know."

"Okay. What don't you know?"

She scrambled for an explanation. "We're

different."

He raised one of his eyebrows. "Like how?"

A little spurt of frustration zigged through her. "You know how."

"You mean I'm a cop and you're not too fond of cops?"

Once more, she reassessed her grasp on who this man was. Way too smart. "How do you know that?"

He raised both eyebrows. "You think you don't give off that vibe?"

Because, yeah, she had and smart guy that he was, he knew. Provoked, she said, "Could you please stop doing that thing with your eyebrows? And seriously, if you'd just wax them you could avoid having a unibrow when you frown." She slammed her mouth shut. But really what else could she expect would come out of it when her brain was a gerbil on a treadmill?

Humor sparked in his eyes. He took a step backwards and leaned against the island, folding his arms across his chest. And smiled.

He wasn't going to help. She was on her own. Flailing around, she said, "You wanted to arrest me."

She waited through his too long silence, and then he said, "No, I didn't."

Her gerbil brain seized up. "What does that mean?"

He gave her a look, one of those impenetrable ones. "It means what I already told you. I didn't want to do it at the courthouse. I didn't want to do it just now. You should be paying attention."

How ludicrously teacher-like. She ought to laugh. If it weren't so serious, she might have. She flexed her hands. "I'm 50 years old. I have a body that goes with my age. My breasts, though the inevitable hasn't started yet, are moving in the direction of my navel. My tush is not far behind."

He gave her a half smile. "Nice pun."

She waved away his funny. "I don't want people to see either."

"People? What people? Who are you planning to get naked with besides me?"

"I'm not planning on getting naked with you."

"You're not?" There, in his eyes, sudden doubt. But then determination. "Why should I care about your age? Or about those things you're saying about your body?"

"How can you not care?" A ball of anxiety lodged in her chest.

"Because even if I was looking at your—" He motioned toward her ass— "which I'm not, right this moment, it wouldn't matter."

"It matters to me."

"Well, yeah. You're a woman. Women have issues." His lips curved into a slice of a smile. "This is your issue, right?"

He was teasing her. She didn't want to be teased. She wanted to be sure. "It is and it's important."

"Tootsie, you're not the most beautiful woman in the world."

"What!" A laugh threatened to cough itself up. "That's so insulting. First I have issues, now I'm not beautiful? Are you looking to commit suicide by homicide?"

"I didn't say you weren't beautiful. Just not the most beautiful."

She should have been insulted. There was something so honest about it that calm overtook her anxiety. "I should feel good about that?"

His eyes shone. "Don't you know what they say about beauty?"

"Yes, that it's skin deep. But I'm talking soon-to-be-ugly-sagging skin."

"Don't talk about yourself like that." He held out his arms. "Come here. Please."

She wanted what he was offering. But did she want to upset her already imperfect life any further? If the last few days told her anything, it told her that it had been that way for a while. That was a truth she had to stop hiding from.

"I have hot flashes," she blurted. There, a deflection.

He straightened. "Are you having one now?"

She scoffed. "I don't know why I'm not. I should be."

"I'm sorry you have them. I'm glad you're not having one now." As if she were breakable, he folded her into his arms, bending his knees so he could reach all of her. He buried his face in her curls. "Listen carefully," he said, voice muffled. "I don't want to screw up my career. And if I do, it's not going to be with someone who the one thing you can say about her is men notice her bust and her butt when she walks down the street."

"That's terrible." She let herself melt into the warmth of his body. "I think." But it didn't feel terrible. And she didn't leave his arms in protest.

"You're a lot more than a beautiful woman."

"I am?" She pressed her nose against his black shirt.

He tightened his arms around her and sighed. "Why is it never enough to pay a woman a simple compliment?"

Rubbing her cheek against the shirt's rough texture, she inhaled the comforting, clean scent of him. "What makes you think that was a simple compliment?"

"Hope against hope it was?" He pressed one hand against the back of her head.

She wound her arms around his waist and kissed his shirt placket. The scent of fabric softener tickled her nose. "It wasn't. But, I'll let it slide. This time."

He ran his hands down her back, to her bottom, the one she'd said sagged, which the way he stroked it, didn't seem to register with him as a bad thing.

He said, "You are some challenge."

"I've never been called a challenge."

"I like that you are. And you're going to test me big time." He brought them mouth to mouth, and began to kiss her. Not kiss. Envelop.

There was no teasing intro this time. There was no question, if there ever had been one.

And that, right there, was when she stopped thinking about her imperfect life.

He ravaged her mouth. He bound her with his arms. He cradled her head and tunneled his fingers into her curls. He pushed a thigh between hers, pressed and slid, all long, iron-hard muscle. Back and forth.

*Exactly.*

She went up in flames, spasms so deep, they were frightening.

There was the sound of breathing, hers and his, heavy and fast.

"Hot damn," he whispered. "I haven't done more than touch you. You and I, we're in for—"

The lights dimmed. Then went out.

"No", she groaned and sagged against him. "They fixed that." She clutched handfuls of his shirt. As if *that* would keep them in the moment.

But he straightened, and the moment passed.

Still she held on. "It's the Glen Allyn transformer."

His eyes, usually so laser sharp, appeared bigger, softer, blacker. He ran his hands down her arms and squeezed her hands. "I'm going to walk outside. See what I can see."

Like he could get a visual on electricity.

She shook her head back and forth, resigned while also ticked off. "The thing used to fail on a regular basis. Back a few months ago, they had a crew out to repair it. They said it wouldn't go bad, again. How wrong they were." She banged her head against his chest.

He cradled her in his arms. "I know what you want. I want it too. He ruffled her curls. "Let me make a phone call."

It wasn't fair, him expecting her to think, her body still humming from the first orgasm she'd had in years that wasn't self-induced. "Make your phone call. Go ahead."

He unwound her hands from his shirt front, pulled his phone from his pocket, and keyed in a series of numbers. Then he walked toward the front door, opened it, and stepped outside, pulling the door toward him. He left it open a mere crack.

Tootsie barely heard him, but what she did hear sounded a lot like 'yeah, it's me.' She turned to look out the floor-to-ceiling doors that led onto her deck and her backyard. The blizzard in process, the snowflakes, the size of small snowballs, splatted against the glass.

Which gave her time to gather the shattered remnants of her self-control. She'd never experienced anything like that orgasm. What orgasms she'd had with her college boyfriend, and then Arlo, were a whole lot of blah-blah. Then there'd been that one man she'd dated for a few weeks after her divorce was final, just to prove she could, and in hopes that her long dormant sex life could be revived. There'd been a lot of adolescent fumbling on his part. When she laughed at his attempts to get her hot and bothered, that was the end of that relationship and PS...no orgasm in the offing.

She could hear the faint murmur of Steve's voice. The front door shivered in the wind.

Maybe the power failing was a good thing because it had stopped her from tumbling further into a maelstrom of emotion that had already frightened her half to death with its intensity. She needed to keep that in mind and slow things down. As in be more mindful.

He walked back into the kitchen. She opened her mouth to respond. And closed it. He stopped in the space between her kitchen and the foyer and ran a hand across the top of his head. Snowflakes flew in every direction. She could just about feel the cold radiating from his body. She wanted to rush across the room to take him in her arms and make all that cold go away. So much for mindfulness.

"It's not only your transformer. It's every transformer everywhere. All the lines down, they're closing the highways. The snow's coming down so fast, the plows can't keep up. Plus the accidents. A lot of them. They need everybody to come in who can get in. That includes me. The trouble is they can't spare anybody to come and pick me up. That means for the next while I'm stuck here. With you."

He came all the way into the kitchen and laid his cellphone on a counter.

They would? And that would be when? But in the meantime... She pressed her lips together. He was stuck here.

Her thinking got stuck, too. "So what do you think we can do to pass the time?"

His bottom lip twitched. "Build a fire?"

As if it had never taken a break for commercials, desire came roaring back, and concern for body issues and whatever went out the door. "What kind of fire did you have in mind?" she asked, her breath catching.

"You know what kind." He focused his intense gaze on her. It flicked from her face to her breasts, lower, and then back to her face. "The kind you build in the fireplace."

"So..." She had to pause. To catch her breath. "We could make that fire pretty hot, don't you think?"

"Tootsie." He crossed the few steps that separated them. "Babe." He put his hands on her shoulders and gave her a look that, if she were kindling, she'd already have burst into flames. "I'm going to be inside you. Don't doubt it. But I'm a big boy. I can wait. We are not starting anything that's going to be interrupted."

Her jaw fell. "What does that mean? Didn't you just tell me it'll be a while until someone can pick you up?" Was this her bargaining with him? Uh, yeah. Should she be embarrassed? Uh, no.

"Listen to me. If you're going to be alone in this

house until the power comes back—which I'm not in favor of, but we'll talk about that, later—before we take care of each other, we need to prep this place." He took one of her hands in his. "What room's the warmest in this house?"

He was taking care of her, in a way that was new and which she didn't recognize...because no man had ever taken care of her creature comforts. What a novelty. She savored the moment for a moment, until she straightened, pointed, and said, "The great room."

"Is it away from all your glass doors?" He pointed at the doors leading out to the deck and began moving toward where she pointed. "Does it have a fireplace?"

"It does." She followed him out into the foyer. "While you check it out, I'll go upstairs and get some towels to roll up against the bottom of the kitchen doors, the front door, and the bay window in the living room. That'll keep some of the cold out."

"Have you got flashlights in this house?"

"I have one."

He gave her a look over his shoulder. "That many, huh?"

She had no problem interpreting that look. "It's in my junk drawer in the kitchen. The batteries are probably dead."

He turned, hands on hips. "Not much in the way of being prepared, are you."

"I have plenty of candles," she said, defending her lack of flashlights.

He frowned. "You ever hear candles start fires?"

"I make it a habit to light them in safe places, like inside a glass chimney."

"Do you have one?"

"Um, no."

He shot her a look of disgust, which tickled her silly. "I'm going to get the towels," she sang out. "And the blankets, okay?"

"Before you do, turn the light off under the soup." He gave her a nod. "I'll check out your fireplace."

Watching his retreating back, she realized she should have known, once the guy used to giving orders took over, he would officially become Charles in Charge. And he'd remember every little thing that had to be done.

She dashed into the kitchen, and did what he'd ordered her to do. And then she ran up the shadowed staircase to her linen closet in the equally shadowed upstairs hallway, she was amazed at herself. She'd never liked being told what to do, especially by a bossy man. Somehow, this man's bossiness didn't bother her. She grinned. Maybe because he was adorable?

She threw the closet door open and gathered towels to keep out drafts, and blankets for sharing body heat. Her own flashed into full life, as she fantasized about what kind of sharing they'd soon be doing, considering she'd already had the appetizer. In her haste, she almost tripped coming down the stairs.

He was waiting for her at the bottom. He held out his hands to grab her. "What's the big rush?" Relieving her of the entire pile, he turned back toward the great room.

She followed him, thinking she could tell him what the big rush was. But *she* was a big girl. *She* could wait. Except she wasn't sure that was true.

He deposited the pile of towels and blankets on one of Tootsie's oversize armchairs. He stood in front of the fireplace and pointed to it. "Have you had the flue checked recently?"

"Just after Thanksgiving." And wasn't she proud she could give him an answer he would approve of?

"It ought to be all right." He half-turned toward her. "Do you have logs? Or do I have to go outside and chop a couple of branches off the tree that killed my car?"

She made a face at him. "I've got a huge pile in the garage from last year that I never used. They're all full of leaves and dirt."

He looked at her askance. "I think I can handle leaves and dirt. But before I do, I'm going to move your couch in front of the fireplace." He made a sweeping gesture in its direction, where Tootsie had placed the couch, with a grouping of chairs, against the other side of the oversize room.

"How smart." She eyed the space between where he was shoving the couch and the fireplace itself: the perfect place for a tryst. "I'll help."

"No, you won't." The master had spoken. What

he had to say and how he said it still didn't bother her much.

*Because he was taking care of her.*

He had the couch in place in an instant. "Let's get some logs." He touched one finger to her shoulder.

She felt the touch tumble through her body. Before he could incapacitate her, she turned and walked fast through the foyer into the kitchen, and then into the narrow hallway leading out to the garage.

He was right behind her, touching her again. This time, it was a spot between her shoulder blades. She shuddered and stopped. There was no escape. Why exactly was she trying to?

The light inside the house was fading fast, with the combination of the day winding down and the heavy snow-laden clouds thickening up further. The cold had begun to seep into the house. With all the body touches Steve had been treating her to, her body staying warm...make that hot...wouldn't be a problem.

He slid his arms around her. She turned and stared up into his dark-as-the-falling-night eyes, breathed in his scent, faint laundry, mid-day earthiness, and skin. She slid her arms up between them and ran her hands over his chest to his shoulders. "This is so nice," she whispered.

He pressed her back against the wall next to the hooks where all her brooms and mops hung. Her eyelids fluttered down. She felt his breath on her face. Felt him bend toward her and sensed his lips hovering over hers. Goosebumps broke out all over her body. She stood on her toes to touch her tongue to his bottom lip.

He pressed against her, their bodies so close there was no separation. The part of him she wanted to become better acquainted with nudged against her belly. She tried to get closer to it, but their clothing was in the way.

"Oh God, I want you," she whispered. "Now." She pushed him and he went, stumbling against the opposite wall. She stepped up onto his feet and there. Proper contact at last. She fought to catch her breath. She took in great lungsful of air. She could hear the sounds she was making: harsh breaths overlaid with the shushing of her sweater against his shirt.

He made an inarticulate sound and lifted her away, setting her feet on the floor. At first what he'd done didn't register.

She looked up at him, dazed. "Did I misunderstand something? Didn't you just say you were going to be inside me? So why are we stopping?" She thought it amazing she could make her mouth work and speak actual words.

"I didn't say here."

"Why not?" She slipped her hands under his shirt and hooked her thumbs in the waistband of his jeans, sliding them along until she found the snap at the center. "No one can see."

"That's not it."

"It's not?" There was a lightness in his voice that was ticking her off. She needed him to take this seriously. "What is?" Her head was clearing and with it came irritation. "If this wasn't going to work for you, why did you let me start?"

"You want to tell me how I could have stopped you? You push pretty hard, shorty."

"I'm sorry you're such a wimp that you couldn't figure out how to do it against a wall. And stop laughing." To show him how hard she could push, she did.

He didn't budge and he didn't stop laughing. "Don't hurt me. All I mean is I'm no twenty-year-old and I don't need to fuck standing up. Plus, I don't know when there'll be a knock on your front door, and one of my guys will be standing there to pick me up. For damn sure I don't want it to happen when I've got a condom in one hand ready to put it on." His eyebrows came down in a concentrated frown. "Are you with me on that?" He gave her a little shake. "Say yes."

"Yes," she whispered, her fantasies, her ego, and her libido in happy check because now that he'd told her, in more graphic detail than she'd needed that she was about to get what was coming. Oh my…another pun.

He spun her around and pushed her toward the door to the garage. "So let's hop to, get those logs, and build that fire. I want us to be just as busy as you want us to be and soon." He reached around her to open the door to the garage. It practically blew back on its hinges. "What the—! The garage door's open!"

Well, yeah. She'd forgotten, so intent had she been emptying her car of her groceries to close it. "I left it open in case the power went out and I needed to get away quick," her smart ass-self improvised.

"What, you have the Texas Rangers after you?"

"You're the only ranger after me." Which was more than fine with her.

He took her arm and set her a few steps back in the hallway. "You stay here. I'll close the door manually."

Taking the one step down into the garage proper, he followed words with action. Then, he hunched his shoulders and gave his arms a brisk rubbing against the cold, crunched through the leaves that pooled around the logs delivered last autumn and stacked in a corner, and took four off the top. He deposited them, leaves and all, at her feet. And was back at the pile again.

He was such a Sir Galahad. Maybe because he'd always been a Sir Galahad, and she hadn't given him credit for it? He worked at the pile, brought another four logs inside, and then came in, pulled the door closed behind hm. "This should be enough."

Stepping around the pile he'd made in her hallway, he brushed his hands off and gave his arms a brisk rub.

"Here. Let me help get you warm." She pushed

aside his hands and replaced them with her own.

"Thanks, babe," he whispered, as she ran her hands everywhere across his upper body. He reached for her and pulled her to him. "You're doing a great job. I'm getting warmed up real fast."

He began to do a little massaging himself. Of her. Of her arms, her sides, and oh yes, thank the stars, her breasts. Her hands faltered in their warming task, as she concentrated on the feel of his fingers doing their magic on her. "Is this foreplay, because if it is, I like it a lot."

"It's the fore in foreplay." He abandoned her breasts and wrapped her closer in his arms. He pressed his lips to the side of her neck.

Again she stood on her tiptoes so she could reach some of the important parts of him better. Somehow one of his feet had ended up on top of hers. "Yeah, I know but you don't have to do it back to me, and you don't have to step on me to hold me in place. I'm all yours."

He chuckled. "I'm not stepping on you."

She answered his chuckle with one of hers. "Are you so far gone you don't know a foot when you feel one?"

He lifted his head and looked down at her, a quizzical expression on his face. "Babe. I'm not stepping on you."

She drew her head back, confused. "Well, if you're not stepping on me, who is?"

And then she made the mistake of looking down.

Curled around her foot was a snake. A long, dark ugly snake.

# CHAPTER TWELVE

Tootsie was sure she'd shrieked in her life, but never like an unhinged maniac. In the moment after she looked down at that dread shape, that winding, evil creature, the moment before it prepared to sink its fangs into her poor, just-last-week-waxed-and hairless leg, she lost the whole enchilada. She was alone, in the deep, dark divide between life and death.

"Shit, Tootsie—" Steve's hands on her arms were vise-like. But no grip could hold her in that existential moment. She wrenched herself away, shook the horror off her foot, and shrieked again, the sound ponging around the narrow hallway. She stumbled over a log and then sped Mach 3 toward the great room.

Quaking, she threw herself into the corner of the couch Steve had just shoved in front of the fireplace.

She grabbed one of the blankets she'd brought downstairs and threw it over her head. She drew up her legs, drummed her feet against the couch cushion, and clenched her toes tight against her soles. Her heart banged against her rib cage like a barn door left open in a windstorm.

Sometime later—she wasn't sure how much later because her eyelids were sealed shut over her eyeballs and her brain had gone to the brain shop for repair—Steve sat down on the sofa and placed one of his big, warm hands on her hip. She flinched.

"It's okay." He smoothed his way down her thigh to her knee and back. "It's gone."

"Did you kill it?"

"No."

Her eyelids unsealed themselves and snapped open. "You didn't? Don't tell me you put it outside so someone else can get bitten and die."

"It's not poisonous." He kept soothing her with that magic hand of his.

"If you did put it outside, I hope you put it in the street so when a plow comes by, it'll get flattened into a belt." She turned so he could soothe more of her. Like her belly. And her breast. Maybe both breasts.

"Nah, I didn't." He got himself set more securely and slid his hand up her side. He missed the key points she wanted him to address.

"You really didn't?" She concentrated on making her mind move his hand, like a planchette on a Ouija board.

"I didn't. I put it in a box in the garage."

"I have a snake box in the garage?" She sat up straight, grabbed a corner of the blanket and, with a clutch of its Dacron and wool blend in her hand, shoved his hand away. "Did you wash your hands? Did you leave some food for him? Did you line the box so he doesn't get cold? And did I ask you already if you washed your hands?"

His shoulders began to shake in silent laughter. "I washed my hands."

She glared at him. The glare didn't work, or at least not as she intended it to, because then he burst into full laughter. He laughed so hard, tears came into his eyes.

She pushed him. He was immoveable. "This is not funny." Said weakly. Because she, too, was beginning to see the humor.

Which made him laugh harder. This time when she pushed, he slid off the sofa onto the floor. Still laughing, he turned toward her, came up on his knees, and slid his hands up her thighs to her hips.

"Being all romantic with me is not getting you off the hook, officer." But her hands said otherwise, when they lifted and she ran them over his close-cropped hair. Her heart, which had been slamming in fear against her lungs, kept at it. But now, it was a different kind of beat.

"It's Detective Lieutenant. That's my title. You can use it if you want."

Right now the only title she had for him was

snake handler. "Seriously. Was it a he?"

"I don't know. I'm not into studying the sex of snakes." He began to laugh again.

"Why didn't you check?" But even as she asked, she knew she was losing interest in the snake. She trailed her fingers across his neck.

He grabbed her hand, folded it into a fist, and nuzzled it. "It's not poisonous. It's a garden snake, less than six inches long. When you threw it off your foot, you probably gave it a heart attack." He placed her fist on her knee, leaned up and kissed the side of her breast.

That kiss was a nice kind of progress away from thoughts of the snake.

"I'll take it to a pet store when I've got wheels," he whispered. "Kay?"

She shivered. "I'm impressed by a guy who wears a big, black gun on his hip who is so gentle with living creatures. Although I wish you weren't so gentle with reptiles. They're not human."

"Don't make me laugh again." One side of his mouth kicked up. "I haven't laughed like this since…" He looked puzzled, and then shook his head, as if trying to jiggle something loose.

He lifted the blanket off her legs, pressed her knees apart, pulled her toward the edge of the couch, and buried his face against her belly. In a muffled voice he said, "I've never laughed like this."

No doubt his memory was playing tricks on him. At some point in his life he must have let loose and laughed like a lunatic. What did it say that he'd let himself with her?

He lifted his head to stare up at her, his fathomless black eyes glowing soft. "Tootsie. What's with the name? Don't bother telling me you were named after the movie. You're too old for that."

She didn't have the strength to be insulted, not when she was otherwise occupied running her fingers back and forth over his close-cropped hair, which was as silky as she thought it might be. "You don't buy that I was named after the candy?"

"No. Give it up. Remember. I can find out easily. All I have to do is look."

She knew he would. Sighing, she gave him what he wanted. "My birth name is Esther. We Jews name babies after the deceased to honor them. I was named after my maternal great-grandmother." She stopped. She would not bring her family grief into this moment.

And he didn't ask for more. He gave her one of his rare smiles and pulled her down on the floor. "Now I know exactly what to call you when I want to annoy you."

Up so close, she could see the start of the beard he'd have to shave tomorrow morning. She saw the sheen of his skin, the wrinkling around his mouth, and the fan of smile lines around his eyes. The thirty-eight-year-old did have some signs of age after all. Which was reassuring.

She put her arms around him and closed her eyes

to concentrate on how it felt to lie in his arms. The heat of his skin and the heat of hers. The ripple of muscle as he pulled her off the couch and arranged her body on the floor in front of the fireplace.

"Why don't you lie back," he murmured. "You're all upset about the snake. You need to rest." But what his hands were doing wasn't promoting any kind of rest she was familiar with.

She took one of them and placed it on her breast. "I do need rest. After that terrible experience."

He slipped his hand underneath her sweatshirt and smoothed it over her bra, then ran a finger beneath. "What, you think there's a problem with this? I can't find a thing wrong with this part of your body. And whatever the rest is like, I won't find anything wrong with it, either."

When put that way, she wondered if, she'd overstated the importance of her body issues. She arched into his hand. "So, you think the body thing won't stand in our way?"

"That's what I think." His gaze changed a fraction and it dropped from her eyes, to her mouth, and then traveled back to her eyes. He slid both hands underneath her sweatshirt.

The adrenalin began to flow.

She reached out with one hand and cupped his cheek. She let her gaze rove across his face, his high cheekbones, his sharp blade of a nose, his stern mouth, now softened. She closed the small distance between them and touched her lips to his.

It was all he needed. He pushed her back to lie flat beneath him. "Esther," he whispered against her mouth.

She invited him in anyway, and he took it. His tongue skimmed across her lips, touched the corners, and entered to play with her tongue. At first it was as if he was testing to see what would happen, see what she would say. And then with increasing boldness, he pressed and sealed her lips with his.

Tootsie's skin heated. She wanted it—and him—and she wanted it without a moment to spare.

He began to kiss her with deliberation, to press open-mouthed kisses across her cheeks, to her ear, to take a lobe in his teeth and first, bite down, and then soothe the bite with his tongue.

He wrapped one arm around her back, anchoring her more firmly to him. He ran his other hand up her rib cage to cup her breast.

She shivered. Her breath began to come faster. Her brain went on a dizzied journey. Her heart pounded in anticipation. She knew what she wanted. Action now. She pressed one hand against his nape, across his short, neat hair. "Steve," she whispered, and nudged the side of his face with hers to dislodge his lips from beneath her jaw. "Enough, please. Stop making me wait!"

He had the nerve to chuckle. "Lift up a little."

And she did, which was when he pulled his hand out from behind her, eased it under her sweatpants and panties both, and finally hit the spot. The nub they called it in some books when they didn't want to go all clinical and call it by its anatomical name. She didn't care what *they* called it. She called it Shangri-La. He took care to treat it without respect, which was exactly what he was supposed to do. Her eyes rolled back in her head. "Yesssss."

"Noooo."

"Not noooo. Anything but noooo." She pounded his shoulder. "Whyyyyy?"

"No condom."

Blang! All of a sudden she was shivering and thinking too clearly.

He stood and reached up on the mantel to grab the flashlight. Crouching back down, he wound a finger around one of her curls. "I have some condoms in my car. Let's hope that when that tree fell, it left me enough room to get the door free." He kissed her. "And into my glove compartment."

Before she could ask why he had condoms in his glove compartment, he was gone. She heard the front door open and close, and felt the whoosh of cold air swirl around her. The flames in the fireplace swayed sideways and then came upright again.

She pressed her legs together against the fading throb of an orgasm of mammoth proportions. She had a feeling it would have been one for the record books…well, at least her record book. With their clothes on! What was going to happen once they got naked—except for his condom? If the next orgasm was anything like the last one, she was destined to die.

She hoped he found his condoms.

But what if he didn't? Suppose he couldn't get inside his car? Suppose he could get into the car but couldn't open the glove compartment? What if there were no condoms inside? You weren't supposed to have unprotected sex with a stranger but did she care about that?

And did she care whether he found a condom? It wasn't like she could get pregnant.

*Why was he carrying condoms in his car?*

Before she could examine any of that, the front door opened and closed. There were the sounds of him brushing the snow off his clothing and then steps as he entered the room.

"Well?"

He came around to the front of the sofa. "I need to take some of my clothes off. They got snowed on."

She cast a critical eye over him. "Good idea. While you're at it, take off what didn't get snowed on. Cold seeps through and does a job on body heat. We don't want to waste any of your body heat."

"Don't you worry about my body heat," he said and started shucking.

"Did your trip have a good outcome?" She held her breath.

He stepped out of his pants and squatted down next to her.

He was... Her brain took a moment to regroup before it could describe the message her eyes were delivering to it. The gloss of skin on his shoulders, adorned with muscle, glimmered golden in the light from the fireplace. Crisp black hair covered a muscular chest that had to owe its shape to genetics. And working out.

A smile played across his lips. Slowly, he held up his hand and there a gold packet, very shiny. And then he twitched his fingers, and like magic, there appeared another. And another.

She snorted a laugh. "Optimistic, aren't you?"

He angled forward onto his knees and planted his hands on either side of her. "Any reason I shouldn't be?"

She placed a hand on his chest. He may have just come from outside, but he was furnace hot. She pressed her hand against his heart. It beat steadily. His eyelids had fallen halfway shut.

She lay back, bringing him down with her. Her heart began a deliberate, resolute thud.

He bracketed her with his body and brought his mouth close to hers. "This is where I'm supposed to say we don't have to do this if you don't want to. Except I'm not into that noble bullshit."

"There's no need to be noble." She looked up to where he'd laid the condoms on the sofa cushion above them. "After so much planning, going out in the blizzard to retrieve your special equipment, it would be cruel and inhuman punishment to say anything else."

He chuckled. "I'm glad we're on the same page on this. Or the same floor." He lifted the hem of her sweatshirt. He frowned. "Are you cold?"

She guessed he'd seen her goosebumps. "The only way I would be cold is if you stopped doing what you're about to do."

That was all the urging he needed to skate her sweatshirt up over her head.

As Tootsie pulled her head out of the neck, Steve began to smooth his hand over the lace covering her breast. "This is a very pretty bra."

She felt his touch deep inside her body. "I got it on sale at Nordstrom's."

He reached behind her, unsnapped the clasp. The bra slid down her shoulders, down her arms, and off. "You're one great shopper." He threw it over his shoulder and it landed on the sofa's plush arm.

"You're efficient," she said, panting.

"I don't have a second to lose on this task."

"Oh." She barely heard the sound, which was something, since she was the one who'd made it. But that was because she was concentrating on what his hands were doing. Because her breasts weren't the only place they went. True, they spent a good deal of time learning everything about them. But they traveled down her back and up. Then to her shoulders, down her arms, to her rib cage and her belly.

"Wait a minute," he said in a voice grown hoarse. He scooted down and tongued her belly button. Tootsie had never known she had nerve endings in her belly button. But perhaps nerve endings elsewhere in her body were having such a celebration, her belly button decided it needed to join in.

He placed his hands on the elastic waistband of her sweats. "These have to go."

For a millisecond she had a moment, recalling her sagging tush, the one she'd told him she worried about. But it was a thought in a millisecond and then gone. "Why are you making statements about the obvious?" She clapped her hands over his to urge the downward trajectory of her remaining clothing.

It came off almost as fast as her bra. He threw it all behind him, and somehow, like magic, everything landed in the same place: on the arm of the sofa.

He placed one hand flat on her belly. "Are you cold now?" He moved his hand downward. "I'm here to fix that."

That was the last thing he said for a long time. Until they were too tired for anything but sleep.

They didn't wake until the sun streamed through her glass doors leading out to the deck. What it told her was the storm was over.

As that first beam of morning hit her face, she squinted into the light and turned away from it back into Steve and the heat of his body. That brought her fully awake and remembering. She'd done it. Something so far from what she ever thought she, Tootsie Goldberg would do. It felt…what?

He stirred and tightened his arms around her. She wasn't sure she was ready for him to be awake. Because then? There'd be conversation. She stilled.

As if that would keep him from waking.

He touched the tip of her nose. "Are you cold?" His voice was raspy with sleep.

Blankets up to her chin, she said, "No. It's just my dog nose."

He shifted around and just like that they were back to where they'd been last night. The two of them. And his condoms.

So, no conversation. At least for a while.

But then, she surprised herself, because it seemed she needed *some* conversing. "I've got a question."

He sighed. "Even first thing in the morning you've got questions?"

"Why not? Is there a time of day when asking questions is not a thing?"

He looped one leg over her hip. "Not for you, I guess. Ask."

That leg. His arm around her back. Her wide-awake body. She had to focus and he was making it difficult. "Why do you have condoms in your car? Do you go places to satisfy the urge and want to be ready at all times?"

"Is that what you think?" He began to sift his fingers through her hair.

"I asked because I don't know."

"And your imagination is working overtime trying to figure it out."

At the moment she was imagining a repeat of last night. Or was it the middle of the night? Or just now? She, 50-year-old mother of two grown sons and all around responsible middle-aged woman, had had hot sex not once but three times with a younger man.

*Raowwwww!*

In her life with Arlo, there'd never been one occasion where they had sex multiple times in one night. There were nights when she wished they hadn't had sex once.

She threw Arlo out of her head, one of many places he didn't belong. "Well, I think you keep them in there so your daughters don't know about your sex life. And responsible, because you make sure you always have safe sex."

He pulled her on top of him. "That's a good story."

As he ran his hands down her body, she lost track of why she wanted to know. Almost. "But not true?"

"Nope."

Again with the one word answers. If this man was going to be in her life—surely she shouldn't think about going there, even if she just had—she would have to get used to one word answers. Or train him to use more.

"Then what?"

"I used to work the juvenile division. I don't anymore but there are these kids who hang out at a rec center in town. I still check in at the place. Some of those 12 and 13- year-old boys are sexually active. They have no idea what happens when they fuck some girl the same age. I explain how babies are made and why they don't want to be fathers at 14."

"And that's why you have condoms in your glove compartment."

"Yup."

She felt warmth come over her. Not the hot flash kind. Just the heat of pleasure being with a human being who didn't *talk* about doing good things but did them. Black Windbreaker was a man who had a heart he hid away in case someone saw it. And he had to embarrass himself explaining why.

She wound her arms around him to get closer although they couldn't have been closer than they already were. It was more an emotional closer than a physical. Which was kind of odd, but she was too busy to think about that.

She wriggled her naked self against his naked self. "I'm ready. Again."

"You're one surprise after another." He chuckled. "Esther."

This time, calling her Esther, annoyed her. "Don't call me that name."

"Why not? I like it. It's different."

"Too different."

"Have you got a middle name?"

The urge to merge was going bye-bye. "I do. Ruth."

"How did you get two biblical names?"

"My grandmother's influence." She pressed her lips tight together.

He leaned away and canted his head to the side.

Studying her. Then he said, "Remember when you were making soup?"

"And you ate it. Yes, I remember." Between sex act number one and sex act number two…to give him strength…or so he'd said.

She pressed her face against his chest and rubbed her cheek against the soft pelt of hair that covered it. His body was like a safe haven. So much better to just be than talk about what she didn't want to talk about.

He turned on his side, turned her, too. His dark coffee eyes all serious, unblinking. "I told you about Penny. I knew I could trust you not to say empty words back at me you didn't mean."

She tucked her arms around his neck.

He kissed her, then. There was no sex in the kiss. "Losing Penny is a part of me. This thing you won't talk about… It's a part of you. If there's pain involved in remembering, you have to lean into it to live with it." He stroked one curl back off her forehead. He smiled. "If I remember the Purim story, Esther was a heroine."

Startled, she said, "You know about Jewish holidays?"

He shifted onto his back, taking her with him. "Listen and learn. I grew up in Brooklyn. My first job, when I was sixteen, was at Sol's Deli on Roebling Street. It was twenty-two years ago, but I can still make a mean pastrami on rye and a great cholent. If you want either, say the word." He tapped her nose. "Speaking of… I bet I know more Yiddish than you do."

"Considering the Yiddish I know is from my grandmother, words only, and considering where you worked, I imagine you do." She wrinkled her nose. "I bet you'd do well schmoozing in some of those Brooklyn neighborhoods even today."

"I would. Now, stop ducking and tell me about the Esther you were named after."

No one had ever pushed her this hard about something she didn't want to talk about. What did it say about him—and her—that she was willing to tell him what he wanted to know?

"The Esther I was named for died the summer of 1942 along with my great-grandfather, two of their three daughters, and their son. My grandmother, Hannah, the third daughter, was the only one in the family who survived."

He sighed and brought her into the protection of his body because the man who, as a kid had worked at Sol's Deli in Brooklyn would know about the ones who survived and the ones who didn't. "In a camp?"

She rubbed her face against his chest. "The biggest, the best, Auschwitz. They got off the train and that was that."

He hugged her closer.

"How did your grandmother not end up with the rest of her family?"

"It was when the Nazis came to their village, rounded up everyone and took them by truck to the nearest train station. While they were busy pushing everyone onto the Auschwitz Express, my grandmother slipped away. She was 13. And really quick on her feet."

Steve soothed her with his hands. "She must have been."

"She ended up in the woods. With partisans. Where she became a champ at making a Molotov cocktail. She knew her way around dynamite and helped blow up a troop train or two. And kill Nazis?" She snapped her fingers. "Easy peasy."

Tootsie shifted over to stare into the glow of the now-banked flames in the fireplace. "I wanted to know for the longest time about all of it, but she wouldn't tell me. I peppered her with one question after another."

"How many times did she say, '*Mammele, why do you want to know, because believe me, it wasn't so wonderful'.*"

"And me? I didn't give up. '*C'mon Grandma, it's history. I want to know your history. What happened with my aunts and my uncle?*'"

She pressed a hand against her mouth. "I didn't consider the pain it caused her to talk about her sisters and her brother, all gone. All murdered."

Eyes closed, as if she could shut out that memory of her own failing, she said, "Even now when I think of how I badgered her to tell me, I'm angry at myself for being so heartless."

He stroked her arm, a small comfort. "You were a kid."

"My life was boring. I wanted to spice it up. In

an unforgivable way I enjoyed it when she told me what it was like to kill as many Nazis as she could as payback. But now when I think about it, what was I doing? Now, I know what those thoughtless questions did to her soul."

He pressed a cheek against the top of her head and Tootsie grew silent. Then she said, "I think it's why, when I got a little older, I followed her lead, did what she did. It was my way of honoring her, of understanding when I hadn't before."

Nestled in Steve's arms, her back against his chest, her hands over his arms wound around her waist, she went on. "I'll tell you that she wasn't a ballaboosta in training. You would know if you ever ate one of her potted meatballs. They were rocks. Her roasted chicken was so overdone, it was fossilized."

"Babe, I shouldn't have asked. I—"

She raised a finger. "It's okay. I want you to know. The eighteen months my grandmother spent as a partisan in the woods told her something. Never again would she remain silent if silence gave monsters license to be monsters, and bastards license to be bastards."

"Sounds like she was a badass."

"She was a hell-raiser. That was my grandmother. I wanted to be nothing more than exactly like her."

Tootsie went silent. Her grandmother's picture...the one Snedeker had destroyed that day in her office. It was good Tootsie had duplicates. Because no way did she ever want to forget what her grandmother looked like. How even when she was in her 50s, when the picture was taken, her hair was still black. She had great bunches of it, worn in a bun at the back her neck.

One tear trickled down her cheek. "My grandmother had blue eyes. They saw everything. They could snap with anger. They could go still and hard. But never at me."

Except they did go hard when they gazed at her own daughter, Tootsie's mother, Francine. Something Tootsie would not talk about, now.

Steve slid one, warm hand around the back of her neck. She shifted in his comforting arms.

"My grandmother's eyes sparkled, with just a little bit of tease in them as if she was saying, Y*ou and me, mammele, we can always find something to care about, yes?*"

Tootsie swallowed against the lump in her throat. "Mammele is kind of like sweetie, or little mommy. It's what grandmother types say to their granddaughters."

He shook her a little. "Remember? Worked at Sol's? If I heard that word once, I heard it a thousand times. The old guys who worked the counter called every girl who came in to shop mammele."

Tootsie's chest felt heavy. "So, yeah and…" she cleared her throat. "How she got to this country…she and my grandfather—he was a GI—met and married in a displaced persons camp in Germany."

He planted a kiss on her neck. "Nice."

"They lived in the Bronx before moving to Tenafly, which is where my mom and my aunt Marilyn were born."

"You have an aunt?"

"She lives in Hawaii and kind of divorced herself from the family, so no, I might as well not have one. Anyway, I don't know what happened to make my grandmother decide, but that's when she made up her mind."

"To do what?"

A dying ember popped in the fireplace. "To be a nuisance."

"And you followed her."

She craned her neck to look back at him. He stared back, his gaze liquid warm, accepting. His hands stroking her back said the same thing.

"You think I'm a nuisance?"

His smile broadened. "Do you care if someone calls you a nuisance?"

"Yes…No." She shook her head. "I don't know. If I could measure up to her…" She looked away from him, remembering. "You would have admired her…she was short, shorter than I am. Even so, big guys, and especially bad guys backed down because when she gave them one of her looks, they knew not to tangle with Hannah Wald." Tootsie smiled. "She was the strongest woman I ever knew. She was my north star. She taught me what was wrong. She taught me what was right."

She sat up. "Hold my place."

He held the blankets back so she could rise. "I won't give it away. I promise."

She stumbled out of the blanket cocoon into the frigid cold air. On bare feet, shivering, she ran into the kitchen to her desk and pulled the drawer open. In the back of the drawer, there it was. The letter. She grabbed it up and running, dove back into Steve's arms.

She held it up between them. "She wrote this the year I went away to college. I was overwhelmed, alone. Maybe in the tiniest of ways me being alone was like her being alone in the woods back in 1942 and she knew it. My grandmother knew I needed to be held, even if only with her words." Tootsie slipped the letter out of its envelope, handed it to Steve, and watched him read.

> *Tootsie, mammele, you lovely girl, named for my mother, may her memory be for a blessing. I know, darling…being in a new place where you don't know nobody, that's hard, and yes, even scary. But you are safe, my darling girl and that gives me peace. Never forget you are a wonderful girl with a big heart. You will find your way. The schoolwork, soon you'll see it won't be so hard, because you have an offeneh cupf, a smart mind. You will be with the ones who are like you, who care about important things, not empty-headed ones like your*

*mother. Always remember to be who I know
you are, a girl who does the right thing.*

*Sending kisses, Grandma Hannah*

He gave the note back to her. "She loved you."

Tootsie's eyes filled with tears. There was a boulder in her throat, so big it almost stopped up her words. "Yes, she loved me and I loved her. It was why I followed her, did what she did. I wanted to be like her."

"Was your mother jealous of the relationship you had with your grandmother?"

Was she? If she had been, the teen-aged Tootsie wouldn't have noticed. The adult Tootsie? "Let's just say my mother doesn't have much depth of understanding about the things that truly matter in this life."

Steve shifted so he could hold her against his side. "Okay, bad mom-daughter thing. And it's safe to say it wasn't your mom but your grandmother who told you it was okay to stand up on a chair and cause a riot."

*Yes.* "She might have gotten on it with me."

"Well, then." He cupped her face in both hands and face close to hers, fixed her with an intent stare. "You need to be a girl who does the right thing, don't you?"

"Yes," she whispered. Though she was still trying to figure out what the right thing was. And why, though she'd been named for a biblical heroine—two, really—she had never felt like one.

After, they fell asleep.

Until the rock came through the window.

# CHAPTER THIRTEEN

The sound was unmistakable. By the time Tootsie had lifted her head, Steve was up on his feet and out of the room, gun in hand. Tootsie hadn't noticed a gun last night. But then, she hadn't been thinking about a gun.

Moments later. he was back and she let herself stare. She would have to deal with something unpleasant in moments. But now, she'd let herself admire the sight of the naked man she'd had in her makeshift bed last night. He was all sleek muscles, and slim, powerful body. He glowed in the reflection of embers from the fireplace. And he was circumcised. Well, she'd known that, long before the insertion of his tab A. But for a tick of time, she'd wondered, when the moment came, if she'd get distracted by the sight of an uncircumcised tab A— him maybe not being circumcised like Jewish boys had to be—since she'd never seen one up close and personal.

"Stay right here," he said, voice curt, bringing her back to the present. In the light from the dying fire, and what little came in from under the drawn drapes and towels, he showed her his implacable cop face.

With spare movements, he pulled on his clothing: trousers, shirt, and boots. Gun in one hand, with the other hand he pushed her down on the sofa. "Don't move until I come back."

A second after he disappeared, she reached for her clothing, still across the sofa's arm where he'd thrown it last night. Even if he thought she'd follow *that* order—uh, no, not happening —it would be better to be dressed.

She slid into her things, and patted around on the floor for her socks. Finding them, getting to her feet, she stepped over the blankets, into the foyer, around the corner to the living room to peek in. And gasped. Her curtains billowed in the arctic air pouring in through a jagged-edged hole, about two feet in diameter in her bay window.

"What did I tell you?" came Steve's angry voice at her elbow.

It was questionable which jumped more: her heart or her feet. "You scared me half to death."

"Being scared to death would hurt a lot less than if I tackled you thinking you were the mutt who threw the rock through the window." He spoke in a fierce undertone. "You don't listen, Tootsie."

"I wanted to see the rock. And where were you just now?"

"I was checking the house."

He bent and came up with the rock. "Whoever threw this had plenty of muscle. A guy. Unless it was a woman who's an Olympic shot-putter."

She spared it one glance, shivered, now both unnerved *and* cold, and took a step into the living room to study the hole.

He grabbed her arm. "There's glass everywhere. You're barefoot."

She looked down. Yup. Shards. Visible in the light from outside. "I better get a broom. Or are you telling me I should wait on that, too?"

"Yeah, go get it. After you do, you're going back to sit by the fire."

"Boy, are you bossy," Tootsie said. There was no heat in her words, just a tinge of resentment.

"I don't care what you call me."

Words Tootsie knew to be one thousand percent true.

"Someone doesn't like you, Tootsie." He hefted the rock. "This is their message."

"Let me see."

He held it out to her.

It weighed heavy in her hand. Turning the rock face up, she read.

**Leave it alone.**

Goosebumps rose all over her body. "Leave what alone?"

"That's the question." He skirted around her. "Get me that broom and I'll sweep." He headed for the kitchen. "I saw a piece of plywood against the wall when I was in the garage yesterday. It's big enough for me to cover this hole. I'll be right back."

She heard the door to the garage open and shut. She looked at the rock again. Who'd thrown it?

The door to the garage banged back against the wall. She hurried behind him to get the broom before he could ask where it was.

Broom in hand, she waited in the foyer as he came back, plywood hefted in hand. "What are the chances you have a hammer and nails?" he asked, throwing the question over his shoulder as he strode toward her now ruined bay window.

She didn't like the way he asked the question. She was beginning to get ticked at him for being so high-handed.

"That hammer? Those nails? You going to get them for me?"

She gave him a look. But he didn't see it, since he'd already turned away. Which left her to lean the broom against the wall and go into the kitchen to rummage through the drawer where she kept her paltry supply of tools. Which included the hammer, and a small box of nails. Supplies in hand, she handed him the broom.

Working fast, Steve made thorough use of it,

sweeping the glass into a pile by the living room entryway. He hefted the hammer in one hand and took the box of nails from her in the other. "This is all you have?"

She looked at the box on his palm. "Sorry. Had I known we were going to need them, I would have gone down to Glen Allyn Hardware and asked for nails in every size and weight. That way I would have been ready for what you might have needed, while covering up a hole in a window I didn't think was going to be smashed into smithereens, like a punctuation point right after a snowstorm."

With a snort, he turned away from her and tramped back to his plywood. "Since you didn't, and because my phone is low on juice and I don't want to use my flashlight app, how about getting a flashlight."

Since they weren't going to be able to recharge her phone or his, she got his point, though she didn't like how he'd said it. "Now we need a flashlight? It's getting lighter out."

"Uh huh, and when I put this board up over the window, we'll lose the light."

A duh moment, courtesy of a hot man making cool sense, though she'd begun to think he was more annoyingly alpha than adorable.

She turned and went back to the great room where they'd left the flashlight on the sofa. She flicked the on switch just as he got the plywood in place over the window, plunging them into darkness.

"Anytime you're ready to shine that light over

here would be good."

She pointed the weak light in his direction. "Wouldn't it be more helpful if I were standing next to you shining what light there is right onto your hands, and you could get done quicker?"

"No." He began hammering.

"Seriously, you swept up the glass, and I'll look where I'm stepping."

"No."

"I could go upstairs and get a pair of shoes."

He stopped hammering. "And I could wait for you to get that pair of shoes, but I'm still not going to let you in here."

She huffed a breath. "Did I by some chance mention you're annoying? I think I should say it again. You're annoying. And getting on my nerves."

"What *I* think is you're not thinking."

He turned back to his self-appointed job and began to hammer away again. In the faint light cast by the flashlight she could see the quick, angry movement of his arm, as he drove one nail after the other into the plywood panel now covering the window.

There was something about how he worked that had her thinking. And then knowing. "It's those phone calls I've made, right?"

He slammed the hammer hard against the plywood and turned to point the thing at her. "And that guy at the radio station seeing you."

"It's the snake, too. That was a warning."

"Forget the snake. It's probably been hibernating in your wood pile since the first cold day this year." He put his hands on his hips.

The knowledge that maybe she'd gone too far looking for information from people who didn't want to give it to her, she said, "Some people might be unhappy with me."

"Might be?" He snorted. "They are."

"I didn't make that many phone calls."

He folded his arms across his chest. "One was too many."

"I needed some answers," she snapped. "I wouldn't have called if..." She petered out. In the cold light seeping in around the edges of the plywood, she could see that what she'd done might have been provocation.

"You can't keep on doing these things, Tootsie."

Feeling the heat of his criticism, she raised her chin. "Are you telling me to back off and let someone else take on whoever threw the rock?"

"Yeah. Someone official." He went back to hammering.

This time she didn't bother to hide her irritation. "Like someone official would care about the rock that went through my window? Or what happened at the radio station?"

He swerved around. In the flashlight's increasingly weak light, it was easy to see his eyes blaze with outrage. "You have a problem with authority that I don't like."

227

Her spine stiffened. "Ya think? Just as an FYI, it's for a good reason." She turned on her heel. "I'm going to change into fresh clothing."

As she tramped up to the second floor, he went back to hammering. Only when she got to her bedroom did she connect the way she'd stomped up the steps with the cold knowledge that she should have never let herself fall for Black Windbreaker. Because she *had* fallen for him, more than a little. She didn't like cops for a reason. He'd just reminded her why.

"Nice interlude," she gritted out. "Time to get over it, Toots."

Except that didn't explain why beneath the righteous anger that simmered through her body lurked disappointment.

And as she rubbed her chest, it didn't explain her sore heart. "I don't care," she repeated.

*Be a girl who does the right thing.*

Tootsie squeezed her eyes shut. Like that was a way that would help. Except whatever it was that was right, she knew it didn't involve telling herself lies.

"Someone's coming for me," he said when she got back downstairs, fully clothed. She'd put on her warmest sweater. Which did not keep her from feeling the cold that seeped through to her bones, a cold that wasn't about the temperature in the room.

But nobody showed up. After he'd paced back

and forth like her house was a cage at the zoo, he made a call…and came back ticked off. "It looks like nobody's coming to get me anytime soon."

"And isn't that something we're both unhappy about."

He ignored the snark, but sat down next to her on the couch. "I need to know. Now's a good time for you to tell me."

Tootsie picked at a cuticle on her thumb that no matter how many times she got a manicure it grew back to annoy her again. "Tell you what? Or is this just a random question you need to ask because if you're not poking at me you'll keel over in boredom?"

"What is it with you and this hate-on you have for cops?"

Her heart was no longer in it. By rote, she said, "I already told you. I guess you didn't think I meant it. It's all about civil disobedience. There should be no need for further explanation."

"Is that what you called it when the Lodi police arrested you back…what, those thirty years ago?"

She abandoned her cuticle. "How do you know that? The record was supposed to be expunged."

"You think I couldn't find out? I've already told you I can find out anything I want to find out."

She leapt up. "What gives you the right to invade my privacy?" She darted over to the fireplace and pressed her back against the rough, brick facing. "I've spent my entire adult life steering clear of law enforcement, and you just reminded me why."

He gave her one of his inscrutable looks that she was so not fond of, then rose, stepped over to where she stood, took her hand and pulled her to sit back down with him.

He turned her to him, one hand cupping her cheek. In a soft voice, he said, "I want you to stop whatever it is you're doing. You're scaring me."

She leaned away from him as best she could, a hard thing since he wouldn't let go of her hand. "I should care that I'm doing something to scare you? You must be confusing me with someone who cares about that, which is not me."

He shook his head at the words, stroked her cheek with the back of his fingers. "Tell me why it happened."

She pried her hand from his and slid across the couch to the other side. "If you've already nosed your way into my record, you don't need me to tell you what happened. You know."

He slid across to her so they were hip to hip, body to body, and took her hand back. "I know why you got arrested. I want to know what that cop did that made you hit him."

Mouth open, ready to deliver another snappish answer, she shut that impulse down. "So…you think I might have been justified?"

"You might have been."

She blinked. "Excuse me. I think some master manipulator just took over your mouth and these un-cop-like words came pouring out."

He had the nerve to laugh. "No, that was me. See, the reason I ask is because, Esther Ruth Goldberg, I already know you." He looked down at their fingers, linked together.

And then he picked up his head and looked deep into her eyes. He raised her hand to his mouth and turning it over, pressed his lips to her palm. "What I know about you is you never start anything. But you sure as hell finish it. So, c'mon. Tell me what he did."

The weirdest thing…she couldn't catch her breath. Of the very few people who knew what happened that day, they all assumed she was arrested for a good reason, because she'd assaulted a cop. But not this black and white issue guy, sitting next to her, holding her hand, looking at her, waiting with patience for her answer. For the nuance. Which she'd never thought cops saw.

Looking into his luminous, dark eyes, all the resentment melted away…and this need to tell him bubbled up, choking her as it rose into her throat.

"My grandmother had her following by then, people who believed what she was doing was righteous. There were five of us that day, all holding signs…" She had to clear her throat… It was hard to go on.

"This company, C&K Chemical, had been dumping waste from their manufacturing processes into the Ligonier River, which runs through about ten towns in Bergen County and then on into the Meadowlands, which didn't need any of that crap making its way into its waters. No matter who tried to stop them, what laws were put forth, C&K got their lobbyists to keep all of it from happening so they could go on with their business, so they could keep poisoning the environment. And people."

He rubbed the back of her knuckles. "Go on."

"Since they'd refused to make any changes, my grandmother decided they needed to be shamed in hopes that would work." She licked her lips. "Local media knew all about Hannah Wald and her causes. They were there and took plenty of shots of our signs. The signs said things like 'Honk if you think C&K Chemicals should be shut down', and 'When was the last time you saw a fish in the Ligonier River?' But my favorite was 'C&K doesn't care if you get cancer'.

He huffed a laugh. "The reporters must have loved that."

"They did." Tootsie swallowed hard. "But then we didn't expect to happen what did happen."

She took her hand from his and rose. "C&K had by this time had it with all the lawsuits and the demonstrations. They hired security to keep people like us away from their gates. So within five minutes these big guys came out and started pushing us back off the sidewalk in front of the plant. But that sidewalk was public property and we had a right to be there. So one of the people in our little group called the cops and they came, though all they did was stand and watch."

That soothing movement of his thumb against her hand…the feel of it was lodged in the back of her mind, now, comforting her as she told her terrible story.

"Given her history, my grandmother was not a fan of men telling her what to do. So she stepped back up on that sidewalk and shoved her sign up in the eyeballs of the biggest of the security guys. He pushed her. She stumbled back off the sidewalk and went down. She got right back up in his face. She didn't say a word, mind you, just brandished that sign at him."

Tootsie paused. "The three people from that environmental group ran. I stood there like someone had cemented my feet to the pavement. I did nothing to help my grandmother."

She began to rock. "That's when this one cop…he was a real porker…grabbed my grandmother's arm and yanked her off the sidewalk, again, and pulled her clear across the street."

Tootsie took a breath. "She fell a second time, this time into the street. The cop laughed."

A moment of silence. Then, in a quiet voice, Steve said, "And so you hit him because when he laughed at her, he disrespected her and you weren't having that."

She took her hand from his and wound her arms around herself and rocked. "No. I should have but I didn't. I should have stood between him and my grandmother, but I did nothing. Because I was scared."

"Tootsie," he whispered.

"Don't even try to make an excuse for me. I should have done something. It was only when that cop laughed that all the guilt I felt broke loose, and I went overboard, slamming him on his back with my sign over and over again. Until he turned around and grabbed me, threw my sign to the ground, and another cop put handcuffs on me, put me in a squad car, and took me down to the station. The last I saw of my grandmother she was sitting on the curb, a hand to her head. I left her, and yeah, I know. I didn't have a choice. But the cops left her. How could they do that?"

She laughed, not a funny sound. "You think I'm a heroine because Esther is my name, worse my middle name is Ruth? In that bible story Ruth never left Naomi. But me? What I should have done was stay by my grandmother so she never fell, the first time or the second. I shouldn't have let myself freeze up and then lose control." She swiped a hand across her nose because whenever she had to work at not crying, her nose ran. "If I'd done the right thing, my grandmother wouldn't have died that night."

He pulled her back into his arms. "I'm so sorry."

Tootsie shook her head. "She died because she hit her head when she fell. Or maybe it was her heart that had felt so much pain in her life that she gave up."

She sighed. "For years after, I never forgave

myself. Because I couldn't count on knowing what the right thing was, I decided I wouldn't try to figure it out. I told myself someone else could go out on a limb for whatever it was they believed in. And I?" She snorted. "I kept my thoughts to myself."

He exhaled a quiet breath and pressed his lips to her head.

She burrowed herself into his arms, giving him the right to comfort her and trying not to think about the guilt and pain she'd carried for so long. "Until Monday. At the radio station. Something broke loose then and I knew I couldn't keep quiet anymore. I can't decide what it was. Maybe me seeing the pain on Fern's face, knowing what was going to happen to her when she lost her job, knowing what would happen to some of my other colleagues, none of it good? I don't know."

"Yeah," he said, the word, corroboration.

He swayed a little, the movement, comforting. "At least now I understand why you've got a thing for cops." He kissed the top of her head. "After all these years? Maybe it's time for you to let that go."

Maybe she should. Maybe this thing between the two of them was telling her she didn't need to hate every cop. After all, now there were two she knew…Brian and Black Windbreaker…who didn't fit the description she'd forever attributed to men and women in blue.

He sighed again. "You can't go it alone, Toots. You know that, don't you? Most of us are not like that asshole who put his hands on your grandmother. Most of us do what we do because we want to protect people. But that said, even when a cop is an asshole, it's not a reason to operate outside the system. That's called anarchy, insurrection, vigilantism."

When she stiffened, he put her away from him with hands on shoulders stared down into her eyes. "Let the system take care of the Petrocellis. They could already be in a shit ton of it, if what that reporter at the *Daily Mouse* uncovered is true. Let things run their course."

"And who benefits from that?" Her frustration level kicked up again. "The wheels of justice grind away at the pace of a snail and if you've got good lawyers…and you know the Petrocellis have lawyers at the top of their game…justice gets delayed indefinitely. My friends will see justice maybe in the next millennium. When they're dead."

He sighed. "Whatever you think, you making your phone calls is not getting you anywhere. So far, from what I can see…" He pointed toward the living room… "All you've done is make yourself a target."

She rubbed her face, tired to death of the frustration that had been with her since she'd walked into the promotions closet to find Robert in there. "And now that I've become a so-called target, what will you do? Some guys from the detective division in the Glen Allyn police will come by, look at the rock and the hole in my window, and write a report?"

"Yes. And then you'll move on, leave it alone like

I want you to."

"I can't. That rock means there's something somebody doesn't want me to know."

"I'll say it again. You're not a professional." He pointed at the rock where she'd laid it down on the floor. "Leave it to the people who know what they're doing."

Tootsie's insides tightened. She'd left it alone for thirty years and what had that gotten her?

"That wouldn't be me doing the right thing."

He shook his head. "I think you don't know what the right thing is. I think you're putting yourself out there because some bastards turned your friends' lives upside down. You're angry. You want to get back at them for that."

That stung. She swallowed her disappointment. "Is that what you think?"

He came to his feet as she did. "I don't think there's anything wrong with standing up for people who need standing up for."

He put his arms around her. For the split of a second she resisted.

He gave her shoulder a squeeze. "How about putting on your coat and boots and coming with me. Maybe the mini mart in that strip center—it's about five blocks down isn't it—might have power."

Getting out of the house suddenly seemed the right thing to do. "And if they don't?"

"Let's just take it one step at a time. How about you go get your boots. You do have boots, right?"

She thought about sticking her tongue out at him.

He gave her tush a pat and sent her in the direction of her fleece-lined boots, which she put on along with her coat and gloves.

On their tramp through the hushed streets, they saw the occasional person, out to observe the state of their sidewalks. By the time they got to the mini-mart, Tootsie was tired of tramping. And thinking about where in her life she'd gone wrong. But she gave up on any existential thoughts when her eyes told her the mini-mart had power. After knocking the snow off her boots, Tootsie hoofed it toward the tall carafes in the center of the store, and poured herself a cup of coffee, hot, strong, and black, while Steve called his office.

"They're going to pick me up in a few."

Over the lip of her cup, she said, "You've been saying that, but so far it hasn't happened."

"It will this time." He looked down at her, that cop face on full display. "I don't want you going back to your house. Until the power comes back to your street it'll be cold as a witch's tit in your place."

She snorted. "And where would you like me to go?"

His mouth quirked up in a suggestion of a smile. "You could go with me."

Could he have said anything else that would send her brain in five directions at once while giving her that smile that made her knees go weak? It *so* wasn't fair.

"I suppose you want me to go with you down to the courthouse to complete the paperwork so you can throw me in the lockup." There, snark. Snark was an easy thing for her to handle.

He raised an eyebrow. "Jail."

"Slammer."

He looked around him at people coming into the 7-11 in twos and threes, no doubt thrilled to get out of their powerless burrows. Then he looked back at her, bent, and whispered in her ear. "Jail."

She caught her breath at the scent of him. "I say pen."

He ruffled her curls. "Jail."

"Hoosegow," she whispered, and canted toward him.

He leaned toward her. "What's a hoosegow?"

"I think that's what Wyatt Earp and his friends called jail."

There was the sound of a horn that had them both turning toward the plate glass window fronting the mini-mart. They straightened away from each other.

"That's my ride." He wound an arm around her shoulders. "Go with me because I don't want to worry."

"Oh ho!" She snorted a laugh. "Now I get it. This is all about your peace of mind, huh?"

"It is and too bad. I don't want you back at the house. And because I think, no matter what I've said, once you have a phone in your hand again, you'll do what I told you that you shouldn't."

She held her hands up. "You convinced me. I'm done with all that."

"We'll see." He squeezed her arm and pushed her out the door—after she'd paid for her coffee—into the mounded snow, blown into drifts as high as the door in places.

He gave her one of his sweet smiles, the perfect kind because it was so unexpected on such a stern face.

Happiness that made no sense cascaded through her. Not with her life in turmoil and her heart telling her she needed to chill.

She let herself be bundled into the back seat of one of those pickup trucks that was so high it needed a running board to get in. Steve introduced her to the driver, a friend of his, a county cop named Mike, who said "Hey", and promptly ignored her.

For a minute she listened to them talk, not that she got more than a smidge of what they were talking about: the snow, the disruptions all around the state, the accidents on the roads, people stranded overnight in their cars. And then they began talking so softly that all she heard was the drone of their voices.

She was doing some serious zoning when she realized Steve was trying to get her attention.

"Sorry. What?"

"Power's back in Bergen County. Do you know anyone who lives in Bergen?"

She took a breath. "My mother lives in Tenafly."

"How about if I dropped you off there?"

# CHAPTER FOURTEEN

Tootsie bolted upright. "When did you get the idea I'd want to be dropped off at my mother's?"

"A minute ago."

"So take another minute, turn around, and drop me off in Glen Allyn."

"We don't have time."

"Says you."

"Yeah, says me. Besides there's no place in Glen Allyn you can go right now."

"You could drop me off at the 7-11. I'll hang out in the automotive aisle."

He turned halfway around. "I didn't think this was going to be more than a quick run to pick up a guy who needs to be at a county task force meeting Mike and I are on. But the meeting site and time got changed and we need to get there a-sap. I can't be running back to Glen Allyn to drop you off."

"You know just because I shared my personal history with you this morning, doesn't mean I elected you my guardian," she argued.

"Say what you want, but it is what it is."

Hot as she was that Steve was carting her around like she was a package, she'd forgotten they weren't alone. When Mike began to laugh, she slammed her mouth shut.

"You kids," chuckled Mike.

"Shut up, asshole," said Steve, not bothering to raise his voice. Mike got the point and shut up.

*She* wasn't ready to, though. "Maybe there's a warming center somewhere."

"I thought about that and I checked the one that's closest. But it's jammed. You really want to go there?"

Did she? There'd be complaining people, crying babies, and children with too much energy, running around like vilde chayas. No, she didn't want to go to a warming center. "What about your office? Drop me off at your office. I'll sit in a chair in a corner and be quiet."

He snorted. "It's not on the way. Besides, knowing you, I'd come back and find you going through my files."

She zipped up her lips. She probably would go through his files for want of anything better to do.

Mike turned onto Route 4, which looked like a snow tunnel with the mounds of snow piled high on each side of the highway. "There's got to be someplace," Tootsie mumbled.

"There isn't."

"So I'll wait in the truck."

"I don't know how long we're going to be."

Was that true? How would she know?

She stopped trying to come up with options for where Steve should take her other than her mother's. And then it was too late.

And now, here she was. Steve's hand on her upper arm guiding her up the unplowed, front walkway of her mother's townhouse, bought after Tootsie's dad died—, Francine was fond of saying she moved because she didn't need that big house where Tootsie had grown up—she dragged her feet. As the front door opened, she took a breath, and made first eye contact with her mother, whose smile, plastered on her face, told Tootsie she was getting ready to be charming, and it wasn't because she was happy to see her daughter.

Tootsie came to a stop.

Leaning in, Steve said, "I know this isn't what you want. But there was no choice, once our plans changed."

"Now he comes clean," she mumbled, pretending she was a ventriloquist so her mother wouldn't see her talking and wonder what she could be saying.

"You'll be fine. My meeting won't be long. I'll be back to pick you up before you kill each other."

Oh, he of too great faith.

"Darling, how lovely to see you." Francine Wald Schiffman, as she was known on Facebook, held the door wide open. "What a nice surprise. After such a big snowstorm, I didn't imagine you might come for a visit. If I had, well I would…" She stopped and shrugged.

Right from the get-go Tootsie's stomach was tied in knots.

Francine stepped back. "It's so cold." She hugged herself and shivered as they trudged up the three steps to the door.

It was probably not a good way to start things off if Tootsie pointed out that she wouldn't be so cold if she wore something other than what Francine called a Florida outfit: a turquoise, short-sleeved blouse and white, summer pants. It was the kind of thing Francine wore at her apartment in Del Ray Beach where she spent February and March…before Passover when she came back north for the Seders.

"And who is this handsome man with you," Francine simpered, fingering the strands of blue and green beads around her neck. She fluttered her fingers at said man.

"Hey, ma'am. I'm Steve." And he gave her one of those smiles he rarely gave Tootsie.

Wasn't that reason enough for her to want to wipe it from his face.

Tootsie said, "Do you think we can come in? My boots are filled with snow."

Francine patted her perfectly-coifed gold-blond hair. "Of course you two can come in." She stepped aside. "I hope you'll stay, Steve."

"Thanks for the invitation, ma'am but I need to go. I'll be back to pick up Tootsie after a while. I hope you don't mind letting her stay here until then."

"Well of course, I don't." Francine fluttered her eyelashes at him.

Sliding his arm around Tootsie's shoulders, Steve turned her to him and bent to kiss her cheek. Like she wasn't who he'd spent the last few hours with, limbs entwined, lips on various body parts. "You can do this," he whispered into her ear.

Before she could cook up a fitting answer, he was off, slogging back down the walk to Mike's truck.

Francine waved as Mike gunned down the street, leaving them in a world of white, the sound of snow blowers doing their thing in the distance. Watching the truck disappear around the corner, a glum Tootsie thought it was like watching the last ship sail for the New World.

"I'm so pleased to see you, Tootsie, but why after a snowstorm instead of a more normal day?"

If it was normal Tootsie would never have been here. So she limited herself to a sanitized version of the last two days. She left out the parts about the snake, the rock, and the interlude in front of her fireplace.

"That sounds like a lot."

More than Tootsie would ever tell.

"And it's too bad your new friend couldn't stay," Francine went on.

"He's busy."

"Oh? He has to work on a day like this? What does Steve do?"

Here it came. "He's a cop."

Francine's feigned pleasure morphed into calculation. "Knowing how you feel about cops…?"

Like Tootsie wanted to explain how Steve had come, with an arrest warrant in hand to her front door, only to have his car crushed in her driveway? And that was only part of the story?

"For me it doesn't matter," Francine said. And then after a strategically placed beat, she added, "Like I always thought it mattered to you. Oh, well, that's old business."

It wasn't old business. It was unresolved business.

"So, how are the boys? Did they call on your birthday?"

"They reached out. I exchanged messages with Josh. I'm sure I'll speak to him over the weekend sometime."

"And Sam?"

Yes, Sam. Her problem child. "He sent me a What's App."

"I don't know what that is, but that Sam…" Crafty gaze fixed on Tootsie, Francine said, "I don't know why you two don't get along. I don't have that problem with him."

Which made Tootsie feel guilty. Which Tootsie knew was her mother's intention. How great was that?

"I see you still wear black, Tootsie."

As if that put her in league with degenerates.

"I especially like to wear black in a snowstorm. The contrast, you know."

Francine gave her the side eye, not sure Tootsie wasn't taking a shot at her. Because as Tootsie knew too well, her mother didn't get subtleties. "Since you've been out, maybe you know how the plowing is going. Of course, they won't plow our street anytime soon."

Great. Whining. Francine's go-to. "Do you have someone coming to shovel out your walk and driveway?"

Francine sighed. "I have a service. And I ask you. Where are they?" She made a motioning gesture. "But let's not talk about my problems. Come. Let's have a cup of something hot." She began to walk toward the kitchen. "What do you like? Earl Grey? Or perhaps something decaffeinated?"

"Earl Grey works." Tootsie trailed slowly through her mother's compact living room with its white wicker furniture, and throw pillows in shades of turquoise, salmon, and yellow...a weirdly-expressed wish to find herself in southern climes when her climes were north of the Mason Dixon Line. From there they walked into Francine's miniscule kitchen with its white table and white chairs, the white-faced

248

cabinets, and the white marble countertop.

In a couple of minutes Francine had a cup of tea set in front of Tootsie and one for her. Sitting, she said, "While you're here, we should catch up. I'll tell you what's going on in my life and you can tell me what's going on in yours." Francine gave Tootsie a coy look. "Won't that be fun?"

Like bungee-jumping without the sling. "Okay."

"Oh Lord, Tootsie." She touched her artful curls, which were sprayed into a holding pattern. "This snowstorm is so inconvenient."

As if it had occurred just to annoy her. "How so?"

"Well, I had planned to go to the big sale at Chico's. Now, who knows if they'll have anything left I want." Francine's colored-to-perfection lips turned down.

"Chico's will have another sale tomorrow. Besides, everyone else can't get there either, so chances are you'll find what you're looking for."

"Yes, I suppose, but..." Francine's voice trailed off. "There was this one pair of pants..."

"Oh, like these?" Tootsie angled her chin toward what her mother wore.

"No, indeed. The style on sale isn't always available in my size." She sighed. "If I don't get them...? I suppose I'll have to find something else similar to bring with me."

"To?"

"To Turks and Caicos. Renee and I are going

with the Jewish Community Center Seniors."

Renee Glassman. Horrible human being. Francine's BFF. She of the heavily-lined eyes, lipstick the color of plums, and oversize diamond ring the glow of which could banish the night.

"You're still friends with her?" The words came out sharper than she'd intended.

Francine's eyes opened wide. "Why wouldn't I be?"

Maybe because Renee Glassman had played a role in her grandmother's death?

When Tootsie didn't respond, Francine added, "Can you imagine if this snowstorm was next Thursday when we're scheduled to leave? I guess I should be grateful."

Tootsie told herself not to pursue the subject. It would get them nowhere except into the heat of an argument she needed to avoid. All she had to do was keep Renee from her mind and she'd get through the next however long it took until Steve came back for her.

"So, Tootsie." Her mother made a face. "My therapist told me something she suggested I share with you."

This was going to be interesting. "What?"

"According to her, I need to unburden myself of the things that bother me so I can feel better about myself." She gave a girlish giggle.

"I thought when you see a therapist you're supposed to keep it all to yourself."

"It concerns my mother," Francine said.

Tootsie stiffened. This was territory more dangerous than talking about Renee.

"According to my therapist, Holocaust survivors dealt with their kids in different ways. Some were overprotective. Some saw their kids as replacements. Some, like my mother, were entirely hands off because they were too busy trying to right wrongs no one could right."

"So what does your therapist say you need to do now? Dig up your mother and tell her how ticked you are that she wasn't what you wanted her to be?"

Francine reddened.

Tootsie took a deep breath to center herself. "Let's not talk about this. Your relationship with your mother and mine with you has been a bone of contention between us for a long time."

"That's true." Francine clenched her jaw tight and took a breath. "So, tell me how your birthday was. Did you celebrate? It was a big one."

"It came and it went, like all birthdays." Hands in her lap, Tootsie linked her fingers together. Hard. "Tell me, anything good going on in your life?"

"Well, if you really want to know, it's been one terrible thing after another. On Wednesday, I had my usual mani-pedi."

"What's terrible about a mani-pedi?"

"It shouldn't have been, but my usual girl quit, and the girl who did my nails? I hope they fire her. I have two bubbles in the polish on my left pinky."

"I hate when that happens." Tootsie said, eyes on her cup. Calm, she told herself. Remain calm.

"Exactly. I had her do it all over again. And didn't give her a tip."

Tootsie was surprised her mother hadn't suggested the woman be banned from the profession forever.

"And after I left the salon, I headed up to the Club for canasta and Dot Rehnquist was there for the first time in months. I'm going to insist upon a new rule. You cannot miss more than two sessions. Either she follows the rules or that's the end of her."

"Hmm. Make sure you hide the body." Tootsie took a sip of her tea, and wished it was something with calming properties. Like chamomile.

"Very funny. As if I would do something violent."

Not with her own hands she wouldn't.

"So enough about me. What about you?"

Tootsie knew she was going to have to deal with it sometime. "Actually, the radio station was sold. We found out on Monday."

"What!" Her mother made a sound of horror. "Oh, Tootsie, I'm so sorry to hear that. You worked at that radio station a long time."

"Yes, I did." The look on Francine's face spoke of sympathy. Was it possible her mother felt concern for what had happened?

Francine prissed up her lips. "I told you, didn't I? You should never have taken that job. Maybe that man gave it to you as a kindness."

Nice. Suggesting Tootsie didn't have the chops to do said job.

"You should have taken your degree in education and become a teacher, like Beth Freeman, so you'd always have something to fall back on. Beth…Mickey Freeman's daughter…you remember her."

Like Tootsie could forget Beth Freeman. Her mother had been throwing the sainted Beth up to her all her adult life.

Tootsie exhaled on a frustrated breath. "Here's a newsflash, Mom. I was never going to be a teacher, which was a good thing. The kids would have hated me."

"You're being silly."

Tootsie was beginning to sweat. "Can we pick something else to talk about?" Except they were running out of what to talk about.

Francine's mouth turned down. "You didn't want to hear about my therapist, you don't want to know about Renee. Be honest. There's nothing in my life you find interesting. I'm trying to make things better between us, but I don't think you want to."

And just like that, the hounds were let loose.

"I'll tell you what I do want." Tootsie sat forward. "An end to listening to your litany of complaints about your life and how sad and terrible it is. You have a good life if only you'd look at it that way."

"Well! That's not very nice." The over-the-top

happy tone Francine had started this conversation with transformed into her default bitterness. "It seems no matter how I try, there's no pleasing you." She folded her arms, and color high, looked away. Jaw working, she said, "How did I get so lucky? A daughter who's as uninterested in my life as my mother was."

Tootsie felt an adrenalin surge. "Your mother would have been interested in your life, if you'd been interested in hers."

"Naturally, you would say that. From the time you were a little girl, you liked all that nonsense she involved herself with."

"It wasn't nonsense. Grandma did the right thing and I wanted to as well."

"Oh, good Lord, Tootsie, do you hear yourself? *That* is nonsense."

The furious tremble in Tootsie's voice took over. "She made it her life's work to call out suffering. Are you telling me there's something wrong with that?"

Francine made an inarticulate sound of contempt.

"Your mother stood up against those who'd take away women's rights, civil rights, against those who would destroy the environment. How could you think that was nonsense?"

"Because I did!" Francine's eyes flashed with anguish. "I wanted my mother to be like other mothers. I wanted my mother to pick me up after school instead of expecting me to walk home no matter what the weather was. I wanted my mother to take me on shopping sprees for cashmere sweaters and go on day trips to spas. But no. My mother said no one needed cashmere sweaters, and my father, who gave in to anything my mother said, agreed. And day spas? She didn't have time for that."

"Because lives mattered to her. Not things." Tootsie slapped a hand on the table for emphasis. "Didn't you understand?"

"I understood that she didn't understand me. I never forgave her."

Tootsie took in a sharp breath. "Is that why you did it?"

Francine looked wary. "Did what?"

"Didn't go to grandma's house that night, the night after the demonstration at C&K Chemicals. The night she died."

Francine made a wordless protest. But Tootsie wasn't finished.

"You know, looking back, I get why you didn't come to the police station to bail me out. I was trouble, just like your mother was trouble and you'd thrown up your hands over both of us. That is, until later when you and Dad realized it made you two look bad to have a daughter with an arrest record and you found a judge to make it go away."

"It wasn't like that—"

Tootsie silenced her with furious eyes. "What I still don't get is why, when the police let me call you, and I pleaded with you to go over to grandma's house to check on her, you didn't."

Nostrils flaring, her jaw clenched hard, she finished with, "Don't bother answering. I know why. You were too busy playing mah-jongg with Renee Glassman. And Renee convinced you to wait until the game was over. After which it was too late."

Tootsie came to her feet. "Don't you ever feel guilty?"

Francine came to her feet, too. "Don't you speak to me that way!" She drew herself up as tall as she could. Affronted.

In Tootsie's mind, Francine had no grounds for that. More than anything, she wanted what she said next to wipe that self-righteous look off her mother's face. Except, she couldn't say it, the thing that would scrape away whatever tiny mother-daughter thing that was left between them.

Because for the first time ever, she'd seen something in Francine's eyes, something about the way she recounted growing up, not having the things other girls had, wanting them, knowing she wouldn't get them. Something sad.

Even if she'd loved her grandmother in ways she could never love Francine, Tootsie knew. Everyone wanted to be loved. And cherished. And yes, maybe even pampered. Her mother hadn't gotten any of that.

She began to speak when her phone rang. Tootsie snatched it up.

It was Steve. The man was a savior because right

there in that moment before she picked up, she'd been about to express…what…sympathy? Understanding? No, she didn't want to do that. "Hey," she said, turning away from the table. And from her mother's hurt eyes.

"Tootsie."

"Yeah. Who else would be answering my phone?" She caught her breath on that spate of sarcasm. Like he was responsible for the corrosive argument she'd been having with her mother?

Before she could apologize…and give him a heart attack because she was pretty sure he thought she didn't know how to apologize, he said, "I need to come back to pick you up, now. Can you be ready to leave in fifteen minutes?"

"Absolutely." Ending the call she glanced across the table at Francine…her mother…still standing, looking for all the world, lost.

God, Tootsie hated this feeling that she was…no, she wouldn't say it even to herself. But she couldn't help thinking it. She'd thought she knew everything there was to know about her mother. Apparently, she was wrong. "Listen, I—"

Francine cut her off with a chop of her hand. "Just go."

As Tootsie said goodbye and walked out the door, she thought there for a moment, maybe a second, she could understand how Francine felt. Forgive? That was never going to happen.

# CHAPTER FIFTEEN

She waited outside, though it was cold, clomping down the still un-shoveled front walkway to Mike's truck, when Steve pulled up to the curb, no Mike with him.

"Where's your friend?" Tootsie heard the tremble in her voice, the after-effects of the scene she'd just walked away from.

"At that meeting."

"You didn't need to stay?" She hoisted herself into the truck, fastened her seatbelt, and pressed one hand to her chest against her still racing heart.

"Nah, I dropped off my report and they released me."

That wasn't a moment too soon. Deep breaths, she told herself. Deep breaths.

He looked straight ahead, concentrating on his driving. His silence lasted until they turned onto a now-plowed Route 4. "How did it go with your mother? Is she still alive?"

She knew he'd ask. "I learned things about her." She had. And now she was struggling with a compassion she didn't want to feel for Francine.

"Anything good?"

Of course he'd follow up question number one with question number two since Tootsie had given him a non-answer. She hadn't been able to forgive Francine forever. Perhaps she'd called her Francine all these years because she didn't deserve to be called mother.

Maybe it was time to think about trying to forgive?

*Not yet.*

Having no idea that there was a whole conversation going on inside her cranium, because how would he know since he wasn't inside there with her, Steve said, "Okay. I won't ask." She was grateful for that, considering how her brain was roiled with emotions she didn't want to deal with.

Without taking his eyes from the road, he nodded. "I've got some news."

"Oh?" Tootsie perked up. She had a need to be seriously distracted from the tumult in her head. "You do?"

"You wanted to know about Elizabeth Comstock, right?"

She stared at him. "What reason did you have for looking up Elizabeth Comstock. I didn't tell you I wanted to know about her."

"Yes, but you left that folder out when you put all the others together. I decided when I had a moment, today, which I did, I would see what I could find out about her. It seems she was a very good friend of your boss, Stan."

"That's news of a sort." She eased a hand out of a glove and tapped her chin with her index finger. "But why are you helping me? Is this you being the professional?"

At the look on his face, she bit her lip. Mouth open, brain not in gear. "I meant I'm happy you're helping. But so what, that she was a friend?"

He changed lanes to get out from behind a lumbering plow. "She was the friend who donated land for the radio station's transmitter site."

Tootsie blinked. "You mean the land where the transmitter and tower sit now?"

"Yeah, there. The radio station's original transmitter site turned out to be a sink hole. The Comstock woman donated land for it to be moved to where it is now. The FCC approved, the move got made, and that was that."

"So the donation was just a donation."

"It was a donation."

Tootsie chewed on her lip. Like The Committee was just a committee.

"Did you hear what I said?"

"I'm listening." And thinking that this was one more trail that led nowhere in the quest to find something that would nullify the station's sale to the Petrocellis.

"This means you don't need to make any more phone calls to anyone else associated with the new radio station."

"Except…what about the rock?"

Steve speared her with one of his tight-lipped cop looks. "You need to wait for the Glen Allyn police to get to it. They're a little busy wouldn't you think with fender benders, blocking off streets where electric lines are down. In the meantime, you could do us all a favor and try not to piss off more people than you already have."

She ignored the insult. Not that she was even thinking of insults when she had a revelation to deal with. He'd looked into Elizabeth Comstock's background. His answer didn't satisfy her.

"So you think that's the whole enchilada, that I'm grasping at tortillas when there truly aren't any?"

"I don't know what you mean about enchiladas and tortillas, but yeah, that's what I think. You're going to have to figure out what other right thing to do with your life."

The sun was shining brightly now. As they swung onto Martling Avenue, the main drag that led to Glen Allyn's downtown—such as it was—she said, "So where are we going? I assume not to take me to jail." She crossed her fingers, a hard thing to do with gloves on.

He gave her that look that said that joke's getting

old. "To your house. I need some papers I left on the seat of my car."

"If you can get them out of the car, that is."

The buzz they heard as they turned onto Tootsie's street told them his chances were good. Ben Hart's tree had fallen not just on Tootsie's property and Steve's car but the street as well, a reason for there to be that big tree removal truck, with one of those big winches on the back at the end of her driveway. Two men were already cutting Ben Hart's tree into a lot of cute little logs.

"Ben is going to be ticked off that he's not here to get the lion's share of the wood," Tootsie said. "The tree roots are on his property." Getting out of the car, admiring the work, she tramped up toward her front door...just as Steve grabbed her, all but yanking her off her feet.

She tried to wrestle her arm away. "What is the matter with you?"

Voice curt, he said, "Your door is open."

It was, an inch, maybe two.

They had not left the door open.

As he disappeared inside, she swallowed her unease and followed him, at least up to the door but not in. With one tentative gesture, she pushed the door wide.

If the rock had been a warning, what she saw in her foyer was an exclamation point. Her curio cabinet, all smashed glass, was lying on its side on her gray slate floor. Its contents were strewn everywhere.

Tootsie's first reaction was no reaction. And then reality whooshed in like a hawk swooping in for the kill. All those little Meissen monkeys she'd bought on a trip to Prague a few years ago, the ones she had to have because they were so silly, were no more than chunks of porcelain. Her beautiful Royal Doulton princesses, and lovely Limoges hand-painted boxes lay on the floor like so much garbage.

Worst of all, there in the midst of all that destruction, her grandmother's turquoise-blue vase with the bird design, the one thing, other than the precious picture, that she had of her grandmother. It was broken into three big pieces.

She gasped. Steve put an arm around her shoulders. It was then that the tears began to pour down her face. Not tears of grief, but of rage. "Those bastards," she gritted between her teeth, struggling to wrench herself out of his grip. "Those damn bastards."

He steered her back outside. "I need you to step outside the house."

She stood on her top step, eyes on the crack of the door where he'd left it open, as if she could see inside, clutching her arms to herself and shivering. The obscenity of it…her mind tried to grapple with what someone had done. To her things. To her.

So much for The Committee only being a committee, and Mrs. Comstock only donating land to Stan for the transmitter and tower. The instant she saw that obscenity in her foyer she knew all of it was connected.

She'd wiped the tears from her face by the time Steve came back outside. "I've got a couple of officers on the way."

"I'm not waiting for them to get here." She pushed him aside. "Unless there's someone in there with my meat cleaver in their hand and it's dripping with blood, I'm going in to see what else has been wrecked." She matched words to action and stepped around him. He gave way.

She looked into the living room where everything looked as it should, even the plywood over the window. Then she moved on to the great room.

The couch was where they'd left it in front of the fireplace. Arlo's recliner, which she'd always hated, stood where it had always stood. Tootsie turned to Steve. Pointing to the recliner, she said, "This they couldn't have destroyed?"

He grunted, but she was already moving on to the kitchen, which was as neat as she'd left it. The one big pot she'd used to make soup sat on the counter ready to be hung up on the hook where it belonged. She turned around. "I'm trying to make sense of this. Why didn't they wreck the whole house? Why just the foyer? Why just my curio cabinet?"

"Whoever it was probably would have done more but stopped when the tree removal guys showed up and he left out the back door. I found prints in the snow. This with your curio cabinet? It looks like malice and that someone I keep telling you about having it in for you. If you don't stop, they won't. Next time they'll do the whole house, maybe with you in it."

She rounded on him. "So you think this is all because I'm annoying?"

"Whatever, that's more reason for you do to what I'm telling you. Back off. Now. At last."

She gave him a ferocious frown. "Maybe we've slept together, but that doesn't give you the right to tell me what to do."

His lips pressed so hard together, a white line showed up around them. "If you're doing something you shouldn't be, yeah, it does."

"I'm going into New York. To the Petrocelli's corporate offices."

"Now, that's one hell of an idea. What's your plan, then? You going to break down their office door? Scream so you'll scare someone into opening it for you? Or are you just going to stand there until Petrocelli calls the NYPD to escort you out of their building?"

"I'm not a screamer."

He huffed in disgust. "That's one good thing."

"So what do *you* think I should do? Just step aside and let you and your pals investigate this when we both know exactly who's responsible?"

"Yes. That's right. There's nothing for you to do here."

Through gritted teeth, she said, "You're wrong about that."

He turned and walked toward the front door and opened it wide as two plain-clothes detectives and a couple of others in uniform tramped their way up the snow-covered front walk. "Let these guys process the scene."

She sighed hard. "Fine. They can do their job. Then they have to leave. You too."

He turned away from her. "Just what I was thinking."

He...what? She frowned. But then she was distracted by the cops and their questions. The whole time, arms folded across his chest, he stood next to her making only an occasional comment. Was he there to make sure she told everything the way it needed telling? She wouldn't snark at him if she thought so. Not while his so-called colleagues were there.

After an hour or so, the cops left. As they pulled away, a truck arrived and backed into her driveway. The driver hopped out of his cab and approached Steve's smooshed car, just as Steve did. The two men had a short discussion about how to get the thing up onto the flatbed, and then Steve started back up the walk.

"In case you're wondering, now's not the time for me to bring you in for processing. It'll have to wait." He reached into a back pocket and pulled out a card.

She took what he handed her and stared down at it. "What's this?" Like she'd never seen a business card before.

He backed down the walk. "You do your thing, Tootsie. I'm tired of trying to convince you to act like a normal human being who quits when she should. If you've got something you think you need me for, reach out." He started to walk away and then turned back. "Do yourself a favor. Stop being your own worst enemy."

His gaze left her and he was back down the walk to help the truck driver load up his smashed car.

She stood and watched him, shocked. He was leaving? Yes, she'd told him to. But all she'd wanted was to be alone for a moment over her private space being invaded and her precious items being destroyed. She didn't want him to go away.

The car loaded up, Steve got into the truck. The driver drove out of Tootsie's driveway and ten seconds later was down the street and gone. She stared at the spot where the car had been. There was nothing left but a few bits of plastic and metal and piles of leaves from Ben's tree she supposed she'd have to hire someone to get rid of, which there was no time better to do that than now.

She called a salvage company and arranged for them to come and take the mess in her foyer away. She called the insurance company and then made a reservation for herself at the local Marriott, because no, she couldn't stay in a house with no heat and a hole in the front window.

It wasn't until she was packing her suitcase that

she let it sink in and she had a moment of disorientation. One moment they'd been joking about her going to jail...and yeah, it had become a joke...and the next moment he was implying it was over between them. Not that she knew what "it" had been. Not that she knew what he'd expected "it" to be. Except she did. Because he'd just now told her. If he'd met her on one of those dating apps, he would have taken one look at her. And swiped left.

Sighing, she closed up her suitcase and rolled it downstairs. Before walking out, she checked each room, making sure all the doors and windows were locked. Which was a joke, with that hole in the front window being the horse that had already gotten out of the barn.

She fingered a plastic bag she'd left on the island in the kitchen. It had the pieces of her grandmother's vase in it, the ones she'd picked up before the rest of the mess got carted away. She couldn't throw them away. Not yet.

A heaviness settled in her heart. For someone who'd wanted to figure out what doing the right thing was, she sure had gone about it the wrong way. The question was how was she going to fix it? And she didn't mean the vase.

# CHAPTER SIXTEEN

She left her suitcase on one of the two queen beds in the hotel room. After taking a shower and washing her hair, she fell into a disturbed sleep in the other one. The next morning, she woke with a bleary head that cleared somewhat after a really sinful breakfast consisting of a couple of eggs, sunny side up, a rasher of crispy bacon, whole wheat toast and a bowl of luscious fruit. After her third cup of coffee, Tootsie concluded there were some things she *could* fix. Or at least she could bring closure to. Best of all, it wouldn't involve her getting in Jim Petrocelli's face. Which would make Black Windbreaker happy. If he'd still been in her life.

Her face reddened with shame. Though she'd said it, she wouldn't have stormed into Petrocelli's corporate offices in New York to confront him over the destruction of her things. She'd been caught up in the moment and said something she didn't mean. Steve wouldn't have known that.

She'd figure out how to explain and yeah, apologize. Which she rarely did. But would make a big exception for him.

Even if he wanted her to back off, though, she needed to give her hopeless enterprise one more try. She would call Angie Driscoll, who according to Fern knew more about WCLS than anyone. If she couldn't get Angie's unlisted number from Elwood—and no, she would not call him again—she'd get it somewhere else. Like from Fern, who, when she rang her number, picked up almost immediately.

"Arizona is fabulous," she crowed. She and Marc Antonio had made it there before the snowstorm could cancel their flight. "If I thought Marc Antonio was going to make this his home base, I'd move here in a flash."

Tootsie was thrilled that things were working out. After Fern prattled on about what they were working on, Tootsie asked her question.

"Gee, I wish I could help. If I had Angie's information, it would be at home and obviously I can't get to it from here."

Strike one. Tootsie called Jolisa, who had been Angie's assistant.

"I don't think Angie liked me very much," said Jolisa. "She would never have given me her phone number."

Strike two.

Tootsie wasn't sure who she could call next to make it strike three.

Until, she gave herself a figurative slap upside the head and remembered *she* had Angie's number. Getting it meant making a trip back to Glen Allyn. Parking in her driveway, she noted the plywood over her window and laid her head against her steering wheel.

It was more than the physical thing that had been between her and Detective Lieutenant DiLorenzo, her very own Black Windbreaker. The connection was scary strong. And there, for that little flash of time he made her think he liked her the way she was. Well, without the drama.

She banged her head once against the wheel and sighed her misery. Drama, it turned out had him walking away.

She sniffed once, threw the door open and marched up to the house.

As she opened her door, she noted the cold. Well, yeah. No power did that. Tromping upstairs she opened her dresser drawer where she'd stashed a list of WCLS employees with their contact information, and there it was. Angie's phone number.

Sitting down on her bed, she slipped her cellphone out of her purse and keyed in the numbers.

"Hello?"

There it was: Angie's high-pitched, scratchy voice.

"It's Tootsie, Angie. I was calling to find out how

you made it through the storm. Do you have your power back?"

"Well, how nice it is for you to call me out of the blue. No, I don't, not yet, but I'm just hunky dory. My niece is with me and she's got the fireplace going and hot water on my gas stove for tea."

"That's good. Hopefully your power will come back on soon."

"Now tell me the real reason you're calling, because we both know you didn't think oh wait, let me call old Angie Driscoll to find out if she didn't freeze to death in the snowstorm."

Leave it to Angie to bypass the niceties. And didn't that free Tootsie up to bypass them, too. "You know the radio station got sold."

"You're not telling me anything I don't know."

"Almost everyone got let go."

"That must have been terrible. Kind of like when I got let go."

And wasn't this a reason why expecting Angie to help might go nowhere? "Here's the thing. No one has the institutional memory of WCLS that you do. You know things."

"Well, it's true."

Tootsie crossed her fingers. "Would you mind if I came over to your house to talk? I have a couple of questions you'll know the answers to. I wouldn't stay long."

There was a long silence during which Tootsie thought Angie might have hung up. Until Angie said,

"I don't know why I should help. No one said boo when Robert fired me, including you."

There was no point in explaining, something Tootsie had long since acknowledged to herself with more than a little shame. "Angie, you were such an integral part of the radio station for so long, I feel like you've forgotten more than most of us ever knew."

There was a long-suffering sigh. "Well, if you put it that way. When will you come over?"

Tootsie gave herself an imaginary, one-sided, high five. "Hoping your roads are good, I can be over this evening."

"Make sure you stop and get some ice cream. Get something good, like chocolate peanut butter."


It was a challenge to find a store that carried chocolate peanut butter. She finally scored at the Stop & Shop in Clifton, which was fortunate, since Angie lived just a few blocks away in Bloomfield. Tootsie was stashing the bag in her back seat when a car pulled up in the space next to her. She didn't give it more than a glance, not until the person stepped out. And then not until he spoke.

"Hey."

He was wearing a ski-parka and heavy gloves. Both black.

She could barely keep the pleasure she felt seeing him from her voice. "Hi."

He looked over her shoulder at the bag on her

back seat. "What's in there?"

And the pleasure died. "No hello and isn't that special? Nothing else, like I really didn't mean it when I walked away. No, look Tootsie, I'm back in your life, even if it's in a parking lot. No, you're worried about what I have in my back seat. Like it might be a gun."

She punched the button on her car door opener. "You are so smart. I didn't know, but you did. I would never have thought I could buy one right here in this store."

He leaned a gloved hand on the roof of her car. "Actually I was hoping there was some food in there. I haven't eaten all day."

She folded her arms, a flimsy lock, on her temper. "It is food. But I'm not sharing it with you." She wasn't about to after his buh-bye with the business card. "Excuse me but aren't you the guy who left me to fend for myself because you wanted me to cease and desist in my battle with the Petrocellis and besides, as you so lovingly pointed out to me, you don't like high drama?"

He lifted his hand off the car roof and shrugged. "It wasn't permanent."

"It wasn't…" She tried, really tried. But no amount of grappling with what *that* meant got her insight into his annoying thought process. She speared him with a look. "I don't understand you."

"Yeah, I know." A slow smile curved his lips. "So are you glad to see me?"

She forced an iron grip on her jaw. She tried to resist smiling, though it was impossible. "It's more I don't know what you're doing. You told me you were done with me. Out of my life."

"Get your story straight. I said I was tired of the drama. There's a big difference there." As if to prove his point, he took a step into her personal space.

She backed up, which wasn't far because she was up against her car door.

"You want to explain what you think I'd conclude? You handed me your business card. Isn't that the same thing as saying this is a formality because though I'm giving this to you, please don't call me?"

"No."

She wanted to hit him. But that would be assault. "If I've got it wrong, why don't you explain."

A look of frustration passed over his face before he put his hands on her shoulders. "I've met a lot of crazy people in my life. But I've never met someone who refuses to give up and should even when common sense puts her in harm's way."

"What common sense?" She tried to wiggle out from beneath his hands. He wouldn't let her. "Common sense told me not to rock the boat after my grandmother died because my thoughtlessness might have caused her death. Common sense told me to stay married to a man I shouldn't have married who I should have divorced long before he pulled the plug on me. Common sense told me not to keep working for that worm, Robert, when I should have quit."

With a sudden spurt of strength she finally dislodged herself from Steve's big hands. "What has common sense ever gotten me? So that's why my new common sense tells me that if I'm the only one who cares enough to keep on looking for the answers to what really happened at the radio station, that's what I'm doing. Yes, because of my friends and what's happening to them. But more because I'm tired of letting the bullies in life win. So if that puts me in harm's way, so be it. And no. I'm not listening to your common sense anymore."

She folded her arms tight across her chest, cold in spite of the heavy coat she wore. Or maybe she wasn't shivering from the cold. She swerved around on a heel and turned away from him, as much as it was possible slammed up against her car.

He turned her back and pulled her into his arms. "I told you once. You didn't believe me," he said, voice muffled because, lips pressed to the top of her head, he was talking into her hair. "So, listen up. In my life, people do what I tell them to do."

He pulled her even closer. "It's because of who I am, what I do for a living, and yeah, what I look like. I'm big. When I get a certain look on my face, even friends and family pay attention to me." He shifted a little. "Well, not my daughters."

As miserable as she'd been feeling, Tootsie couldn't help but smile into his coat at that little addendum. "And not me."

He ignored that. "I thought I needed to be as far away from you as I could get. But there's been something about you that made me ignore my own advice from the get-go. Even when you kicked me. Even when you wouldn't give me your keycard. For sure when you broke into the radio station and argued that you had every right to be there. It was like I kept putting myself in a position where I needed to be where you were. It was like I was a…" His voice trailed off.

"Like you were a moth to my flame," she prompted, not so angry at him the more he spoke. "You kept wanting to burn yourself to a crisp." She put her arms around his waist. "What a dodo moth you are."

He shook with silent laughter. "Maybe. But see, then what happened is I started to care about what you were doing, putting yourself in danger and it scared me."

He put her away from him then, and hands on her shoulders again, said, "I guess you didn't believe me when I said it the other day. I guess I have to tell you again that I don't like being scared. There for a moment when you told me you were going over to the city to get in Petrocelli's face, I thought I was crazy for sticking around you. I was the one who was worried you'd get hurt. You weren't. I never wanted crazy in my life. So I needed away. Until I could figure it out."

There was one reason someone like Black Windbreaker would worry she'd get hurt and she was pretty sure she knew what it was. He liked her. Maybe more than liked. And it melted her like snow on a sunny, seventy-degree day. Because she more than liked him, too.

"So you gave me your business card. Now you're back because you figured it out. Have I got that straight?" She slid her hands under his and brought them down to clasp them between their bodies.

"Yeah."

"Good."

He gave her a shrewd look. "So we're starting all over again. From the beginning."

"I wouldn't go that far."

He pressed against her. "How far would you go?" He played with the zipped closure of her coat, pulling it down an inch.

Her back came up against her Volvo. "I think we've established how far I'd go."

He cradled her face in his big, glove-covered hand. "Yeah, you did." And he kissed her. "Dammit, Tootsie," he whispered against her lips, his so cold, all she wanted to do was press hers against them, to warm them up with her breath. If need be, with her tongue.

"Dammit, what?" she whispered back.

"You're up to something, again, aren't you?"

She drew her head away from his. "How did you guess? And while I'm thinking about it, how did you find me?"

"Don't get all squirrelly. Just listen. I've been following you since you left your house. And this store is not on the way to your hotel. So where are you going?"

It was hard to think when he held her in his arms and especially because now she understood what had been going on in that mind of his. "I'm going to visit a friend."

"Didn't you hear me?" He got the cop look, which might have made his friends, family, and assorted people take note of and retreat. As she'd just pointed out, she wasn't his friends and family.

"I heard. And your point would be…?"

"You need to stop playing games. This is about your safety."

"I can take care of myself," she retorted, even as her other self said, what, are you a teenager?

"I'm not going to debate with you. Wherever you're going, I'm going with you. Since you're not using your head, get used to me being your keeper."

That sounded good to her. Though she knew it shouldn't. She leaned her forehead against his parka and under it the faint, welcoming warmth of his body. "Okay."

One hand slid beneath her jaw. "Could you say that again?"

"I said okay."

He gave her one of his special smiles. "Just making sure, babe." He took her hand. "Grab whatever's in your car you need and get in." He opened the passenger door. "In case you were wondering, I'm driving."

She hadn't bothered to wonder.

"Where are we going?" He said as he pulled out of the parking lot.

And she told him about Angie.

"Why do you think she'll know anything you'll find useful, whether it's about this Elizabeth Comstock or not? And remind me. The reason you're doing this is to get some information. No funny business."

"I'm not calling Petrocelli to share it with him."

He snorted.

After a few minutes, they pulled up in front of Angie's tiny Cape Cod. Which, when they did, it was apparent Angie and her neighbors had gotten power back. The whole neighborhood was awash in light.

Steve pulled into Angie's cleared driveway. He helped Tootsie out of the car. With the bag with ice cream in it in one hand, he took her arm with his other. "Hold onto me."

"How can I do that when *you're* holding onto *me*?"

That left him nothing to say.

As they picked their way up the just cleared walk to the front door, Tootsie said, "Listen, Angie's a little strange, so if she says anything crazy, don't look like you're surprised." She rang the doorbell.

They waited and waited until they heard a lock

turning, and then another, and another, and Angie's muffled voice saying, "Hold on, I'll have this damn door open in a minute." One more lock turned, the door swung open and there Angie was. She was short and shapely and naked. Except for a shower cap.

"Angie," Tootsie said her voice trembling with nervous laughter. "Um…how are you?"

But Angie wasn't interested in Tootsie. She was too busy making eyes at Black Windbreaker.

Angie slapped one hand on a bony hip. "You didn't tell me you were bringing someone with you."

Steve said something under his breath and took a step behind Tootsie.

"Can we come in? We're letting in a lot of cold air and you're—" Words failed her.

Without waiting for Angie to give the okay, Steve put a hand against the small of Tootsie's back, and pushed. Then he closed the door behind them. "You do what you need to do, ma'am." He looked up at the ceiling. "We'll be here."

Angie simpered, "I hope you will be, honey." She batted her eyelashes at him. "You make yourself comfortable." She waved one hand in the direction of the love seat and chair in her small living room, turned, and pranced away.

The moment Angie disappeared up the staircase, Tootsie slapped a hand across her mouth. To keep from howling with laughter.

Steve's expressive eyebrows shot up. "Was that real?"

"She probably didn't know I'd have a man with me."

"That's why she answered the door, bare ass naked? Because it would be just you girls?"

Before Tootsie could explain Angie—not that she could—Angie was coming back down the stairs.

"All righty, then," came Angie's trilling voice as she reappeared, no shower cap, wearing a white robe that covered her to the neck. It was trimmed with a white boa that fluttered in the air. On her feet were matching white slippers. The long red hair she wasn't born with flowed down her back.

"What a pretty robe," Tootsie said, pleased that there was no tremor in her voice.

Angie glided into the room and sat herself down on the love seat. She patted the cushion next to her. "Why don't you come sit next to me, gorgeous."

Like a man who had probably been in a whole lot of hard-to-believe situations, he did what Angie expected of him. He sat, as far from Angie as he could, not so easy on a piece of furniture that was called a love seat for a reason.

Sitting down on a chair opposite, Tootsie said, "I thought your niece was here. Are you all right being alone in the house?"

Angie smoothed a hand over her hair. She leaned toward Steve and gave him a little nudge and a coy smile. "Yes, I'm fine. I was fine by myself. I let her think she was doing me a favor." She gave Steve another nudge and this time a wink. "If you know what I mean."

Steve didn't react to the nudge or the wink. Or at least Tootsie didn't think he had. But then she caught the gleam in his eyes. Despite the shock of seeing an 80-year-old answer the door buck naked, he was settling in to enjoy himself.

Belatedly, Tootsie remembered the ice cream. She popped up out of the chair and grabbed the bag out of Steve's hand. "I'm going to put the ice cream in your freezer."

"Well, I'm sure you can find your way to the kitchen while I just wait here with...what did you say your name was, honey?"

As Tootsie made her way into the kitchen, she heard the murmuring of the two voices. She wasn't sure Angie wasn't propositioning Steve.

The freezer was jam packed with lots of things wrapped in foil. There were no markings on the packages. Tootsie couldn't imagine how Angie knew what was what.

As she came back from depositing the quart of chocolate peanut butter in Angie's freezer, she caught a blush on Angie's face. Was Black Windbreaker flirting with her? The humor that danced in his black eyes told her that yes, he was. After his initial shock, he was enjoying himself to the fullest.

Angie said, "Now, how 'bout you tell me what you're all so fired up to find out from me?"

Tootsie sat. "Did you ever hear of a woman named Elizabeth Comstock?"

"Well, of course I did."

Into the silence, Tootsie said, "What do you know about her?"

"Well, for one thing, she loved classical music." She lapsed back into silence.

"Angie, I know you're mad because Robert fired you. You do know if he hadn't, it would have delayed things just a few months. The Petrocellis would never have kept you, just like they didn't keep most of the rest of us."

"There are some real bad people in this world, don't you think, sweetums?" She gave Steve an arch look. He gave her one of his better smiles.

Then, to Tootsie she said, "I don't know why you want to know about Mrs. Comstock, but if what I know will help y'all make trouble for Robert, I'll do my part."

"Okay. Good." Tootsie relaxed, not bothering to point out that it was the Petrocellis she wanted to make trouble for. "Tell me everything you remember."

"Mrs. Comstock and Stan were friends back in the day, both of them in the real estate business. They both made a lot of money. After he made oodles, Stan got out and bought himself the license for the radio station. Mrs. Comstock kept on doing real estate and made even more oodles."

Now that Angie had jogged it, Tootsie had a vague memory of seeing the Comstock woman once. "Didn't she come to the station for some kind of catered buffet that Stan held to honor her?"

Angie crossed one leg over the other. When she did, the skirt of her robe fell open, exposing one bony knee. It was slathered with lotion. "You remember right."

"When I was looking through some files at the station—"

Steve cleared his throat.

She gave him a look that would be impossible for him to misinterpret. "As I was saying, one of the files had her name on it. Why would she have her own file?"

"Well, that's because she donated the land for a new transmitter site when Stan needed one."

"We know about the transmitter. But what else there is to know about it, we…" Her voice trailed off.

"Oh Lord, Tootsie, don't you know anything?" She leaned her shoulder into Steve's and gave him doe eyes. "Maybe you should be taking notes in case she forgets what I'm telling her. She may be losing her mind now that's she getting older."

Everyone in her life seemed hellbent on mentioning age…hers. "We know your mind is totally there, Angie."

"Well, yes, that's true." She patted her lips with one long finger, the nail painted fire engine red. "The way I remember it, she had some stipulation or another."

"What stipulation?" Tootsie's brain began to fire on all cylinders.

"Well, now that's something I'm not sure of. Maybe Robert knows. Or Elwood."

"Do you think that was on Robert's mind when he..." Tootsie cleared her throat. "...Fired you?"

Angie had been swinging her leg back and forth. She stopped. "Robert didn't fire me because of the seven veils."

Tootsie frowned. "He didn't?"

"It was because he was afraid if I was around when he wanted to sell the station, I might have had something to say about that."

Tootsie leaned forward. "Like what?"

Angie made a sound of disgust. "That little shit. What a Robespierre. He thought I'd let him get into that safety deposit box."

Tootsie glanced at Steve. He raised his eyebrows. "What safety deposit box?""

"It's the one with the information you're looking for. What Mrs. Comstock got for donating the land for the transmitter." She sniggered a rude laugh. "You want to know something else?"

Steve had long since stopped smiling. He watched her with an intensity Tootsie was familiar with. Speaking for the first time, he said, "If you're willing to tell us, we want to know."

"Well..." She fluttered her eyelashes at him. "Not only do I know where that box is, but I have the key. Would you like me to give it to you?"

# CHAPTER SEVENTEEN

"We'd love you to give it to us," said Tootsie, all her neurotransmitters humming. "Have you got it handy?"

As if that question hadn't come from Tootsie, Angie continued to lavish her attention on Steve with a bright, come-hither smile. "Well, I wouldn't have thrown it away, now, would I?"

Ignoring the feeling that she was being ignored—because what did she care if Angie made goo-goo eyes at Steve as long as they got that key—Tootsie said, "No, you wouldn't. That would be crazy, and we both know you're not crazy."

"That's true." Angie patted Steve on the knee. He didn't betray in any way what he was thinking. His standard operating procedure.

Shifting around in her chair, Tootsie said, "I bet, if you have it here in your house, it would be somewhere no one would think to look."

That got Angie's attention slewing back towards Tootsie. "Even a genius wouldn't find where I hid that key."

As if she was now done with that subject, she turned back to Steve. "So honey, you sure I can't get you something to drink? Or to eat? How about some of that ice cream Tootsie brought me?" She patted his knee for the second, or maybe it was the tenth time. "Someone as handsome as you, I'd be willing to share."

"You're a generous woman, Angie. But we're good. We ate before we got here." On the heels of telling that whopper, he took Angie's hand. "Do you think you'd mind getting that key for Tootsie?"

Angie simpered. "Well, if that's what *you* want." She got to her feet, the boa's feathery collar waving like white palm fronds in the heated air in the room. "Y'all wait right here. I'll just head into the kitchen to the freezer."

Steve glanced at Tootsie. "Angie," he said. "Thanks for the offer of that ice cream, but really—"

Angie stopped and came around. "Did I say anything about ice cream? Didn't you just tell me you didn't want any? Do you think I lost my hearing?"

As she flounced into the kitchen, she muttered something Tootsie couldn't hear...or cared to hear...not if Angie brought back that key.

There was the sound of rummaging and then the slam of a door. Moments later, Angie was back, with one of those foil-wrapped packages Tootsie had noted when she'd stowed away the ice cream. She handed it to Tootsie.

Looking down at the odd shape, Tootsie said, "What's this?"

"You wanted the key. I'm giving you the key."

"It's in…this?" Holding the package in one hand, she held it out as if corroborating that it was what Angie said it was. "This doesn't feel like a key. It feels like… a piece of steak."

A look of horror came over Angie's face. "You think I would do something like that to a good piece of steak? I'm on a budget, Tootsie."

"Okay." Tootsie nodded, not trying to understand because most everything Angie had said tonight made her think she'd fallen down a rabbit hole. "And the key is in here because…?"

"Isn't it obvious?" Angie gave her a look filled with disdain. "If someone came looking for the key, why would they think to look for it inside a package of calves' liver?"

"That's…probably…true." Tootsie's hands were starting to sting with cold from holding the frozen package of… Her stomach began to do little flips.

Calves' liver…blech.

"Just be careful. The key might be stuck. Wait before you try to pry it out, because otherwise you'll get liver blood under your fingernails."

Tootsie's gorge rose, thinking about a piece of slithery organ meat in her hand, blood seeping out everywhere. "That won't be a problem." She handed the package to Steve. "Where did you get the key?"

"Well, you know Stan and I went way back. I worked with him at that realty company. After he made all those millions. left there, and bought the radio station, he asked me to come with him." She stroked her boa. "I was WCLS's first employee."

"That's great. But Angie, the key?" Tootsie prodded.

"Stan trusted me more than anyone at WCLS. Including Robert."

Rabbit hole... Tootsie told herself. "Indeed. Why didn't Stan trust Robert?"

"Robert hated the station. Stan knew that."

That sounded right. "I do have one more question."

Angie gave Steve a wink. "She has another question. Isn't that cute?"

Steve gave Angie's hand a gentle squeeze. "You've been so helpful. Will you answer this last one?"

Angie rolled her eyes. "I will for you, handsome, even though I'm tired of answering questions."

Tootsie didn't wait. "So Stan trusted you to know what he wanted for the future of the radio station. But you never shared it with anyone else who might be interested in the future of the station. Why is that?"

Angie pouted. "I told you. No one came to my defense when Robert fired me. A couple of those silly interns even laughed at my seven veils. Why would I want to help anyone at the radio station when no one wanted to help me?"

That made unfortunate sense. "Then why have you told me, now?"

"Because you brought me ice cream. And because I'm tired of inviting my nephew, Jake, to sleep over every time that big guy comes lurking around my house."

Steve straightened. "What big guy?"

"Why, the one who keeps trying to break in."

In a quiet voice, Steve said, "Have you called the police?"

Angie made a scoffing sound. "Like I would. Have you seen Jake?" She snatched a framed picture that sat with its mates on the table next to the love seat and handed the picture to Steve, who took one look at it and handed it to Tootsie.

Big didn't begin to describe Jake. He was a true big boy, but the smile on Jake's face said he was a nice big boy.

So someone was after Angie too. And if Tootsie was guessing right...and she was pretty sure she was...they were looking for what Angie had hidden in the liver. "So, let me get this straight. Stan gave you the key..."

"Yes, he did. But then it got stolen."

Tootsie just resisted clapping a hand to her head. In measured words, she said, "How do you have it, then?"

"I stole it back, didn't I, when they weren't looking the day Robert fired me. From Elwood's office," she added.

Tootsie opened her mouth. Elwood was involved in the key business, too? Everything began to fall into place. She exhaled a short breath. "Why did Elwood need the key?"

"Why would you ask, Tootsie? It was so he could get into the box and get what was there."

"What bank is the safety deposit box in?"

Angie opened her eyes wide. "Well, let's see... I need to think." She tapped her cheek. Then hummed. Then frowned. "It's one of those small ones."

"You don't know which? Who does?" Tootsie asked through her teeth.

"Why, Elwood, of course. When I stole the key back, I left the envelope in his desk drawer. The name is on the envelope."

*Of course.*

"Good luck getting it from him. He's a secretive one."

Tootsie nodded.

Though Angie tried to get them to stay, Steve was Johnnie on the spot with an excuse. "We had a really good visit, Angie. But the roads are icing over and I'd like to get Tootsie home before they get bad."

"Well, aren't you the gentleman," Angie said, batting her eyes at him, again.

Later, in the car, Tootsie said, "Okay, Mr. Windbreaker. Is that what was going on with the rock through the window, my house almost getting trashed and the snake? They were looking for that key?"

"Forget the snake. About the rest? I don't see how anyone would have thought you had the key."

"Except they knew I was in the radio station that night. Couldn't they have thought I snatched it out of Elwood's office? And I'm not forgetting the snake."

"Yeah, maybe. Especially if Elwood didn't look in the envelope until after he found out you'd broken into the station and saw it gone."

"Then why would they have gone on to Angie's after? She'd been gone from the station for months. Why would they suspect her, now?"

"It's possible she said something. Maybe she taunted them with the key and didn't bother to tell us she had.'"

Tootsie threw her hands in the air. "This is one Alice in Wonderland moment."

He grunted.

Which meant, even if Steve had a thought there, he wasn't going to tell her.

She shifted in her seat. "What's to be done about Angie?"

He gave her a quick glance, his attention on the dicey road with its patches of ice and piles of plowed snow spilling back into the street. "I'm calling the Bloomfield cops. Angie's nephew isn't always going to be there. He wasn't there tonight when we arrived. I want a car driving by checking things out."

"That makes sense." She eyed the tinfoil package

on the floor, careful that her feet didn't touch it. "Didn't you feel like we were being whipped back and forth like a ball at a tennis match?"

"She was having a good time at our expense. But now we have the key to a safety deposit box we didn't know existed. It's more than what we came for."

"A safety deposit box which contains the information about what Elizabeth Comstock got for giving Stan that land. And if it meant something to the sale of the radio station."

"You have to wonder what was in your friend, Stan's will."

"Wills don't get read anymore. They go through probate. Because I agree with you. I think it matters." She sighed. Tapping her foot against the package at her feet... and then pulling it back, remembering what was in it... she said, "So what's the next step?"

"First let's see if there really is a key in the package. If there is, then we think about a next step. A legal next step."

She stewed. And he continued to be silent as he drove back to where they'd left her car.

After a minute, he said, "I don't like that look on your face."

"How do you know what look I have on my face? Your eyes are face front, paying attention to your driving."

"I don't have to look. I can hear your look." He pulled into the lot, right next to where Marge sat by her lonesome. the store closed, no other cars in the lot but her.

Steve beckoned for Tootsie to give him Angie's package. "Let's get that key."

Snatching it off the floor with two fingers she said, "It's defrosting. It feels a little spongy. Yuk." She shivered and gave it to Steve.

"That's because it's been on the floor underneath the heater vent."

"I hate calves' liver."

"You've said that at least five times since we left Angie's." He began to unwrap the plastic underneath the foil.

"Wait." Tootsie held up a staying hand. "Don't you think it would be better if we did this outside? If that disgusting piece of meat falls anywhere inside your car, you'll have to sanitize your carpet and the floor beneath."

Steve sighed and stepped outside. Tootsie followed, and came around to stand next to him. Under the white lights that made the parking lot bright as daylight, she waited, breath held, as the last piece of foil came away. And there. One big dark, red, almost brown/purple piece of meat. With veins. She began to breathe through her mouth. In case there was liver odor in the air.

She made herself lean closer, though it was the last thing she wanted to do. "Do you see a key? I don't see a key. Angie was putting us on, which makes me wonder how much of that story she told us about a safety deposit box was true."

He turned the liver over. It drooped over his fingers. "She wasn't putting us on."

There, pressed into the meat was the familiar shape of the kind of key that would unlock a safety deposit box. Before she could comment, he extracted the key and with a flick of his wrist threw the liver away. "I'm holding onto this."

Eyes on where that ugly piece of meat landed in a snow bank a few feet away, she said, "You're doing this just to stand in my way, aren't you?"

"Yeah, I am. Because you're planning something that involves this key."

"Maybe. Maybe not."

"After everything I just said to you, you're working overtime trying to figure out how to get into the radio station to get that envelope from Elwood's desk, aren't you? That's what you're thinking. Tootsie, there's no way."

The door code at the radio station had been changed, and an alarm installed. Tootsie wouldn't tell him about the window at the rear of the building that was low enough to open and climb through.

As he got in his car, leaving her to stand next to hers, he gave her that look that said he knew something was on her mind. "Do not, under any circumstances try anything funny, especially if it involves the radio station. If you do and you get caught, I won't be able to protect you this time."

He closed the door, started the engine, and drove off, leaving her by herself to contemplate what had just happened.

She was willing to bet that last thing he said he meant. Which was fine. She understood. There would always exist a big divide between a man who believed in the law and a woman who believed in justice.

She huffed a breath and looked down and there, right by her feet, the key. She'd seen him put it in his pocket. Or at least she thought he'd put it in his pocket. She bent, and with two fingers, she picked it up.

The right thing to do was to call and tell him she had the key and he should come back to get it from her.

She did not take her phone from her purse.

*Be a girl who does the right thing.*

Was breaking into the station the right thing? Was not telling Steve she had the key the wrong thing? Nope. It was much cleaner. And simpler. Doing the right thing was putting herself out there, maybe even in danger, so the bullies and bastards of this world couldn't always get off scot free.

Because she knew most times they would.

That would not stop her.

A cascade of memories flooded her mind, of things she'd stood up for with her grandmother. There was the time they'd picketed the town library in a neighboring town that had given in to ignoramuses wanting to ban *The Handmaid's Tale* and *The Bluest Eye* from their shelves. Their protests had seen the reopening of a home for disabled men in Warren

County that had been closed down by a NIMBY crowd. And yes, the picketing of C&K Chemicals...even though a personal tragedy came out of it. These were the right things. More than that, they were the righteous things. She'd forgotten. No, that wasn't true. *She'd made herself forget.*

She was not going to let herself forget ever again. And yes, whether Black Windbreaker approved or not, she was going to break into the station and ransack Elwood's office until she found that envelope.

The first thing she did when she got back to her hotel room was scrub the key and her fingernails...with scalding hot water. And then she waited. Because naturally her keeper had a squad car stationed outside the hotel. For her safety, he'd said. She loved that caring part of him. But she knew it was more he knew she was planning, and it didn't involve what show to watch on TV tonight.

What she didn't get and what she was still trying to figure out was how had Black Windbreaker dropped that key in the snow. Even for the short time she'd known him, she'd never known him to be careless. The more she thought about it, the more the only thing she could come up with was he wanted her to have it. So when she broke into Elwood's office, she'd have the location of the bank and the way to get into the box and that would go a ways towards getting the answers she was looking for.

But why would he do that? Her brain was sore, wondering.

It wasn't until after three in the morning that the patrol car left. Just to be sure she went downstairs and walked the Marriott's perimeter. Calling it the perimeter…she snorted a laugh. What was she, some paramilitary commando? But the car was gone, and she was free to do her thing.

She went back up to her room to find something she could use to break the window at the back of the station. She found what she needed down the hall: the metal scoop in the icemaker.

As she drove up to the radio station, she glanced, often, at her rear view mirror to see if she could catch lights, which would indicate that someone was following her. By the time she parked—this time across the street in the Starbucks lot instead of down the block—she decided she was home free.

It was a chore to get to the window. The alleyway had been plowed, yes, but the back of the building had not. There, the snow was up above her knees, blown in drifts by the wind off the Hudson River. Worse, there were things underneath, things thrown there that weren't being used anymore. She hoped there wasn't anything jagged she could cut herself on. If she was breaking and entering, she didn't want to leave her blood—and its telltale DNA—for detective types to know she was the culprit.

The window was one filthy sheet of glass. Not

that dirt had anything to do with it but she knew the scoop would make a loud noise when she whammed it against the glass. Which was why she'd brought a towel to wrap the scoop in.

Bracing herself up against the window ledge, she reached into her bag and removed the scoop. She hefted it up, preparing to smash her way into the station when her phone vibrated in her pocket. Robo call, she told herself, although she knew even robo callers didn't annoy people at 4 o'clock in the morning. This was Steve. And he knew where she was. She took one glove off, stuck her hand in her pocket, grabbed the phone, and looked and yup.

**I'm here.**

She blinked. He wasn't just checking on her from wherever, he was here at the radio station? Black Windbreaker had followed her.

She threw her gloves onto the snow and texted back.

**Go away.**

**I'm not leaving.**

In a weird way, she felt a kernel of respect for him for not giving up.

**There's nothing to talk about. If you don't want to destroy your career helping a criminal, you need to go away before someone sees you.**

The little dots danced for a couple of seconds before his answer appeared.

**I'm going to help you.**

Of all the things she thought he'd say, this wasn't it. She dropped the scoop on the windowsill and shuffled back around the corner to see him there by the back entrance to the station. She stepped on something underneath the snow and stumbled before righting herself.

"Watch yourself," he said.

"I can't. I'm too busy watching you and wondering. Did you have an awakening of your conscience?"

She stared up into his normally deadpan face not so deadpan this time. Nope, even in the dark she could tell his eyes were seething with emotion. "I knew you wouldn't listen."

"Forget that. How did I not see you? You didn't drive all the way here with your headlights off."

Anger poured off his body. "You think I didn't know what you would do the moment that squad car left the hotel?" His laugh held no humor. "I drove up here to wait for you."

"Well, good job," she said without heat. "Now, please leave."

He exhaled a heavy breath, condensation in the air hanging between them. "Forget it. You wouldn't listen and you wouldn't do what I told you to? Now you will. You're not going into the station for that envelope. *I am.*"

"You…what?"

"I want you away from here and in your car. No matter how long I take, don't come to investigate. Are we clear?"

It was a struggle not to grin. Or salute. "Yessir," she called out to Detective Lieutenant Steve DiLorenzo. Who was a law-and order guy who was more in favor of justice than he'd ever admitted.

He turned her around and gave her a not so gentle push in the direction of the street. She went.

Her car had already lost a good deal of its heat, so she cranked up the heater, sat, and prepared herself to wait.

The sound of the heater humming lulled her into a doze, deep enough that she was startled by a sharp knock on the passenger side window. She flipped the lock, letting him in. "Here," he said and slapped a small, reinforced envelope into her hand. "Elwood didn't bother to hide it. It was in the top drawer of his desk, right there in the front."

"How did you get in his office?"

"Don't ask me that."

Taking the envelope from him, she looked. He'd snagged the right one. This was the envelope from which Angie stole the key. The name of the bank was on the piece of paper—Garden State Savings Bank. Someone had also written down the branch address. Probably Angie.

"There's a problem," he said. "Unless you're a signatory, no way is anyone at the bank going to let you into that box."

"Crap. I didn't think that far." She sighed. "What now?"

But the answer came clear to her when the next morning, she called Angie to tell her she had the envelope, and knew the name and location of the bank—not that she told her how she'd found out—and was ready to go to the bank to get into the box and did Angie know who was a signatory.

"Well, Tootsie, I used to think you were a smart girl."

It had been a long time since anyone had called Tootsie a girl. She hadn't ever liked it. Now, at fifty, it seemed like she needed to reconsider. "Tell me why I'm not."

"Because I wouldn't have that key if I weren't a signatory now, would I?"

Well, duh.

"Wouldn't you like to come pick me up and take me to the bank so we can see what's in that box?"

# CHAPTER EIGHTEEN

S he called Steve. When he picked up, she said, "Problem solved. Angie can sign to get into the box."

He was silent for a moment and then said, "That doesn't make sense. Why would your old boss trust Angie with such responsibility? Even if she was his first employee."

"I'm going to pick her up and take her with me to the bank. I'll ask. Do you want to go with me? Oh, and by the way. You dropped the key. I picked it up."

"Yeah, I know I dropped it. And no, I don't need to go with you. Besides, you've got it under control."

"Aren't you the least little bit afraid that I'll skip town," she said, surprised he was being so chill about that key. Which made her know she'd been right and didn't that warm her heart about the man all over again. *He had dropped it on purpose.* "Then you won't be able to throw me in jail like you've wanted to."

"It's taken care of. I spoke to a judge about vacating the arrest warrant. She agreed."

A zing of pleasure winged through her and she grinned. "That's such a relief."

"You're a passionate woman, Tootsie."

Her smile faded. "Now I'm passionate? Isn't that the same as being a drama queen? Either way, are you too wimpy to deal?"

"My life was a lot less complicated before I met you."

"Your life was a lot duller before you met me," she retorted.

"You're making the assumption that there's something wrong with dull."

"I'm making the assumption the past few days you've had the best time of your life."

He was silent. And then he said, "I like what I do for a living. I arrest people who break the law. I don't let them go. I've let you go twice. I don't want to put myself in a position where I do that, again. That's why I'm not coming with you when you take Angie to the bank."

"I don't think I've ever heard you say so many things you're not going to do all at once."

"Pay attention to them."

"Okay." But it wasn't okay. "Whatever happened to you saying you would be my keeper?"

"You make it hard for me to do that."

She sighed. "I get it." Because she understood.

There was just so far he would go before he couldn't go further. Later, after she hung up, after she'd checked out of the hotel because the power was back on at her house, she reminded herself of how she'd changed these past few days.

She tightened her hands on the wheel, the feel of the hard, cold plastic biting into her skin, keeping her from becoming too emotional. So much wasted time… Because she'd never lived the way her heart told her she should. Why? Had it been so important that she do what the people in her life expected her to?

No. It hadn't been.

Pulling in front of Angie's house, she noted that someone had shoveled out Angie's walk and driveway. Angie was waiting for her on her swept clean front steps. She was wearing a puffy, pink jacket over a pair of cranberry-colored pants. Her red hair, put up in a bun on the top of her head, was a flare against the blinding white of the snow.

As Tootsie got out of the car to help Angie down the walk, Angie waved her off. "I thought you were going to be here five minutes ago."

Tootsie thought she would be, too. But she hadn't expected to have that conversation with Steve, and then feel like crap after. "I'm here, now, Angie." She reached for Angie's arm. Angie pushed her away.

"I'm 80, not 100. I can walk down to the car by myself." And she set off, marching in a pair of brown boots that had seen better days, Tootsie trailing behind.

For the first part of the drive, Angie yakked away, telling Tootsie about her niece abandoning her for a ski trip to upstate New York, about the wonders of her nephew, Jake, and a man who had been bugging her to sell her late husband's 1965 Ford Mustang that had been sitting in her garage since 1995.

"It has 18,000 miles on it. I keep it dusted off. I know that's why he wants it."

Tootsie was pretty sure lack of dust was not why Angie's buyer wanted the car. But she was happy to be distracted by Angie talking about the car, because then it meant she didn't have to think about Steve.

Like that was going to happen. He was there in the back of her head like a big cavity in the last molar in her mouth that didn't quite hurt, but would soon enough.

She'd made him crazy. He wasn't the type of man who liked to live crazy. That was clear to her. But then she'd persisted pushing him, and for a fleeting second she thought she'd won him over. But no.

Now, here she was headed to the Garden State Savings Bank in East Rutherford with a crazy lady who might be the one who could help her figure out if the radio station had been sold the right way or not. And Tootsie was going to have to admit, based on what he'd said about passion, that Steve DiLorenzo might be out of her life.

…And the hits kept coming…

"Oh my goodness," said the sympathetic bank manager, all decked out in a stunning red suit. "I'm very sorry but Mrs. Driscoll is not a signatory for that particular safety deposit box. I looked and didn't see a card for her."

With the bank manager turning away to speak to one of the tellers, Tootsie cornered Angie. "Why did you tell me you were, Angie?"

"I am." Angie's face set in stubborn lines. "Stan made me one and he was the other one."

"Are you sure?" It occurred to Tootsie that Angie could be having a senior moment.

Another 80-year-old's eyes might have dimmed in confusion. Not Angie's. Hers spit fire. She knew exactly what Tootsie had been thinking and didn't like it. "I'm sure."

Just great. Tootsie's level of frustration climbed a dozen notches. She didn't want to think dead end, but this was beginning to feel like one. Except…

She turned to the bank manager, who for the moment was helping a customer. Finally, the manager was available again.

"How can I help you, Mrs. Goldberg?"

"I'm sorry we bothered you. My friend did think she was a signatory for that safety deposit box."

"Oh, no bother. This is not the first time I've had to deal with elderly patrons who get confused."

Hoping Angie's silent fuming wouldn't become verbal fuming, Tootsie said, "I do need to know, though because I have to report back to my boss, Robert Hillman, who wants to know who is, so we can retrieve some papers we need that are in the box. Can you to tell me who is the signatory if there is one besides Stan Hillman?" She kept her fingers crossed as she boldly told that lie.

"Let me check." She disappeared inside the area where the safety deposit boxes were. Minutes later she came back. It's Robert Hillman."

Tootsie pretended surprise. "How weird that Robert doesn't remember that. "I'll let him know."

"According to the records, he's never come in."

That's because, Tootsie was willing to bet, Robert wasn't a signatory. Somehow someone had removed the card with Angie's name on it that made it kosher to get into the sacred confines of the safety deposit box room, and replaced it with one with Robert's name on it. "Thank you." Tootsie was backing out of the bank, taking Angie by the hand. She needed out of there before Angie said something else that would screw their chances of getting into that box. "I'll let him know."


Tootsie texted Steve the moment after she dropped Angie off. He'd want to know her theory. He didn't answer. She waited a couple of minutes and called. She got voicemail. Which left her with the feeling that he might have meant it when he said he wasn't going to betray his oath of office for her anymore. Though he'd slipped it once helping her retrieve the key from Elwood's office, she needed to recognize that he had a different moral compass she'd been too busy to give him credit for.

Gloomily, she stared at her phone before she sent him another text.

**I wish I could have done it differently.**

This time if he didn't answer she wouldn't judge him.

*Be a girl who does the right thing.*

She let her breath out slowly. She was discovering there was a whole raft of things that required her to do the right thing.

Her phone rang and she got excited. This was excitement of a different sort.

As in the freaking out kind.

"Hi, Elwood," she said, making sure her voice didn't betray her.

"Hello, Tootsie. How are you?"

Like this was a social call. "I'm fine. What's up?"

"Well, since you ask, I was wondering if we could meet."

"Sure. But I'm curious. Other than the other day when you came to meet the crew at Starbucks, you and I have never met in a social way. Why now?"

"I know you've still got lots of questions about whether the sale of the radio station to the Petrocellis went off the right way. I want to give you a more complete picture."

"Thank you, Elwood. That's great. I'm wondering if giving me a complete picture will include you answering questions about Elizabeth Comstock. I know she gifted Stan with the land he needed to relocate the transmitter from where it had been."

"Yes, that's true. She was a fine lady."

"And she got something for that gift, right?" And just like that, Tootsie dropped all pretenses and went for the jugular. "The answer is in a safety deposit box in the Garden State Savings Bank. Maybe you can satisfy me by telling me what it is."

Elwood dropped his pretenses, too. "Somehow you got into my office and took an envelope that wasn't yours. I won't call the authorities and charge you with theft if you give it back to me. Oh and while you're at it, you can give me the key that was in it, the one Angie stole the day Robert fired her."

"What is it you'll give me if I give you what you want? And I'm not admitting to taking anything from your office since I didn't." Though true, that was a technicality.

"You'll have the answers. Isn't that what you've wanted all along?"

"Yes. But not just answers. Proof. The sale of the station, Elwood. You and I both know the radio station sale was totally not kosher. If you have proof that it was otherwise, I'll go away."

"When can we meet? The sooner the better."

She just bet the sooner the better. "I'll meet you

at the bank later this afternoon. How about at 3 o'clock?"

That would give her time to get her pals to go with her. Though Black Windbreaker would say she was into drama, she wasn't a dunce. She knew there was safety in numbers.

"I'll be there." And he hung up.

Which was when Tootsie called Fern, who surely was back from Arizona.

"Oh, Tootsie I wish I could."

Tootsie could hear a loudspeaker in the background.

"Marc Antonio and I didn't make our original flight. We're at the airport waiting to board now. Sorry."

"Don't worry about a thing. All is under control."

"Just tell me you're not going to meet Elwood by yourself."

"Of course not. I'm sure Vito will go with me. I bet Jolisa will come along, too. And Lenny. How could I forget Lenny?"

"Promise me if the others won't go with you, you won't go by yourself."

"I promise." Not for the first time did she lie today. Whoever went with her or not, she was meeting Elwood at the bank. Because Elwood wouldn't pull any tricks with the bank open and people all around.

The point became moot. Jolisa and Taryn

decided to take their first few weeks of unemployment—that they hadn't gotten yet—and fly to Aruba, where it was going to be warm enough that they could sun themselves silly on the beach.

Vito, too, was busy. He'd already snagged an interview at WQXR. Tootsie gave him her best wishes for success in getting the job.

Lenny wasn't available. Not that she knew that for sure. He didn't answer his phone, nor her text, nor as a last resort, email.

So that was that. She was on her own. She shivered and reached out to Steve in hopes he'd answer. And he would, wouldn't he? He'd want to know if she was putting herself in danger. He'd said it was important to him that she be safe. Even if he didn't want to be part of her passion or her drama.

**I'm going to meet Elwood at the bank where the safety deposit box is. The meeting is at 3 p.m. He won't try anything, not that I think Elwood is the type to try something, anyway.**

She stared at her phone. But no little dots danced up and down to tell her he was sending an answer.

Maybe he was so busy he couldn't look at his phone. Which was a crap thought. He *always* looked at his phone.

She put hers away. She had a date with destiny and had to be ready for it. Or at least for a man she'd thought had no imagination and hello, how wrong she'd been. Considering there might be other things about Elwood she didn't know, she slipped a paring knife into her purse. If he tried anything funny, she'd whip that knife out to show him she meant business. Forget that it was good for cutting up a hard-boiled egg in quarters, but not much else.

# CHAPTER NINETEEN

Fifteen minutes before her meeting with Elwood was set to begin, Tootsie was already in place, in her car, at the end of the parking lot, waiting. She'd left Marge at home, not wanting to alert Elwood to her presence, and so rented a gray Honda Civic.

The Garden State Savings Bank looked the same as it had earlier: squat, utilitarian red brick, an ATM on the outside and a small lobby with utilitarian desks on the inside, walls and carpet in beiges and blues.

While Tootsie waited, Tootsie wondered. In all the years she'd known him, Elwood had never made waves, like Marc Antonio, or pranced around in designer duds like Michael LeBoff. He stuck to his office, his nose in the radio station's virtual ledgers. Where had the other Elwood who'd showed himself this week come from?

She checked her phone. Still no message from Steve. She pressed her lips together. She was starting to worry. Since when would he, with his rigid sense of what was right, no slicing, no dicing, keep away when he knew she might have bitten off more than she could chew…which was not what she hoped she'd done.

Nothing came back her way.

A dark green car pulled into the bank parking lot. Tootsie knew that car. She'd seen it parked at the radio station for years. It was Elwood's.

He eased into the first vacant spot in front of the bank entrance, and when the passenger side door opened, and Robert stepped out, Tootsie told herself she shouldn't have been surprised. Elwood *and* Robert…frick and frack.

Robert was dressed as his usual schlumpy self. But Elwood? Why had she never noticed? With his suit and overcoat, very Brooks Brothers, and the way he held himself, he was a person of power. Or maybe he always had been but had chosen to camouflage himself to keep his true intent hidden. Until he didn't need to anymore.

Tootsie reached into her purse for her phone. Still no message from Steve. "Where are you?" she muttered.

She steeled herself against the possibility that she was on her own. Anxiety and oh yes, a lovely hot flash, drenched her turtleneck collar.

Gritting her teeth, she got out of the car and

hurried to the bank entrance. She was ready to beard the two lions in the den…bank…although she never did understand what bearding a lion was. Didn't they already have beards?

Inside, no Elwood or Robert. Two tellers were at their windows. The bank manager got up and came over to Tootsie. This time, she was wearing a royal blue suit…also beautiful. "Hello again. Your two colleagues are waiting for you. I gave them our private room for your meeting. They need to be away from prying eyes, they said." She pointed at a door, partially ajar, against the wall next to the vault.

Tootsie looked around. Other than the tellers, and the manager, herself, there was no one in the bank. So much for there being lots of people around.

If it was possible, Tootsie's body heated further. If this meeting was on the up and up, they could have sat at one of the vacant desks, couldn't they? They didn't need to request use of a private space, did they?

Unless they were planning something they needed privacy for.

She reached for her knife and stopped herself. Was she an idiot? Was it such a good idea to head into a room by her lonesome where there were two men, who she was 99 and 99/100 per cent sure had something weasely on their minds? Because even she knew a paring knife was not a prime weapon in anyone's book.

She scanned the bank parking lot, hoping against hope, but there were no vehicles there of an official nature that hadn't been when she'd arrived. If Steve was here, he was hiding himself well.

She sighed. She was tired of this whole mess. She wanted it over with. As for Robert and Elwood? She knew them. She didn't need to go in guns blazing…or in this case, knife sharpened. Surely they hadn't gone over to the dark side altogether.

Tootsie tugged down the zipper on her coat, headed across the lobby, knocked, and pushed the door open to view an interrupted scene. Which confirmed the new dynamic.

Elwood sat at a table set in the middle of an otherwise empty room, hands in his lap, a cold-as-ice look on what Tootsie had always thought of as a colorless, blah face. Not so now. Not when that glacial stare was fixed, unblinking, on her.

Robert hunched over, canting toward Elwood, looked a lot like he was…could it be…groveling?

As she entered, Robert straightened. And Elwood sat back, the chilled stare papered over by the dullness Tootsie was used to. How fooled she'd been.

"Well, Tootsie," Elwood said, his voice in a monotone. "Who would have thought we'd have to meet like this?"

Tootsie gave him her most insincere smile. "Who indeed?"

"Isn't it time we moved on from all this unpleasantness about WCLS?"

"So funny." She flicked a glance at Robert, who seemed to have shrunk back into his collarbones once the conversation started. "Move on you say…nothing to see here. Is that what you mean?"

Robert cast a quick look at Elwood before forcing a laugh. "That's hilarious."

"See, that's the thing, Robert. Weird things keep happening to me. Like when a rock came smashing through my living room window with that charming message painted on it: *Leave it Alone*. And someone invaded my home just to trash some of my most precious things. Then a switcheroo happens on a safety deposit card that used to have one name on it and now has one that's different. I'd call that *not hilarious*." She turned to face Elwood. "What about you? What do you say?"

Muddy brown eyes blank, Elwood stared at Tootsie and said nothing.

She turned her attention back to Robert. "There are so many questions that have gone unanswered. Now, I'm sure you and Elwood—especially Elwood—" She glanced his way… "Are leaving them unanswered because of some simple reasons."

Robert's gaze flicked toward Elwood and then back to her.

She spread her hands wide. "You're both too crazy busy to answer them." She shrugged. "But see…I do need you to explain what you know about all these strange things that have happened."

Elwood's face showed her nothing, no reaction. But Robert? There, for a second, there was shame, before he dropped his gaze to his lap.

Gotcha, she thought.

Elwood cleared his throat. "Well, Tootsie, I can see how, now that you have so much time on your hands, you'd want answers when I don't intend to give you any. But…" Elwood placed his hands on the table. "Whatever. Let's get to the point. You have the key to the safety deposit box. We need it back."

"Okay, so we're getting to the point of what *you* want." She paused. "The key, I mean. Not that it was in my house. Although you did hire someone to look for it and destroy my things while they were about it. But when I came home unexpectedly, they left before they could do more damage. Then they went on to the next place, right? Angie's…except her nephew stood in your way."

Elwood didn't bother to look shamefaced.

"I think I know what's in the box that key opens," Tootsie added, wound up and raring to let it all out. "Whatever it is, it will prove my point that the sale to the Petrocellis was bogus."

The two men looked at each other. It was that question mark on Robert's face, and Elwood's subtle shake of his head that had Tootsie recalibrating. Because considering these two characters were who she was dealing with, she was now willing to bet the Petrocellis had nothing to do with the accidents that had befallen her. Maybe the Petrocellis were…well, she wouldn't go so far as to say they were innocent…but she had an inkling they might, in fact, be in the dark about what was in the safety deposit box. And wasn't that a stunning revelation?

And one thing she didn't have to blame them for.

"So, now that we've established that you know what you know, why don't we do a little horse trading?"

Elwood's tiny, little smirk was a chink in his camouflage. It said he thought he was in the driver's seat. "That would imply that we have to give you something in exchange for what you have."

"Don't you?"

"Not really. And frankly, there's no reason why we wouldn't just take it from you right now."

"That's assuming I brought it with me."

Elwood levered his bulk up from the table. He had something in his hand.

A gun.

It was a miniature affair, dark metal, its barrel barely extending beyond Elwood's fleshy fingers. "Hand it over, Tootsie." He waved the miniature gun in her direction.

The gun's unblinking eye pointing in her direction, Tootsie said, "Wow, Elwood. Who knew? How did I ever think of you as a nebbish?"

She kept her gaze trained on Elwood, while Robert popped up and scurried over to the side of the room. "You do know if you shoot me, that little thing will make a big noise and people will come running. Or they'll call 911. And then someone will take video and you'll go viral on Instagram."

She had no clue why she felt so calm while Elwood continued to point the gun in her direction. If fired, it could do some serious damage to her life expectancy. Suddenly living beyond 50 seemed pretty sweet. She forced a grin because that's what she figured she should do in this situation. "Like I said. I didn't bring it with me."

"Don't bullshit me, Tootsie." Elwood's eyes glittered with venom. He held the gun steady.

Elwood said, "A friend of mine is about to show up. He'll do what I tell him to do. If you don't give me that key."

As if the man heard Elwood through the door, it opened and in came Tootsie's nightmare: A. Snedeker. Her brain took a flyer, remembering that day in her office. A brave person, she told herself, would stand her ground. Her not so brave self took a stutter step away from him and his big, threatening body, and the menace in his little pig eyes.

"You!" He shot his finger out at her. "I lost a job because of you."

Tootsie didn't know which way to look. At Snedeker, the human battering ram. Or Elwood, the not-so-simple simpleton with the Saturday night special. She settled on the not-so simpleton. "Once I give you the key, have you thought about what comes next?"

Which she fervently hoped wasn't a cement overcoat.

"We don't have any intention of harming you,"

said Robert in a voice with a quaver.

That would be a good thing…if Robert was in charge. Which he wasn't.

"Once you give us the key and we retrieve what's in the safety deposit box, you won't say a word. Because you wouldn't want my friend here…" And Elwood pointed at Snedeker… "to hurt you."

To Tootsie it sounded like so much bad slapstick. She risked a glance at Robert, who had gone back to cowering in the corner. "So, Robert, have you thought about what you're going to do, now? You're an accessory to all this not so good stuff."

Robert seemed unable to answer. His eyes widened, his mouth kept opening and closing like a fish on life support.

The silence in the room became deafening. She was alone with three men who were not her friends. She was more on her own now than she'd ever been. Elwood's elevated breathing—yeah, the guy was getting nervous and nervous people with guns in their hands needed to be made nice to.

The upshot was she'd have to do her own saving. "No point in all of us getting all farklempt," she said, a brightness in her voice she didn't feel. "I think I have a solution."

Robert took that moment to come back alive. Making calming gestures, he said, "We should listen, Elwood. Tootsie wants to get out of this situation more than we do."

That was so true. Focusing on Elwood, not

Robert, Tootsie said, "I left the key in my car. I'd be willing to go get it."

She turned to exit but Snedeker blocked her way. "I'm going with you."

"I'm sure you'll be very good company."

He gave her the look of death.

Turning back to Elwood, she said, "Before I go, couldn't you at least tell me what's in that safety deposit box?"

"That's not going to happen." Elwood said.

Robert looked at Elwood and then her. "You can tell her. What's she going to do? Once we have it, there's no record of its existing."

Elwood angled his head to one side, considering. "That's true."

"Yup." She flashed a bright smile all around the room. "My word, your word, yada, yada."

Elwood said, "All right. You've been so emotional over the radio station changing hands that no one will believe you anyway."

What was it with men thinking being emotional prevented a woman from being believable? She wanted to haul off and give Elwood a gezuntah clop. But he was still holding that gun, which meant clopping was out of the question. "Now that we've established I won't be thought of as a reliable witness, what exactly is in there?"

"That woman, Comstock…" Elwood shook his head. "When Stan told me what she'd done, and what *he* intended to do, I knew we couldn't ever let that information come to light. It would be a huge problem. So I told Robert."

"Yes, yes, the background. Every story has one." She gave him an encouraging nod.

"Elizabeth Comstock was a serial do-gooder," Elwood said, as if do-gooding was why the western world was going to hell. "It wasn't enough that she donated the land the transmitter and tower could be moved to. She stipulated that Stan give the employees of the radio station first option to buy the station after his death and before it was offered to anyone else."

And just like that, everything fell into place…*employees first option to buy* rang through Tootsie's head with the mic's volume cranked up into the red zone. She prayed that the look on her face said confusion, not confirmation.

"Of course," she said, nodding. "It would have been just awful if someone found out. What a mess you'd have on your hands."

Nostrils flaring, Elwood took a step away from the table toward her, seeming to grow in spine-chilling stature. "There'd have been no mess. Except for you and your questions."

Tootsie locked her knees in place. No way would she step back and show how now, for the first time, she was scared.

"Yeah," Robert piped up. "And then you screwed it up when you realized Angie had the key."

Elwood didn't look Robert's way. But what he

said, made sudden sense. Though the key had been in a piece of liver in Angie's freezer for months, Elwood hadn't missed it. Until Tootsie started asking questions.

"I don't understand, Tootsie." There was a whine in Robert's voice. "You've always gone along with things. You never rocked the boat. Why did you have to get up on that chair and rile things up?"

Like she was going to share with Stan Hillman's idiot son that her life, going forward, would be all about riling things up.

"Why couldn't you have left it all alone?" Robert's voice got thin and reedy. Like he was about to cry. "Everything was going so well. All I wanted was to sell the station. Would that have been so bad?"

"Except you knew you couldn't, Robert." Tootsie felt a twinge of sympathy for Robert. From the feel in the room Tootsie guessed he had no idea what he'd gotten himself into. "And why did you, anyway? You had plenty of money coming to you that your dad left you. Why didn't you let the employees take the station over?"

"There was one problem," Robert wiped his nose with the back of his hand. "I'm not the sole beneficiary. He left his money to…" His lip curled up in contempt… "Charity. A third of his money went to food banks. A million to the Community Food Bank of New Jersey, a million to the national food bank of Israel, Leket, and a million to the World Rescue Mission. That left a mere two million for me."

"How terrible." Tootsie tried and failed to keep the sarcasm from her voice. Less than that was what she'd left herself after she gave away most of what she'd gotten from Arlo in their divorce. For her, it was way more than enough, considering what everyone else in the world had. Or didn't.

"You can judge if you want," Robert said, all hot now. "But you've never walked in my shoes. You've never had to put up with my trials and tribulations. A father who never understood me. It was just terrible. Why do you think I spent three years in Bhutan?"

Such a problem… "I thought you liked mountain air."

"Enough," said Elwood with a growl that would have won a pit bull's approval. "The key. Go get it from your car."

She hiked her thumb behind her. "I'll go, but before I go, my inquiring mind wants to know why did *you* get yourself involved in this little drama? It wasn't to assure yourself that you'd have a job with the Petrocellis."

"You're right. Robert didn't know what to do. I helped him figure it out. I found the Petrocellis. I found a law firm that would accept on face value everything we told them about the station. To compensate me for my help, Robert gave me enough money so I'd be fixed for life."

The words sounded familiar. They were almost the exact words Robert had used the day she found him in the promotions closet. They must have talked over the 'fixed for life' thing and convinced themselves it was okay to proceed. "I guess you won't work for the Petrocellis too much longer?"

"They knew we were rushing to sell for a reason and the reason didn't bear looking into. They wanted me to stay on for three months to give the appearance that everything was on the up and up." He pushed her toward the door. "And now I've explained as much as I'm willing to share with you. Let's get this charade over with. The key. Get it now. I'm all out of patience."

Not until Tootsie opened the door did it become clear that Elwood was all out of luck, too. Because what else could it be when there in the bank lobby stood so many cops in their black bullet-proof vests, their guns, and their attitude that she was willing to bet any crime about to be committed in northern New Jersey was going to go unpunished.

Especially because standing front and center was Black Windbreaker.

# CHAPTER TWENTY

Things happened so fast that Tootsie felt like she was having an out-of-body experience. With no fanfare to speak of, Elwood, Robert, and Snedeker were in handcuffs, snapped securely behind their backs. Shocking to Tootsie how, for such a big guy, Snedeker went so meekly, which gave special meaning to the bigger they are, the harder they fall.

Black Windbreaker was in charge, no question. He was in the middle of the bunch, kind of like when the important one was always in the middle of group pictures. Still, how crazy was it that the moment she stepped into the main part of the bank, he had his hand cinched firmly around her upper arm and was dragging her off to the side.

"Stay here. Don't move."

Did he always have to give orders? Not that this time she wouldn't listen. Being cooperative...that's how she decided to frame it. Because he was acting in his official capacity as an officer of the law. Because her knees felt like rubber and her head was pounding. Because she knew she'd avoided either being stomped to pieces or shot, neither one of which she would have enjoyed.

In her mind—or at least after watching every episode every week of Chicago PD—the guilty were whisked off right away. They had to be, didn't they? Producers had a single hour to tell the whole story. Well...with commercials about 40 minutes.

Yeah, no...that wasn't what happened because this was reality, not some production that would air tonight at nine on everyone's 55-inch box.

But then she stopped thinking about Chicago PD, the air went out of her, and she sagged against the wall. Suddenly one of the many chatting cops, who seemed to be on site with nothing to do but shoot the breeze, was there with a chair. After thanking the uniform, she looked Black Windbreaker's way to see he was, for that one moment, watching her intently, and she mouthed a thanks his way.

She was proud of him. Which made no sense. Except it did. She wasn't sure what came next between them, but one thing she knew for sure. He was *her* Black Windbreaker...who looked at her with soft eyes, before he again went about the business of being Big Man on Campus, or at least this bank.

The poor manager had been nowhere around

when Tootsie and the three stooges came out of the so-called private room. She supposed the woman and the two tellers had been whisked away for their safety. But she was back now, and being questioned by a cop with a pad in his hand, and she was talking fast. Tootsie hoped she'd been wrong, that she hadn't conspired with Elwood and Robert's in their delightful scheme.

But it turned out the bank manager had. So when she was put in handcuffs, too, Tootsie felt sad. With her brightly colored suits, she was a snazzy dresser.

It took what seemed like hours with everyone still standing around, even the miscreants or was that an old word…out. And then the cop who had been questioning the bank manager came over to her to ask her questions. Lots of them. Some made no sense, but she answered them all.

"We're going to want to speak to you again, Mrs. Goldberg," he said, all deep voice and serious eyes. "Would you mind coming down to our offices so we can get a formal statement from you?"

Tootsie agreed to make herself available. "I have one question."

The cop—his name tag said his last name was Sullivan—said, "Shoot."

Considering that was what she was afraid had been about to happen to her not too many minutes ago, she wished Sullivan could have used a different word. "The reason I agreed to meet the perpetrators was because there's something in a safety deposit box here at this bank. Something important. Could I maybe look at what's in there? I have the key." She pointed outside to where her rental was parked at the end of the bank's parking lot.

"Hold on for a moment," Officer Sullivan strode over to where Steve was talking with a cadre of other cops. When Sullivan interrupted him, he listened, spoke, and then gave Tootsie a long look. His features gave nothing away. As usual. But then he turned away and went back to his conversation.

Was that a no? According to the law, no one could get into that box unless they were a signatory. "Drat," she said, under her breath.

Sullivan returned to Tootsie's side. "He says okay but only if Mr. Hillman consents to open the box, since he's the one who can sign. And I need to go in there with you."

In the end, Robert agreed, though he didn't look happy about it. And why would he? What was in that box would put an end to his dreams of…what was it he said…being fixed for life? His fixed for life would change after today. Poor guy.

Robert, Sullivan, a couple of other cops, and one of the bank's tellers squeezed into the little room. The teller used her key, Robert used the one Angie had given Tootsie, and the box was open. There were two things in it: a number ten envelope, its flap tucked in, and a bigger, flatter manila envelope.

Everyone but Robert and Sullivan left and Tootsie slid the paper out of the number ten envelope. It had a date from twenty years ago. Unfolding it, she spread it out on the table, and began to read.

*To whom it may concern,*

*I, Elizabeth Comstock, have donated land to Stan Hillman for use by the radio station for a new transmitter and tower. It has been in my family since my ancestors came to this country from England in 1737. I am deeding it to the radio station that has made my life so happy these last years. I do not want thanks for my donation. Instead I am doing this for the men and women who work so hard to bring pleasure to so many. I stipulate that should the decision be made to sell the station, at any time whether by my friend, Stan Hillman, or once he passes, by Mr. Hillman's estate, first choice of buying the radio station is to be given to the radio station's employees. I have instructed my attorneys to draw up the documents accompanying this letter to make my wishes legal.*

Those documents were no doubt in the manila envelope. Where Tootsie would leave them for whatever attorney would be hired to decipher them. She slipped the Comstock letter back into place. Glancing at Sullivan, she said, "So, all this time, Mrs. Comstock's attorneys could have let us know what her wishes were and we wouldn't have had to go through this rigmarole."

He shrugged. Sullivan wasn't in the business of having an opinion on that.

At the end of the day when Tootsie was back at the hotel and on the phone with the remediation people who had cleaned out the mess in her house and were ready for her to head over to the house to see if they'd done everything she'd wanted them to do, she was too tired to think about who knew what about what. Or not. She wanted to think about Steve.

On the drive to Glen Allyn, she thought about the strange way back at the bank he'd made sure she was okay, and yet didn't seem to be paying much attention to her. And if he'd been through with her and her drama, why had he shown up with that army of cops anyway?

She knew the answer to that, didn't she?

It was because that was the kind of cop he was. Because he knew what the right thing was. Yeah, he was a black and white kind of guy. He was clear about the law.

When he was talking to Robert and Elwood, when he was questioning the bank manager, how he bent toward her, listened to her intently, and somehow, without one of his sparing—if in this case manipulative—smiles, got her talking. When he spoke to his team, when they came to him and asked him questions, he was aware of everything that was going on around him and that included her. His glance always found her when hers found his. And he didn't look away when she did. It was obvious he didn't care that she caught him looking at her.

She remembered that smile, the one he'd given to Brian the day of the big storm. It was warm and wonderful, and open and accessible. All the things she'd accused him of not being.

Maybe, just maybe he wasn't as far out of her life as he'd said he was? Maybe the breaking and entering didn't matter to him anymore. Or the burglary.

If he was in her life, what was he? Maybe her lover or not, although they'd made love. It wasn't because he was her friend, because she'd never had a friend like him and she wasn't sure they were friends. And it wasn't because he'd fixed her front window, or arranged to have her arrest warrant taken care of, or because he put the snake in a box in the garage.

Black Windbreaker would never betray himself. He had his own moral compass. And a huge heart.

Now, if only he'd take her text or her call so she could tell him she wanted him back, him and his huge heart.

Coming around the corner, she could see the remediation company's truck parked in her driveway, where other things had happened. She hadn't thought to call her gardener, who doubled as snow removal guy, to plow out her driveway. But her driveway was clean. Her walk up to the front door, and the sidewalk were also plowed out neatly from one side of her property to the other.

Though he wasn't talking to her, though he'd

decided she was too much for him to deal with, she was willing to bet Black Windbreaker had made it happen.

She smiled her way into her house to check on what was going on inside.

It was amazing. All the glass in her foyer had been swept up. All the fragments of her pretty Limoges boxes and Meissen monkeys were gone. She felt a pang, a small one, only. One of the advantages of being the wife, ex or not, of a lottery winner, was she could buy more.

What she couldn't buy again was her grandmother's vase. A lump rose in her throat, thinking of its loss.

She made her way through the house to the kitchen, where she found the head remediation guy leaning on her island, making some notes. He looked up as she entered. "We're almost finished, here, Mrs. Goldberg. I just want to be sure. One of my men said that you want me to take away some of the furniture, even though it's not damaged. Is that right?"

He waved a hand in the direction of the great room. "He said it was that brown leather recliner."

"That's right." She'd done a job on Arlo's Pachysandra, or at least a part of a job. Now she was getting rid of his recliner and his leather presence. "Somebody else can make better use of it than I can. I'm not big on reclining."

"We'll take it then. And all's good. You can move back into your house. As long as the police say it's okay."

"I called, and they told me I can."

As he made for the front door, she followed him. Hand on the doorknob, he turned back. "Oh, Mrs. Goldberg. There's a vase sitting on the counter to the left of your stove. It has some hairline cracks, but looks pretty good for something that we might have swept up with the rest of the mess in your front hall."

For a moment, she wasn't sure what he was talking about. But then, her heart jumped into her mouth. "I-it was in pieces the last I saw it. I put it in a bag. How were you able to fix it?"

"We didn't." He swept an encompassing arm in the direction of her island. "It was there, already fixed, when we got here. My guys moved it so someone wouldn't knock it over."

"Thanks," she managed. Somehow, though she wanted to turn back into the kitchen right away, she made herself wait until they drove away. And then, she made a beeline for the counter next to her stove.

There it sat.

It was obvious that it had been glued together. Some of the glued places didn't quite meet. And there was a chunk of porcelain that was missing from the mouth of the vase right by one of the handles.

She squinted her eyes at it. If she didn't look too closely, it looked almost like it had never been in pieces. Like it had never ever been damaged.

Picking it up, she held it close to her. A piece of her grandmother, still with her. "Who did this,"

Tootsie said to the vase. But she knew. Because, at heart, no matter what, what he did better than most anyone she knew was fix things.

She also knew, without hearing a thing, that he was there, behind her.

"You left the door unlocked," he said in his quiet, uninflected voice.

She smiled at the vase, her eyes tearing. "I shouldn't have, should I?" She turned.

He stood in the entranceway between the dining room and the kitchen. He was still wearing his SWAT jacket. It was black. But not unrelieved black. It had yellow letters.

Coming further into the room, he said, "You should have called me before you came back here."

She wouldn't remind him that she had and he hadn't taken her call. Because he was here...and it didn't matter. "There's no danger."

He was here, caring. Wanting her to be okay. Her heart began tripping the light fantastic. "I didn't expect you'd want me to, considering you don't want me in your life anymore."

He came further into the room, coming within inches of where she stood. He took the blue vase, still in her hand, from her unresisting fingers and placed it on the island to stand in glory all by itself. "You're always making statements."

She gave an infinitesimal shake of her head and folded one hand into the other. The touch of his fingers to hers, even for the split of a second made her forget what she needed to say. Almost. But not. "Didn't you tell me you were over my crazy ways? Didn't you tell me I'd complicated your life way too much?"

He shoved his hands in his pockets. Those black eyes of his that saw everything studied every part of her face looking for what he wanted.

"Yeah, I did say that. But so what?" He shrugged.

"Wouldn't you think I'd come to the conclusion that what that meant was what I thought it meant?"

He flicked one of her curls. The skin of her scalp raised up in goosebumps. "After spending one moment with you, I know not to try to think for you."

He put his hands back in his pockets and took a step back.

Silence then, while she looked at the vase. She sighed. "You put this together, didn't you?"

He shrugged. "Yup."

"Why?"

He took one hand out of one pocket and rubbed the back of his head. "Because you wanted it fixed."

"Thank you, Steve," she said, smiling the words. "That was very nice of you." And wasn't that the least of what she wanted to say?

He shrugged again. "No problem."

There was a slight tinge of red on his neck, just at the edge of his jacket. Strong, inflexible Black Windbreaker was blushing. The words might not come easy for him, but he had deep feelings that he did something about. Lucky her, it seemed she was currently on the receiving end. She wanted to wallow in it, but she had a couple of things she needed to know before she did.

She folded her arms across her chest and said, "So where are the four Musketeers? Have you had them transferred to death row?"

The warmth in his eyes iced over. "They're spending the night in the county lock-up and then I expect they'll be arraigned. They'll make bail and go home with ankle bracelets. No death row for them. Sorry."

"Did Elwood or Robert talk?"

"Robert did. He confessed. Your Mrs. Comstock did—and her attorneys confirmed—make the deal her note described. Robert would have been good with giving the station to the employees. He didn't want it. For him, spending one day there was torture."

And wasn't that something Tootsie knew well.

"But then, when he got a look at his dad's will, he found out he'd been stiffed. That's when it became important for him to sell the station for the proceeds."

"Did the Petrocellis really not know about their scheme?"

"Not according to Robert."

"Do they know now?"

"Unless someone told them, no. But they've already got those other problems we talked about.

This will be just one more. A smart prosecutor will be able to show they knew they were getting something they had no right to."

All the pieces were falling into place, proving she'd been right to ask all her annoying questions and showing up where no one wanted her. "What about the bank manager? She did something with the cards."

"Yeah. Destroyed the one with Angie's name on it and subbed in Robert's. Angie was right. She was a signatory. Stan wanted her, once he died, to make sure those papers got to the lawyers because he didn't trust Robert to honor his and Mrs. Comstock's wishes. But he made the mistake of trusting Elwood, who made sure Angie was out of the picture, who saw an opportunity to make a lot of money, and went for it. After, he, Robert, and then the bank manager cooked up their scheme."

"I do like it when all the pieces fit." Tootsie felt lighter than air. "Now, I can call my friends and let them know WCLS might soon be back on air. But making it all right is going to take time. And attorneys. It will be expensive."

Steve stroked his chin and narrowed his eyes at her. "Maybe you can help with that."

When they knew things were going to get rough, money wise, her friends hadn't wanted her help. Tootsie's smile came slowly. She'd never been a big spender. But she was a good investor and she'd invested wisely. So, yes she could help. And they'd accept. "All that money Arlo had to cough up for me in the divorce settlement will pay for some really good lawyers."

"It would be doing the right thing, wouldn't it…paying for something your friends can't afford?"

And wasn't it funny how things came full circle? There would have to be a committee to make decisions every step of the way before and after the station was back in the right hands. Though the first committee, the one Tootsie had thrown in the Petrocellis' face had had no role in selling the radio station, it would have one buying it back. "I guess Elwood will be out of a job."

Steve voiced a dismissive snort. "Unlike Robert, your friend Elwood isn't talking. He said the word, lawyer and clammed up."

"Which proves Elwood is a pretty smart guy."

"Or maybe not." His eyes shone with humor. "If he got caught by a rank amateur."

She firmed her lips up against the smile that wanted to break out, calling her an amateur. "What about the muscle?"

Steve raised an eyebrow. "You mean Snedeker? He didn't say anything either. But we're pretty sure he's the one who trashed your curio cabinet and threw the rock through the window."

She raised an eyebrow, too. "And the snake?"

He cleared his throat and looked away. "I may have been wrong about the snake sleeping off the winter in your garage. We think Snedeker put it there as a joke."

Some joke.

On a slow smile, Tootsie said, "So the snake was a warning, too. Good to know my imagination hasn't run away with me...altogether." She began to pick at a thread on the edge of her sweater. "So there's this one other thing I need to know."

He waited.

"Why did you help me all the time you were telling me I was too much drama for you?"

That red tinge at his neck came back. But his beautiful, black eyes were trained right on her. "Why do you think?"

Naturally, he wasn't going to make this part easy.

"Maybe..." She bit her lower lip... "because you like me?"

He shrugged. His eyes softened.

"So you did that research on Elizabeth Comstock...because you like me?"

His upper lip twitched. "Maybe."

"And you read the *Daily Mouse*...because you like me?"

One eyebrow went up. "Could be."

"And all the rest...dropping the key in the parking lot, following me up to the radio station, going in so I didn't have to...that was all because you like me."

This time she didn't frame it as a question. Because her heart knew, and it sang a hallelujah. "So, now that it's all over, what do you think?"

"For me, it's just getting started."

Another cryptic statement. But Tootsie was getting better at figuring them out and she knew where he was going. "Oh?"

"It's simple. I want to see how it is to be around you without all the drama."

She folded her arms across her chest and gave him a pretend considering look. "I'm not giving up drama."

He took his hands out of his pockets and looked around the kitchen. And then he ambled over to the wall of windows facing her deck. "It looks like you need some work done out there."

Tootsie came to stand next to him, wondering what he saw beneath all the white. Not the Pachysandra bumps for sure. But whatever it was they were talking about, there was subtext in those words. "I have a gardener. He does good work."

"Why pay a gardener when you might be able to find someone to do the work for nothing. Except maybe a bowl of soup?"

She said nothing. Just waited. And her heart began to play jump rope with her lungs.

After a moment he walked into the back hallway, looked at the rake where she'd left it and came back into the kitchen. He walked over to the island and reached up to touch one of the copper pots she'd so lovingly hung on the rack above. The pot swayed and made a tinging sound against its neighbor.

"These are nice," he said. "Although knowing

you don't like to cook, I don't know why you have them. Maybe you were waiting for me to come around."

Maybe she was. She wanted to be in his arms so badly. But he wasn't finished.

He touched a sauce pan she'd never used. Proof of his point. "This one's good for making my famous Bordelaise sauce. Which goes good with a nice steak. Which I can cook on the grill. You do have a grill, right?"

Her brain started a slow whirl. He loved a circuitous path. She was going to have to get used to going down it with him…for however long it took. "Yeah. It's on my deck. Snowed under. Do you really know how to make a Bordelaise sauce?"

He turned her big skillet a couple of degrees and then let it go. It made a sweet, musical sound as it, too, kissed its neighbor. "This one's good for pancakes on a Sunday morning. What kind of pancakes do you like?"

Any kind he wanted to make.

He didn't wait for her to answer…again, just turned and opened the refrigerator. It had not much more food in it than it had at the beginning of the week before everything happened and her life took a complete 180. He looked over his shoulder at her and said, "Somebody needs to make a run to the market."

As he touched things, as he toured the kitchen, she trailed behind him. Though she wanted to put her arms around his waist and lay her head against his back, even more now than before, she waited. "Those are really good observations. What's to be done about them?"

He turned, hands back in his pockets, his face inscrutable, his eyes warm and soft. "I'm thinking someone needs to use those pots more than you do. And you need someone who's good at shopping. You know, so you can be sure every day you eat something from all five of the food groups."

"And who would that be who might do all those things?"

"Not saying I'm moving in or anything." That face of his, so still, not giving anything away…so good at keeping whatever he thought to himself.

He was really dragging this thing out, enjoying himself and she was enjoying herself. "I'd love steak with Bordelaise sauce for dinner. I could go outside and clear off the grill. Once you get to whatever the point is you're making."

He gave her an enigmatic smile and shook his head. "The point… I have obligations. When the girls are home from school. And my mom…she lives next door, and I like to keep my eye on her, in case she needs something."

"You wouldn't want them to worry you'd abandoned them." Because he never would.

She reached up, because she wasn't waiting any longer, and touched her fingers to where his last name, DiLorenzo, was embroidered on his jacket. Over his heart. He leaned into her hand.

"But if I happened to be here a couple of nights a week, maybe three, I could make sure there was food in the fridge, and I could watch while you make soup. And maybe if there's drama, I could figure out how to handle it." He drew her close to him. "What do you think?"

"I'm thinking a lot of things." She raised her hands and pressed them against his chest. His heart beat steady against the not-so-steady throbbing in the tips of her fingers. "First one is, you have nerve thinking I want you around two or three nights a week."

"It is pretty nervy of me, you're right." He raised one of her hands brought it up to his lips for a kiss.

"But I'll let you slide this one time." She kicked off her shoes and rubbed her foot up and down his leg from his knee to his ankle.

"Good." He blew on her fingers. "Because I already made up my mind."

"Well, that's rude." She pushed him back against the island.

He trailed one finger over her lips. "I like planting flowers. The condo where I live, I can't plant anything. Because there's this ground cover."

"I hate ground cover." She pulled his shirt out of his waistband. "It's like cheating."

His black eyes grew intense. "So, what kind of flowers do you like?"

"I don't know." She took his hands and placed them on her hips. "What kind do you like?"

"You know that garden shop up in Fort Lee?" His breaths came faster. One moment he was flexing his fingers against her hips, the next he'd pulled her flush against him. Where what she felt was way more than subtext. "Anybody looking for a place to make flower choices would head up there to see what they like best."

"I'm up for checking the place out." She reached beneath his shirt and flattened her hands against the smooth as silk skin of his back. "What about the Bordelaise sauce? Because I want to remind you. I don't cook. So if you're making Bordelaise sauce tonight we need to go shopping." It was getting hard to speak. But Tootsie pushed on. "If you want to, we could go. But maybe later?"

She sure hoped he voted for later.

He eased one of the arms of her sweater down over her elbow and wrist, and then the other. He dropped the sweater onto the floor. Only for a second did her mind rebel. Because really...in situations like these, neatness was *not* next to anything, godliness or otherwise.

"I took one look at you and knew what kind of shopper you are, which is not too savvy. And as for the cooking? It didn't take me long to figure out you were good for cooking one thing."

"And what exactly is that?"

His answer came much later. And didn't surprise her.

"Soup."

# EPILOGUE

"**I**'m not sure I can come over this afternoon, Mom." And wasn't it amazing that she could now call Francine mom...for the first time in thirty years.

Though it kept slipping, Tootsie had secured the phone between her cheek and her shoulder. She needed both hands to peel and cut the carrots, celery, parsnips, and celery root for her chicken soup. Steve had never had Jewish Penicillin—which shocked her, given that he'd worked in that Jewish deli and could have gotten the good stuff anytime he wanted. Now he was sick, although he'd gotten a little testy when she pointed out that he might want to think about taking at least one little afternoon off to get better.

"Well, you've told me in no uncertain terms that you'll never let me teach you mah-jongg," Francine said. "I don't understand why but then I've never understood you, so…"

"If you expect your mother to change, you're wasting your time," Steve had said in one of the many conversations they'd had about family in the two weeks since he'd sort of moved in. Tootsie marveled at how the taciturn man wasn't so taciturn after all. When it came to certain conversations, he was beyond voluble. Voluble had been what he was when he chastised her for holding on to the three decades of anger she'd held against her mother. "You need to let it go," he said. "Not for her. For you."

"I'm going to start calling you Dr. DiLorenzo with all the advice and psychoanalysis you're doling out. I might even have to get one of those couches therapists have in their offices.

"I do have a master's degree in national security studies and homeland defense. You shouldn't forget that I am a learned man. If you decide to get one of those couches, we could test it out for…well, you know what for."

Like they'd tested out a lot of surfaces in her house where they could indulge what seemed to be an insatiable need for them to…well, the jury was out on whether it was to have sex or make love. Whatever, she was planning to enjoy every minute of whatever it was.

"I'm glad we're finally on the same page," Tootsie said to her mother, who was still droning on about the benefits of mah-jongg…as if there were some. "However, I really wish you would give me that recipe of yours for stuffed cabbage."

"I'll be glad to. It's a recipe I got from your grandmother Sylvia. It was in the family from the old country. And why exactly do you want it? Have you suddenly started to cook?"

It was a sly question asked slyly. "I don't want the recipe to get lost. When Sam and Josh get married, I'm going to be sure to pass the recipe on to their wives."

"Good luck with daughters-in-law. I've heard they're not easy to get along with." Francine paused. "Almost as difficult as getting along with daughters."

Francine would always get in her shots, but that was okay.

"No worries," Tootsie said telling herself to remember that conversation she'd had with Dr. Black Windbreaker. "I have plenty of time to think about how I'm going to cope. Meanwhile, I still want that recipe." Which forget the boys. She had time for that. Right now, she was sharing it with Steve. So he could cook it. She was really jonesing for a good plate of sweet and sour stuffed cabbage—made the Hungarian way—over rice.

She'd already hit END when she felt the man's warm hand on the back of her neck. The moment he touched her or the moment she touched him, she wanted to drop everything and get horizontal. This time she acted with restraint. She looked over her shoulder to find he wasn't looking back at her, though. Instead his gaze was fixed on the vegetables.

"You put all that in the pot with the chicken?"

"Obviously, you've never been around a cook who specializes in amazing Eastern European cooking, Jewish style."

"I never watched when the guys back at the deli made soup. I wasn't so much into soup back then." He took a sniff, not so easy to do with his nose stuffed up. "Although what you're making looks like it'll be as good as that vegetable soup you made the other day. And the split pea. Although I never saw split pea soup cooked without ham."

"Ham isn't kosher."

"I know kosher and Tootsie, you're not kosher."

"In my atavistic brain I am."

He was silent for a mere second. Then he said, "Somehow that makes sense to me." And then he kissed her neck.

Her knife paused mid cut of one of the larger carrots. "Did you want soup today, or are you not in any hurry?"

"You told me your chicken soup is going to prevent this cold from getting worse, so yeah, I'll be in a hurry later. Plus I thought you'd like to know where things stand with your radio station. I've got an update."

When Tootsie had let everyone know about Robert and Elwood's conspiracy, the phone calls flew back and forth, everyone over the moon about the change in direction. Probably Lenny was the most excited.

"I knew you could do it, Toots. You're the bomb," he crowed.

"Now aren't you glad that bus didn't hit you?"

"That bus?" Lenny made a dismissive sound. "It was close but close doesn't count except with horseshoes and hand grenades."

Tootsie wasn't sure what that meant, but she did know there wasn't going to be any need for WCLS's listeners to form a committee to get the station back.

"Anyway," Steve went on, "According to what I've heard, the Petrocellis have seen the handwriting on the wall, and how things would play out in the courts. They've decided they'd rather abandon their new radio station without making any kind of fuss, and return control of it to your colleagues."

Just as Tootsie had thought. There'd be that committee and there'd be a search committee for a new general manager, since obviously Robert wouldn't be it...even if anyone wanted him. He, Elwood, and the bank manager were currently awaiting sentences since they'd all pled guilty. For Snedeker, who couldn't make bail and was too stupid to admit guilt, no such luck. He currently resided in the kind of cell Tootsie had imagined for herself.

Later, when they were sitting down to their steaming hot bowls of chicken soup, they talked more about WCLS.

"The thing is about going back to work at the station, I told everyone it's the last thing I want to do."

She poked at her matzo ball. Pieces of carrot, celery, and chicken floated toward the top of the golden broth. Her ball had sunk to the bottom. "I've never been able to get them to be light. I just don't know what I'm doing wrong."

"Maybe your proportions are wrong. Too much matzo meal for too little chicken fat and not enough egg."

"When did you become Joan Nathan?" she retorted.

"Who's Joan Nathan?"

"The Jewish Julia Child."

"Any YouTube videos of her I can watch? Maybe I can learn how to make matzo balls from scratch."

When she raised her tablespoon at him in a threatening manner, he laughed. "Don't worry. You're in charge of soup, not me. Besides, I like my matzo balls to be like rocks."

Of course he was lying to make her feel better, which she had discovered he did because that was his way.

"So if you don't want to go back to work at the radio station, what do you think you want to do?" He asked as he ate the last bite of the matzo rock in his bowl.

"I'm not sure, but whatever it is, it's going to be for me."

Steve picked up her bowl and his, and brought them to the sink. After he rinsed them off and put them in the dishwasher, he came back to the table. He was about to sit down when the front doorbell rang.

She began to get up. He pushed her back down. "I'll get it," he said, something he said quite often. It seemed that Black Windbreaker made it his business to make things as easy as he could for her in her own house. At first, she'd argued with him. She was no fragile flower and she could do what needed doing all by herself. But by the tenth time he told her he'd take care of it—whatever *it* was—she understood. He was taking care of her the way he knew to take care of her and that was that.

In a moment Steve was back with Brian. Tootsie gave her second most favorite officer of the law a kiss. "How about a cup of coffee? I just made some. Or some chicken soup."

Brian was obviously off-duty wearing not his uniform but a pair of faded jeans and long-sleeved sweatshirt. "I'll pass on the soup, but yeah, I'll have some coffee." He cocked his head to the side. "I gotta say, Toots. You look good. I guess becoming a vigilante agrees with you."

Tootsie ignored the shot—because that's what it was. "So what brings you by? I know you haven't come to impound Marge."

"It's true. I'm not on official business but I am here to ask if you'd be willing to join some of us in the neighborhood to go down to the town council meeting tomorrow night, and see if they'll agree to replace a yield sign with a stop sign on this one cul-de-sac off Martling Avenue. There's an accident there at least once every week. You know, one of the people who lives in that cul-de-sac thinks he has the right of way and ends up in fender benders and almost fender benders. There needs to be a stop sign before something worse than a fender bender happens. We could use your mouth—now why would I say that? I mean your smarts, to get them to agree to the request. Will you help?"

Tootsie handed Brian his coffee. "Is that the cul-de-sac where Chesty Kowalczyk lives?"

Steve shifted in place. "Kowalczyk? I know that name."

Turning to Steve, Tootsie said, "You should. He's that guy who might or might not be on the need-to-know list about where Jimmy Hoffa is buried. He's Glen Allyn's least favorite native son and he's not even native. His wife is."

"We're up against it with Chesty," said Brian. "He's got friends in high places, including the mayor. Which is one reason we still haven't been able to get that stop sign in place. I know because I've given him more than one ticket the way he comes shooting out of that cul-de-sac and he's told me to put it where the sun don't shine. I've tried to arrest him but he bleats like a wounded sheep and then goes to my chief and my chief goes to the mayor and tells me to lay off."

She didn't like to hear that. It made her hot. But not hot enough. "You've got this, Bri. You don't need me to step in."

Steve shifted in place. "Will not stepping in be the right thing?"

Tootsie jerked her gaze up to his. His face told her nothing, but it didn't have to because his words had. Because yeah, that 'you've got this' thing had been her go-to for so many years, it came out of her mouth on automatic.

It didn't take her two moments to make a recovery. "You know, Brian, you can count me in. I'll do whatever you want if it will get that stop sign in place. People's safety matters. Chesty Kowalczyk shouldn't be able to keep it from being put up. I'll get on any committee you want me to be on." She patted her bottom lip. "Maybe I'll even run for the town council."

Steve groaned. Brian's face turned white. But then he did a quick recovery and gave her a thumbs up. "About the town council, I'll leave that up to you. But meanwhile just help us with the stop sign thing. In fact, why don't you head up the committee."

"The committee…there's a committee?" She paused mid-thought. Then with a sly smile, she said, "I've always wanted to be on a committee and now if I can convince the powers-that-be to let me, I will."

Brian said, "I'll put in a good word for you."

In a flurry of motion, Tootsie hurried into the dining room. "Why don't we set up a nerve center right here." She patted the surface of her dining room table.

Steve, who had trailed behind said, "I'll call the

phone company and we'll run some cable. I'll see if I can get a direct line to the U.S. Department of Justice."

He was teasing her. But that was okay because her dining room wasn't really going to be a nerve center. And he wasn't really going to call the phone company to run cable. But getting past Chesty, that was going to be fun. Something to do for someone who liked a challenge. And hadn't Steve said she was a challenge?

The two men got into a discussion on how to rearrange the furniture. She knew they were teasing her some more. Put posters with pictures of some of those fender benders on them on telephone poles around town? There was no teasing about that. She'd have to get busy doing a poster design.

Tootsie smiled as they got more and more into it. How much her grandmother would have loved listening to the two cops who'd come over to her side, go at it. Her eyes got misty. She turned away and walked back into the kitchen where Steve had hung the shadow box he'd put together, the box in which sat her grandmother's vase in lovely majesty. She touched the edge of the box with one finger.

"Hey Grandma. I'm sorry for thirty years of not trusting myself enough to do what I knew I should. But that's over with. I'm going to do what you were so good at. I'm going to raise hell with the bad guys. I'm going to stop them in their tracks. I hope wherever you are you'll be proud of me."

She took a tissue out of her pocket and blew her nose. She marched back into the dining room. "Hold up, guys. Before you start rearranging my dining room, maybe you want to think about consulting me?"

"Yeah Brian, about that," Steve said. "We'd better before we do something she won't like. Because you don't want to be around — *when she gets hot...*"

\*\*\*

Thank you for reading all about how Tootsie gets herself in trouble and out! Want to know the meanings of all those Yiddish terms Tootsie uses to describe what exactly is going on in the story?

Claim your copy of the Tootsie Goldberg Yiddish Lexicon and get the latest news and updates when you subscribe to my newsletter.

https://dl.bookfunnel.com/fn6j2bbsmg

\*\*\*

Honest reviews of my books help bring them to the attention of other readers who are more likely to read something from a new-to-them author if it has more reviews (even if they aren't five star). You can easily leave a quick rating at your online book vendor of choice. Thank you!

# Acknowledgements

Some people I know say that Tootsie is me. I want to respectfully disagree. I would never get up on a chair wearing a skirt. I'd wear trousers instead.

Tootsie owes who she is to a number of wonderful people without whom I would have been just guessing. First and foremost, Tim Scheld, radio professional extraordinaire, former news manager at WCBS-AM in New York, provided me with the puzzle Tootsie needed to figure out the story mystery. With his comprehensive knowledge of the radio business—and a newsman's rich, active imagination—Tim had me focusing on the transmitter and tower at WCLS-FM, not a real station, but one whose calls I made up. By the way, calls is short for call letters, as in WCLS.

I leaned on the divine Captain John Devine of the Paramus, NJ Police Department for anything having to do with law enforcement. He kept me from having Tootsie get arrested for the wrong crime. And told me what Black Windbreaker would and would not do on the job. If there are any errors, in regard to police work, they are mine.

I owe huge thanks to my brilliant critique partners: Jen Wilck, Lisa Higgins, and Nancy

Herkness. They set me straight when I was going down rabbit holes and made suggestions that enriched this book. They kept me from writing Tootsie off the rails. Well, almost.

Thanks go to Sue Grimshaw, editor extraordinaire, who told me when things didn't make sense and suggested ways to rewrite. Thanks also go to Paula Gardner, whose proofing is so excellent she found mistakes that I doubt anyone would ever see and corrected them. Again, if there are others that didn't get caught, I'm the guilty party.

To my husband, Andy, who's let me take over the table in the room where his favorite TV is—because it's the best table in the house—and relegated himself to watching on his least favorite TV. There will never be enough thanks or enough love. In addition to being my perfect companion, who I can't imagine being without, he's a great chef, and an even better shopper, he has always been my chief cheerleader, especially when I didn't think there was much in myself to cheer about. Thanks, babe! I think it's time we took that river cruise we keep talking about.

# About The Author

Award-winning author Miriam Allenson writes about smart-mouthed women and the men who love them. (She's been told she's a little smart-mouthed herself.) Miriam took a dog's age and then some to publish her first book, FOR THE LOVE OF THE DAME. She cut the time it took her to write her next book, A DUKE FOR DESSERT, in half and she reduced it by half again writing WHEN THE DUKE FINDS HIS HEART.

With WHEN SHE GETS HOT, she's writing a whole lot faster. Look for more books in the series coming soon.

When Miriam is not working on a book—which is almost never—she's in the kitchen baking something, gardening on the "huge" 8'x4' deck of her apartment, or adding one more character to her 400+ Pez collection (no, she does NOT eat the Pez candy.). She likes licorice but not chocolate, polenta more than pizza, and baseball, any day over football.

Miriam lives in northern New Jersey with her fabulous, supportive husband, Andy, and near a good number of her seven grandchildren. She's happy to do overnights and serve dessert before dinner to any one of them who requests it.

Miriam isn't the best on social media, but you can connect with her below. Or you can join her newsletter when you claim your copy of Tootsie Goldberg's Lexicon.


Facebook: facebook.com/msallenson
TikTok:    @miriamallensonauthor

Publishing History

Print edition published by MS Allenson & Associates
©2023

Cover design by www.getcovers.com
Formatting by Lisa Verge Higgins
Editing by Edits by Sue.com and Paula Gardner
ISBN: 978-1-7338501-6-2

Made in United States
North Haven, CT
11 January 2024

47323565R00202